W9-CXL-647

"Something Woke Me Up,"

she confessed. "I—I think it was an owl."

Marc had gotten to his feet and Jennifer moved toward him, narrowing the space between them, not even conscious of what she was doing.

"I thought…I thought maybe if I got some hot milk…" she began. But Marc didn't pick up what she was saying.

She saw that he was devouring her with his eyes, and the longing that had been stirring inside her all evening became insatiable. She was hungry for this man; she wanted him. Nothing else seemed important.

"God," he said, rasping the words as if they were being torn out of him, "you're so beautiful."

"In this?" she choked out, gesturing toward the baggy pajamas.

"In anything. In nothing." Marc was walking toward her as he spoke, and she met him halfway. He stretched out his arms, and she went to him. He pulled her close, lowering his head, his mouth brushing her forehead, her nose, then moving on to claim her lips. His kiss became an invasion, an act of piracy, an invitation that branded Jennifer with its heat and urgency.

Dear Reader:

Nora Roberts, Tracy Sinclair, Jeanne Stephens, Carole Halston, Linda Howard. Are these authors familiar to you? We hope so, because they are just a few of our most popular authors who publish with Silhouette Special Edition each and every month. And the Special Edition list is changing to include new writers with fresh stories. It has been said that discovering a new author is like making a new friend. So during these next few months, be sure to look for books by Sandi Shane, Dorothy Glenn and other authors who have just written their first and second Special Editions, stories we hope you enjoy.

Choosing which Special Editions to publish each month is a pleasurable task, but not an easy one. We look for stories that are sophisticated, sensuous, touching, and great love stories, as well. These are the elements that make Silhouette Special Editions more romantic... and unique.

So we hope you'll find this Silhouette Special Edition just that—*Special*—and that the story finds a special place in your heart.

The Editors at Silhouette

SERL-7/85

MAGGI CHARLES
Autumn Reckoning

Silhouette Special Edition

Published by Silhouette Books New York

America's Publisher of Contemporary Romance

For Edith...
and our very special
bridge of friendship,
which has spanned so much.

SILHOUETTE BOOKS
300 E. 42nd St., New York, N.Y. 10017

Copyright © 1985 by Koehler Associates, Ltd.

Distributed by Pocket Books

ISBN: 0-373-09269-5

First Silhouette Books printing October 1985

10 9 8 7 6 5 4 3 2 1

America's Publisher of Contemporary Romance

Printed in the U.S.A.

MAGGI CHARLES

is a confirmed traveler who readily admits that "people and places fascinate me." She is a prolific author, known also to her romance fans as Meg Hudson. Having studied the piano and harp, Ms Charles states that if she hadn't become a writer she would have been a musician. A native New Yorker, she is the mother of two sons and currently resides in Cape Cod, Massachusetts, with her husband.

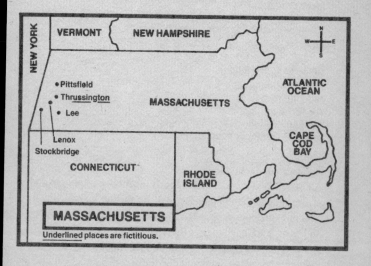

VERMONT NEW HAMPSHIRE

NEW YORK

- Pittsfield
- Thrussington
  - Lee
Lenox
Stockbridge

MASSACHUSETTS

ATLANTIC
OCEAN

CAPE
COD
BAY

CONNECTICUT

RHODE
ISLAND

MASSACHUSETTS

Underlined places are fictitious.

Chapter One

There was a marked beauty to the countryside that October morning. Jennifer had always responded intensely to fall's palette of colors, and nowhere were they more glorious than in New England. As she drove through the Berkshire region of western Massachusetts, she was surrounded by a mixture of shades ranging from tawny-gold to flaming red, the meadows and the mountains brushed with burnished splendor, and she felt herself suffused by a deep emotion.

"Autumn colors are like food for my soul," she'd once told Julia, laughing as she said it because it was one of those things you didn't usually say even to someone as close as Julia was to her.

Julia had smiled quietly, understanding this. But then, Julia almost always had understood, which was remarkable under the circumstances.

It was four years since Jennifer had driven this highway, but the terrain was all too familiar. She swung off the Massachusettes Turnpike at the proper exit, then headed north toward Thrussington. The narrow, winding road was lined mostly with sugar maples, some scarlet, some orange. The area, she found to her relief, was still delightfully rustic. Along the way there had been some changes. A new motel complex. Condominiums. A small shopping center. But most of the countryside was still.

Thrussington was the same charming New England village—a white-steepled church facing the village green, stately old homes, a main business street that was something of a jumble but still managed to be picturesque. Past the town the road began to curve again as it ascended into the hills, but before long Jennifer veered off onto a side road, remembering as if she'd driven this way yesterday the turnoff to the narrow dirt lane that led to Julia's house.

Julia's driveway was off this dirt lane, and it needed attention, Jennifer soon discovered. Her car gave a distressing thump as it encountered one of the many potholes, and she slowed to a crawl. This was neither the time nor the place to have to cope with a broken axle, or even a flat tire. Much as she loved Julia's house, Jennifer's intention was to be in and out of it and on her way again as quickly as possible.

Nevertheless, she hesitated before getting out of the car. It wasn't going to be easy to go through that front door and walk into the wide hall with the curving staircase on the right that swept up to the rooms on the second floor.

In effect, Jennifer knew, she'd be unlocking a trunkful of memories once she unlocked Julia's front door, and none of them was a memory she wanted to pull out of the trunk and examine.

I must remember that this is Julia's house I'm going into, not Roger's house, she told herself as she crossed the lawn to the flagstone walk. It was a cool day, and she was glad she'd decided to wear her gray wool skirt. The matching blazer, piped with a red that matched the leaves on the oaks, felt snug and comfortable.

Tall and slim, Jennifer walked with an easy grace. Her shoulder-length, ash-blond hair swung slightly as she moved. People had always told her that she had the figure, the looks, and the "presence" to be a model, but modeling as a career had never interested her.

When she reached the front door she pulled off the dark glasses she'd been wearing for driving, squinting slightly as her light gray eyes made the necessary adjustment to the afternoon glare. Only then did she take the brass key out of her handbag, fit it in the lock, and turn it, swinging the door open and starting down the hall. Then all hell broke loose!

The rending cacophony tore at Jennifer's eardrums. It was a wailing banshee screaming high tones, then low tones and high again. Until that moment the only thing she'd heard was the chirping of the birds in nearby trees as she approached the house. Perhaps because it was normally so quiet—Julia's house was at least a quarter mile from the nearest neighbor—the hideous howls now violating the peaceful surroundings seemed especially magnified.

Jennifer clapped her hands over her ears, teetering back on her heels as if the assault were physical as well as sonic. It didn't seem possible that the sounds could continue at such a pitch, but they did. It took considerable effort to try to focus mentally. Then Jennifer realized that Julia must have installed an alarm system and had forgotten to tell her about it.

With this realization came the immediate need to find the switchboard for the system and somehow shut it off. With her hands still clutching her ears, Jennifer sped out to the kitchen, then stood in the center of the floor, staring around helplessly. It seemed logical that this might be the place where the system was centered, but it was such a big room. A real country kitchen, complete with braided rugs and a rocking chair and a wood stove to be used on cool fall and spring nights. Julia had never lived in the place through a winter.

There were closets and cabinets, drawers, storage places. Jennifer, having no idea what an alarm system would look like, began to open and shut everything she could find. She was standing directly next to the wall telephone when it began to ring, or she'd never have heard it.

She grabbed the receiver off the hook, the phone's added intrusion more than her ears could bear. She was breathless as she mouthed, "Hello?"

"Bouchard," a deep male voice answered tersely.

"Hello?" Jennifer said again. Then, frantically, "Who are you? I have a problem, I can hardly hear you..."

"Who are *you*?" the voice countered.

It was too much. "Look," Jennifer began irately, but the man cut in on her.

"Can you identify yourself?" he asked coolly.

"What?" She couldn't believe this was happening.

"Can you identify yourself? The number?"

The horrible sound was still cresting and ebbing as badly in the kitchen as it had been in the hall. Jennifer suspected that it would be just as torturous everywhere in the house and all the way through the woods outside. It wouldn't have surprised her if people living in the heart of Thrussington were hearing it too.

Frantic because the noise was actually hurting her ears at this point, she said, "I'm Jennifer Bentley."

"What are you doing there?" the caller persisted.

"I'm here on an errand for Julia Gray." Why, Jennifer wondered distractedly, was she answering this man's questions?

She asked again, "Who *are* you?"

"I told you," he answered tersely. "Bouchard. What errand are you talking about?"

That was enough. "It's none of your damned business," Jennifer sputtered.

"I'm afraid it is." There was a slight pause, then he said, "Where is Julia Gray? Can you tell me that?"

"In Boston, she's a patient at the New England Medical Center," Jennifer snapped, holding one hand over the ear that wasn't covered by the phone receiver. "Look Mr....what did you say your name was?"

"Bouchard. Are you in the kitchen?"

"Yes."

"Turn the alarm off," he instructed.

"For God's sake, don't you think I already would have if I knew how to?" she demanded.

"See that small, numbered panel on the wall over the phone?" he asked her.

"Yes."

"Punch out the numbers three-seven-five-eight. Do it now. Then I'll expect you to come back on again."

Clutching the receiver with one hand, Jennifer followed his instructions with a trembling finger. At once the earsplitting sound stopped as abruptly as it had begun, and she sagged with relief, even though her ears were still ringing.

"Oh, my God," she said half to herself and half into the receiver. "A couple of minutes more and I think I would have gone crazy!"

She became aware of a new kind of sound. A silence that filled the room, filled her ears. Into it this man named Bouchard spoke. "All right," he said. "Now tell me who you really are, and what you're doing there."

The authoritative clip to his voice was abrasive. Nettled, Jennifer stung back. "Let's stop playing games," she suggested. "Who are you, and why do you know so much about the workings of Julia's house?" Her mind was in gear again. Julia had never mentioned anyone named Bouchard. But then, Julia had not said anything about having had an alarm system installed either.

The coolly superior tone of the man's deep, resonant voice rankled Jennifer all the more as he said, "I'm willing, in fact eager, to stop playing games with you. So suppose you answer my questions."

That did it. "I don't see why the hell I should tell you anything!" she shot back.

She could picture him—whoever he was—shrugging as he answered indifferently. "All right. The police should be on the scene within the next sixty seconds. You can tell your story to them." With that, he clicked down the receiver.

Jennifer sank back against the kitchen counter, shaking her head in disbelief. This couldn't be happening to her! She'd come out here today to do Julia a favor, even though she'd had no wish to walk into the Gray house ever again. She'd lived here with Roger during the two summers after their wedding; they'd broken up their marriage in the upstairs bedroom they'd shared. Right after that Jennifer had left, emotionally battered, mentally bruised, wanting only to go off someplace where she could be alone and lick her wounds.

Well…Julia had come after her, and she'd be eternally grateful for that. Few mothers-in-law would have espoused a daughter-in-law as Julia had espoused her. But even Julia had never suggested that she come back to Thrussington until now. She'd done so only because she needed some papers she kept in a metal box in her bedroom, and there were few people she'd trust to come into the house and go through her things.

Because she'd do anything for Julia Gray, Jennifer had agreed to make this particular safari. And she'd walked into a hornet's nest.

It could be explained; everything could be explained, she was sure. But that didn't lessen either the added trauma heaped on top of all the other traumas, or suffering the embarrassment that having the police loom up on the scene was going to cause her. If they did come charging in, that is. Had this Bouchard, whoever he was, been serious? Were the police really on their way?

They were. Jennifer heard sirens in the distance, sirens that came closer and closer. She was at the living room window as the Thrussington cruiser swung around in front of Julia's house, its red and blue lights blinking furiously.

Two police officers leaped out of the car, actually clutching their holsters. Jennifer closed her eyes, wishing she could reopen them to find that she'd stumbled into the middle of a bad movie. But this was reality. The two policemen strode toward the house with a cautious, measured tread that might have been funny in other circumstances. They were so wary, so definitely on red alert. Jennifer approached the open front door more than half expecting them to draw their guns on her.

Instead, they froze. As did Jennifer. She stood in the doorway staring out at them; they stood in position glowering toward her. The tableau was broken only by the arrival of a blue van that careened into the dirt driveway, then came to a screeching stop.

Through a cloud of dust Jennifer saw the writing on the side of the van. BOUCHARD SECURITY AND ALARM SYSTEMS.

So! she thought, and gritted her teeth.

She watched through narrowed eyes as a man got out of the van, a tall man with a shock of black hair that glinted with steel-blue tones in the October sunlight. He was wearing a vivid red wool jacket that highlighted both his eye-catching proportions—he was exceptionally well built—and his dramatic coloring. But as he started across the lawn toward the waiting policemen, Jennifer noted that he had a slight but definite limp. This was a jolt, rather like looking at a picture that was slightly out of focus, perhaps because he was such an otherwise perfect individual—physically.

Jennifer heard him call, "Wait up, Bill!" Even if she hadn't seen the name on the van she was sure she'd have recognized his voice from that single short sentence. It was a deep voice, with a special kind of timbre, an admittedly sexy quality. Even with the banshee alarm ringing in her ears, Bouchard's voice had made its impact…damn him.

She watched as the older of the two police officers turned toward him with a frown. "What is it, Marc?"

"There's been a mistake," Marc Bouchard said. "I plugged in to headquarters before Ms. Bentley identified herself. She's here on an errand for Julia Gray." He added, "I tried to reach you, but you'd already left the station. Sorry about this, Bill. I'm afraid I've let you in for a false alarm."

The police officer nodded. "Okay, if you say so." He turned toward Jennifer. "Is that right, miss? You're here on business for Mrs. Gray?"

Jennifer nodded, unable to trust herself to look toward Marc Bouchard. It was he who'd pushed the panic button, she thought resentfully. He could have made the trip out here himself to verify her story without calling in the police.

She said stiffly, "That's right, officer."

"Excuse us, then." The police officer had a weather-beaten face; now it cracked into a smile. "Nice day for a ride out in the country anyway," he said. As he climbed back in the cruiser he nodded to Marc Bouchard. "See you, Marc," he said amiably.

"Right," Marc Bouchard returned absently.

Resolutely keeping her eyes averted, Jennifer was sure he was looking at her. She wanted to turn on her heel, to walk back into the house, and to slam the door in his face, but she was equally sure she wouldn't get away with it. Marc Bouchard had let her off the hook as far as the police were concerned, but she had a strong suspicion that he wasn't yet finished with her himself.

Thinking this, she glanced toward him despite herself and found herself meeting blue eyes that were several shades darker than the deep October sky. He had gorgeous eyes; no man had the right to have such gorgeous eyes, to say nothing of the thick black lashes that fringed them.

She tore her gaze away to watch the police cruiser swing around in Julia's driveway and then continue on out onto the dirt lane.

Swiftly she decided that the only way to deal with this situation was to take the initiative. But it was only when the cruiser was out from sight that she mustered enough courage to turn toward Marc Bouchard and say crisply, "You had one hell of a nerve!"

He'd been about to speak himself and he stopped abruptly, staring at her as if he hadn't heard her right. Then he countered, "You should thank me for not turning you over to the cops."

"I'd like to know why."

"I'd like to know why, if Julia Gray has enough confidence in you to send you out here on an errand for her, she didn't also tell you how to handle the alarm system," Marc Bouchard shot back.

"Obviously she forgot," Jennifer said coldly.

"People don't usually forget details like that."

"Julia might. She doesn't bother about details most of the time." This was true enough. Julia, bless her, tended to see everything in broad strokes.

He digested this, then shook his head. "That doesn't quite wash," he told her. "Look, Ms. Bentley, you're going to have to answer a few questions for me."

"I disagree," Jennifer informed him. She added with more assurance than she felt, "This has been nothing but a stupid comedy of errors. Why don't we let it go at that?"

"A comedy of errors? Is that what you call it?" he queried. "Well, I don't agree. Shall we go inside?"

"I intend to go inside, do what I have to do, and get out of here," Jennifer informed him. "But I'd suggest that you get on your way."

He grinned at her, and his grin was so infectious, so disarming, that it would have taken an iceberg not to be affected by it. "This happens to be my priority job for the afternoon," he told her. "Whenever one of my alarms goes off, I consider it my first order of business to track down the reason why."

He was moving toward her as he spoke and, again, she was aware of the limp. He said, accompanying his words with a gesture that might have been termed gallant had things been otherwise, "You first, if you please."

Jennifer turned her back on him and strode into the house and down the hall toward the living room, the way she moved conveying complete indifference, as she intended. But she was, nevertheless, acutely aware of Marc Bouchard just behind her.

She sat down on a small love seat, drawing herself up erect, her chin tilted to the determined angle that people who knew her would have recognized as a challenge not easily brooked. Marc Bouchard lowered himself into an armchair opposite her and said without preamble, "Okay. Suppose you fill me in, Ms. Bentley."

"Why don't we call Julia and let her verify what I've told you?" Jennifer countered, her chin tilting up a shade higher. She didn't want to bother Julia. But neither did she want to spend the rest of the afternoon submitting to an inquisition from this man. There were things to be done.

To her surprise, he said calmly, "There's time enough for that."

"On the contrary." Jennifer said, "I'm eager to get back to Boston."

"For any particular reason?"

"I don't need to answer that," Jennifer informed him, "but in the interest of time I will. I have an engagement this evening. Does that satisfy you?"

He grinned. "Satisfy me? Not exactly," he said in a way that made Jennifer feel he was giving the words a double meaning. She stirred slightly, perturbed by this. Perturbed by him. There was a quiet assurance about him, an air of professionalism. It was out of keeping for a man running a small alarm-systems business in a little Berkshires town. City-wise, that's what Marc Bouchard was. Jennifer sensed this about him, recognizing the quality because she was a city person herself. She'd been born in New York and had lived there most of the time until her marriage to Roger. Since, except for the two summers spent in this house, she'd lived in Boston.

It was impossible not to be curious about Marc Bouchard. And equally difficult not to feel a tug of attraction toward him. He had an interesting, rugged face. Handsome, yes, definitely he was handsome. But there was a lot more to his face than well-arranged features and gorgeous eyes. She estimated that he must be thirty-five or so, and there were lines etched across his forehead and around his lips that told their own story. This man had lived; he'd lived a lot, and she suspected the quiet, controlled exterior he presented was exactly that. An exterior. She also suspected that there might be a very interesting person behind that careful façade. But those were conjectures.

Jennifer pointedly glanced at her watch. "Seriously," she said, "I do want to get through with my business for Julia and be on my way. It's a good four-hour drive back to Boston."

He nodded. "True."

Jennifer sighed. "Look, Mr. Bouchard," she said, "maybe you'll be satisfied that I'm bona fide if I tell you Julia Gray is my mother-in-law."

She'd never seen a more skeptical expression. He said slowly, "As I understand it, Julia Gray has one son. His name is Roger, and he's a screenwriter. He lives in California, and he's married to a movie star named Colleen O'Brien. You'll have to do better than that, Ms. Bentley."

A wave composed partly of anger, partly of annoyance, and partly of embarrassment swept over Jennifer. She'd never liked having to explain herself to anyone, and she especially disliked having to do so to this stranger. "I was Roger Gray's first wife," she said, biting off each syllable because she hated having to spell this out. "We've been divorced for four years."

"So Julia Gray's your *ex*-mother-in-law?"

"Yes."

"Interesting," Marc Bouchard drawled.

Jennifer flushed. "Julia is the...the best friend I have in the world," she said, appalled because she found herself choking with emotion over this statement. "We're very close."

"Surprising," he observed.

"Maybe you find it so. That doesn't mean—"

"No," he said, the smile fading. "No, it doesn't mean a damned thing, does it?" He stood. "Perhaps we'd better save ourselves a lot of time and call Mrs. Gray," he suggested.

"Well," Jennifer said rather snidely, "I'm glad you're seeing it my way."

"The phone's in the kitchen, isn't it?"

"One of them, yes."

He nodded. "Would you lead the way, please?"

Jennifer had no doubt that he knew the way to the kitchen just as well as she did, but she complied. And, again, she was intensely conscious of him just behind her.

She handed the receiver to him and said acidly, "I'm sure you'll want to place the call yourself...to be sure it really is Julia Gray we reach."

"Thanks," he said, and took the receiver out of her hand. "Do you have her number?" he asked agreeably.

"She's a patient at the New England Medical Center in Boston, as I told you," Jennifer reminded him. "Yes, I have the number." She fished in her handbag for the scrap of paper on which she'd written the number, with Julia's extension, and held it out to him. "Here."

She watched him dial. He had long fingers, the nails blunt-edged. He also had capable-looking hands; she liked his hands. He was a capable-looking man, this above and beyond his attractiveness. The sort of man it would have been pleasant to know in a different world, at a different time.

She saw him frown, heard him say, "When will she be back in her room? All right, thank you, we'll call again." He turned toward her to say, "It seems Mrs. Gray is having therapy. She won't be back in her room for an hour." He paused. "That does pose a problem, doesn't it?"

"Look, Mr. Bouchard," Jennifer began, but again he stopped her.

"There's no way I can allow you to go through any of Julia Gray's things until I speak to her," he said firmly. "Nor can I let you walk out of here and head back to Boston. That's a rental car you have out there, isn't it?"

She stared at him. "Yes. How did you know?"

"The license plate."

Her lips tightened. "I don't see what my having a rented car has to do with anything."

"It would be pointless to check the registration," he informed her. "I don't imagine you have any papers on you that prove you're who you say you are, do you?"

She didn't. She'd retained her maiden name, even during the years of her marriage to Roger. She'd been Mrs. Roger Gray socially, but professionally she'd been—she was—Jennifer Bentley.

"Your face does give you away," this man standing at her side said gently. "You have a transparent face, Jennifer Bentley. That in itself should prove that you're as honest as the proverbial day is long. But it doesn't always."

She stood very still, his deep, husky voice caressing her with his words. There was a near-hypnotic quality to his voice, and a warmth to his deep blue eyes that surprised her.

Unexpectedly he suggested, "Why don't we go get some coffee? There's a little place a couple of miles down the road. By the time we get back, probably Mrs. Gray will be in her room and we can straighten everything out."

Jennifer shook her head. "No, thank you."

"Look," he said patiently, "there's no point in just sitting here."

"All right. I'll make some coffee, if that's what you want," she said tersely.

"I doubt if you can."

"What do you mean?"

"Maybe there's a can of coffee on the shelf, I don't know. But the water's turned off. So," he added, "is the electricity. Only the phone was left connected, because of the alarm system."

"Great," Jennifer muttered bitterly.

"Mrs. Gray closed up the place just before Labor Day this year," he informed her.

"I know, I know," she said impatiently. "She went to Greece and she fell, somewhere around the Acropolis, I think it was, and did a real job on her ankle. They flew her back to Boston two weeks ago."

"That news hadn't caught up with me yet," he admitted. "I'm sorry to hear it."

"It was rotten luck," Jennifer said. "Julia was supposed to go on to Egypt from Greece and then..." She shrugged. "It doesn't matter," she said, making it clear that there was no reason why this man should have an interest in Julia Gray's itinerary.

He didn't respond to this. Instead, he said, "Would you reconsider on the coffee?"

"All right," Jennifer gave in grudgingly. But as they were walking out the front door together she couldn't resist saying, "Aren't you afraid I may try to run off on you?"

He shook his head. "Even with my gimpy leg I guarantee I could catch you," he told her.

"Oh?"

"Yes," Mark Bouchard said flatly. "Shall we use your vehicle or mine?" he added.

"Why not mine?" she suggested. "That van of yours would probably scare off any other potential thieves who come creeping around here in our absence."

He smiled at this, and she liked his smile. She was coming to like too many things about him, which was irrational to say the least. Jennifer was not usually so easily impressed by a man. Any man. Roger hadn't turned her off to the opposite sex. But he'd done a good job on her ego from which she sometimes wondered if she'd ever recover. She'd lost a lot of faith in herself, and in men as well.

Nevertheless, since the divorce she'd dated. At the moment she was seeing three different men in Boston, including Kenneth Trent, who was her publisher, and with whom she was supposed to be having dinner tonight. Again she glanced at her watch, wondering if she could possibly get through here and back to Boston in time to dress for the dinner engagement.

Marc Bouchard saw the glance and said, "I won't detain you any longer than necessary."

"It isn't necessary to detain me at all, as you'll find out," she told him, but he merely shook his head slightly and held out his hand.

"The car keys?" he suggested.

"You don't trust me to drive?"

"I know the way," he said smoothly, and she couldn't argue with that.

The afternoon sun was gilding the trees with added beauty as they drove down the dirt lane toward the main road, and the autumn foliage began to have its usual effect on Jennifer. For some, spring might be the time for dreaming, for awakening, but for her it had always been this season. Life seemed at its zenith at this time of year, ready to be lived to the fullest, every experience, every little facet of existence to be savored. She sighed deeply, but it was a sigh of contentment, and she suspected the man at the wheel knew the difference.

She stole a glance at him. He had a strong, determined chin, a nose that jutted out somewhat and wasn't quite symmetrical enough for perfection, a broad forehead above those exceptional eyes, and thick hair that, just now, was slightly tousled. As if he could read her mind, he reached up a hand, smoothing his hair back, but it was a wasted effort. A lock sprang forward, brushing his forehead again, and Jennifer smiled.

It wasn't until they reached the little coffee shop that she realized they hadn't said a word to each other in the course of their drive. Then, seated across from each other at a small round maple table, Marc suggested, "The pumpkin pie's terrific here. Would you go for it?"

Jennifer, who seldom ate sweets, found herself nodding, and even agreeing to letting the waitress add a dollop of whipped cream to the pie. Even more strangely, she found herself wishing that this interval could be prolonged. Despite the fact that this man had caused her to have one of the most disturbing afternoons she could remember, despite the fact that he evidently still didn't believe the story she'd told him, she had a nagging desire to get to know him better.

Chapter Two

Marc Bouchard stirred cream into his coffee and warned himself to count to ten, to slow down. This woman sitting across from him was having an alarming effect on his pulse rate.

If she was a thief, she was the most beautiful thief he'd ever seen, he thought whimsically. And he'd dealt with a fair number of thieves in his time.

In a way, it would be interesting if she were a lady Raffles. But she wasn't. He was sure of that. Common sense and experience had convinced him of her innocence even before he'd turned his van into the driveway at the Gray house and had gotten his first glimpse of her standing in the doorway, her proud head tilted at a defiant angle as she faced the two Thrussington police officers.

Thieves didn't linger at the scene of a potential crime. If Jennifer had been about to rip off the Gray house—there was plenty to rip off in it, Marc conceded—she would have been gone by the time the police arrived. Maybe she'd have stayed around long enough to try to shut off the alarm, but he doubted it. Maybe she'd have answered the phone, but he doubted that too. Usually one shrieking wail of the alarm was enough to send unwanted intruders flying. Instead, Jennifer had remained at the scene. Looking at her surreptitiously, watching her take a forkful of the pumpkin pie he'd ordered for her, he was unexpectedly glad that she hadn't fled, for purely personal reasons. And that didn't make sense at all.

Marc had learned a long time ago to resist being swayed by a beautiful woman. Nevertheless, he was enjoying Jennifer. He was enjoying just being here with her, looking at her. Still, there was a stumbling block yet to be faced. Probably it could be resolved easily enough by simply driving back into Thrussington, stopping by police headquarters, and having a brief chat with Chief Andrews, who had been born in Thrussington and knew everything there was to know both about the locals and the summer residents, whose houses were scattered throughout these Berkshire hills. Andrews would know whether or not Roger Gray had been married before to someone named Jennifer Bentley. Andrews would be able to fill him in. Unaccountably, Marc decided that he would much prefer to hear the story from Jennifer herself.

He said ineptly, "Pie's good, isn't it?"

Her eyes were an incredibly clear shade of gray. Looking into them, Marc felt like a schoolboy out on his first date, bumbling, not knowing what to say next, what to do next. This was so out of character for him that he smiled, an odd little smile that quirked up the corners of his mouth. He was acting like an absolute damned fool, he told himself, but telling himself so didn't seem to help any.

Jennifer said sedately, "The pie's very good."

"They make their own pastries," Marc informed her, nodding in the general vicinity of the coffee-shop kitchen.

"I see."

"Ms. Bentley, or should it be Mrs. Bentley?"

"Ms. Bentley will be fine."

"Look, I'm not trying to make your life difficult."

She surprised him by saying, "I didn't think you were."

"I installed the system for Mrs. Gray right after Labor Day. We talked about it before she left here; she wasn't planning to come back till next spring. She's left the house vacant in the winter for years, she told me that, but there's been an upsurge in break-ins and vandalism around here, just like everywhere else. She'd moved a lot of her paintings here from a house she owns in Boston, and they're very valuable."

Why was he telling her all this? Mark pondered. But Jennifer only said quietly, "Yes, I know." Julia Gray was one of the leading contemporary artists in the United States, and her original paintings were each worth a small fortune.

"I tried to phone her after the system was installed to give her the code number," Marc continued, "but she'd already left for Greece. I figured she'd get in touch with me when she got back...."

"She probably would have," Jennifer pointed out. "The accident upset all of Julia's plans. She'll be in the hospital, or near it, for at least another month. I say near it, because they may release her if she can lease a place to stay nearby. She needs daily therapy, and they've told her they'd rather do it there, for the time being. Later, she can be turned over to a therapist who'll come to the house, or maybe I can be taught how to handle whatever's needed." Jennifer paused. "We haven't gotten around to that yet," she confessed.

"Do you live with Mrs. Gray?" Marc asked her.

"No," she said. "I have my own apartment in Back Bay. Julia's still living in the family home out in Chestnut Hill, but she's said for a long time she wants to sell it, especially now that Roger's established on the West Coast."

It seems to Marc that she stumbled slightly over Roger Gray's name.

"That's why she moved her paintings out here," Jennifer concluded.

It made sense. Everything she was saying made sense. Marc swallowed another bite of his pumpkin pie, then asked, "Did you say you've been divorced from Roger Gray for four years?"

"Approximately."

"I see."

"Do you, Mr. Bouchard?" The challenge in her voice made Marc feel as if he didn't see much of anything, he, who'd been at the top of his profession until he'd had his own unfortunate accident, and who'd been known for cutting through expert alibis, red tape, and just about everything else to ferret out the truth.

"Perhaps if you'd been in my position today you'd have done the same thing," Marc found himself suggesting to her. And thought privately, *My God! She's got me on the defensive.*

He couldn't remember when he'd ever been put on the defensive professionally, so he had to hand it to her for this. He'd seldom let himself be put on the defensive privately, for that matter, only Helen had gotten away with it...and that was water long, long under the bridge.

These days he could think of Helen without any feelings surging up at all. The pain was gone.

Jennifer Bentley asked, "How long have you been in Thrussington, Mr. Bouchard?"

"Nearly four years," he told her.

"So...evidently I left, and then you came," she conjectured.

He was surprised. "You lived here?" he asked her.

"Summers. Two summers, when I was married to Roger."

He smiled wryly. "No wonder you know the house so well."

She smiled faintly herself. "Did you think I'd been given a diagram?" she queried. "The safe's located behind the oil painting in the study sort of thing?"

He grinned at this, relieved to see that she had a sense of humor about the situation he'd put her into.

"Is there a safe behind the oil painting in the study?" he asked her, keeping his tone light.

"Which painting?" she shot back.

"You've got me," he confessed, laughing.

"Julia doesn't have a safe," Jennifer offered. Then she added, "I wish she did. It would make my job a lot easier."

Marc hesitated. He hoped she'd fill him in about the job she was referring to without his having to ask her about it, and after a moment she did.

"Julia has some papers at the house she wants me to bring into Boston for her so she can go over them with her attorney," she said. "Her will, among other things. The deed to the house here. Some other odds and ends, all of them quite important. They're documents that should be in a safe deposit box in a Boston bank. Julia tends to be much too casual about things like that. But," Jennifer finished, again surprising him, "that's a part of her charm."

"I don't know her that well," Marc said somewhat regretfully. He was wishing that he did know Julia Gray better, because maybe she would fill him in on some of the things he'd like to know about Jennifer Bentley.

"She's the most terrific person I've ever met," Jennifer told him. "So vibrant, so vital. She exudes life. She hasn't lost her zest, even though she had to cancel the major part of a trip she'd been wanting to make for years because of what she calls her stupid fall. She's been an inspiration to me and...a very good friend."

Again she was surprising him, and he couldn't hold back the question. "Yet, she's your ex-mother-in-law?"

"Yes," Jennifer nodded. "When I knew that Roger and I were going to divorce, I think what I feared the most was that my relationship with Julia would suffer. I hadn't counted on her. I hadn't taken into consideration the fact that she can handle situations that would upset most people. I—"

She broke off, and he was sure she felt she'd said too much to him. He said gently, "Look, why don't we head back to the house so you can look for the papers you're talking about before it gets too dark. There's no electricity on in the place, remember?"

Jennifer's eyes widened. "Are you saying that you've decided to believe me?" she asked him.

"Yes," he told her, and added, "I never really doubted you in the first place." Which, odd though it might seem to her, was the truth.

Jennifer mused over this last remark of Marc Bouchard's as they drove back toward the Gray house. If he hadn't doubted her, why had he insisted that they verify her presence in the house with Julia, after hearing her story? Why had he been so suspicious, so disbelieving when she'd told him she'd been married to Roger?

True, everyone around knew that Roger was now married to a movie star and was living in California. It occurred to Jennifer that Roger had left this scene, just as she had, before Marc Bouchard had arrived on it.

"Where did you come from?" she asked him suddenly, following her own train of thought.

He looked across at her, startled. "What?"

"Where did you live before you came to Thrussington?"

"New York," he said with a brevity that telegraphed his dislike of being questioned.

Jennifer felt a pleasant little twinge of triumph. So...he liked being on the interrogating end but he didn't like being interrogated. So much for that, she decided, and plunged on. "Did you have an alarm-systems business in New York?"

"No."

She waited for him to say more, and when he didn't, persisted. "What did you do?"

He turned toward her at that. "Curious, aren't you?" he asked bluntly, but he softened the words with a smile.

She smiled back. "It's something of tit for tat, wouldn't you say?"

He laughed at this. "Okay. I suppose it is. All right. I was with the New York City Police Department."

"A policeman?" This surprised her. He didn't look like her concept of a policeman.

"In the beginning," he conceded. "By the time I left I was with a detective division involved in some pretty special investigations." His work had been extremely specialized—classified. He'd worked in areas where one pledged oneself to secrecy for the rest of one's life, he mused.

"Didn't you like what you were doing?" Her question broke his train of thought.

He reflected on this. "Like it? I don't know that it was a question of liking or not liking. I was trained for it and...I was good at what I did." Now that it was all over he could say that.

"Yet you left?"

His "gimpy leg," as he'd put it. It came to Jennifer that this obviously was why his career had come to an end. She'd assumed the limp was temporary; now she realized it must be permanent. The realization made her feel foolish as well as inquisitive. She'd stumbled into areas he hadn't wanted to talk about just to get even with him. She wished she'd bitten her tongue first.

Again, as if he could read her mind, he said evenly, "It's okay. I've adjusted."

"I'm sorry," Jennifer said. And meant it.

"That I'm stuck with a lame leg?" He shot her a quizzical glance. "You don't have to be. It's hardly your fault."

"No," she said. "I mean, yes. I mean—"

"There's no reason to be self-conscious, Jennifer," he said, using her name with a deliberation that made her know he knew exactly what he was doing. "I got over being self-conscious about my handicap a long time ago. I'm lucky to be able to hobble around. At first, they thought I'd never walk again."

"What I meant was," she said, trying to match his coolness, "I didn't mean to pry."

"But you were curious?"

She was sure her cheeks were flaming. "Yes," she admitted. "Yes, I was curious."

"I was shot in the course of an operation that involved drugs. Millions of dollars worth of drugs," he told her. "That's about all I can say about it, except that the result was successful, regardless of my injury." He drew a long breath. "Subsequently," he said, "I spent a couple of years in and out of various hospitals. Surgery a number of times, therapy, all the rest of it. So I have a certain empathy for what Julia Gray must be going through right now. Afterward, they retired me at an impressive ceremony where even the mayor made a speech. They gave me a medal, and put me out to pasture. So I came to Thrussington."

"Alone?" she asked.

"Are you asking me if I'm married, Jennifer?" he teased.

Damn it, he could read her mind! "I...wondered," she fumbled.

He laughed. "I'm flattered," he said, only adding to her confusion. "I was married. I'm not married. It would seem that you and I have been travelers in the same kind of boat."

He was turning into Julia's driveway as he said this, and he came to a stop in front of the house, exercising more restraint than he had earlier in the day so no dust cloud rose to blot Jennifer's vision.

He climbed out of the car and she watched him walk around to her side. He'd shrugged off his jacket in the restaurant, giving her a full view of his broad chest, his muscular arms, and a crazy little spiral of something she had to recognize as desire had twisted inside her. Now she felt it again, an emotional corkscrew that reminded her there was still passion alive in people. She hadn't experienced passion for a long, long time. Sometimes she wondered if she'd ever really experienced it at all.

Marc opened the car door for her, then proffered a hand to help her get out. His grip was warm, she let him clasp her fingers in his and, inevitably, their eyes met. Jennifer felt as if the breath were being drawn out of her. It was all she could do not to sway toward this man. *Let yourself fall so he can catch you,* some impish alter ego urged, and she stepped out of the car hastily, mounting a quick resistance in the process.

"I'll come in with you and hang around," Marc suggested, and the joy went out of the afternoon, a cloud come to blot her sun.

"You still don't trust me, do you?" she queried.

"Of course I trust you," he told her quickly. "It isn't that. I don't intend to put through a call to Julia Gray again, if that'll convince you. It's just that time's getting on, and I thought you might be more comfortable out here with someone else around."

Darkness came quickly in the low mountains; Jennifer had forgotten about that. Darkness came quicker by October, too, and they were almost at the middle of the month.

"When we switch the clock back in a couple of weeks, it'll be pitch black by now," Marc said reflectively, glancing up at the sky, gold where the sun had gone behind the trees.

"We should keep daylight savings all year round," Jennifer opined.

"I don't know. It's kind of nice here on fall and winter afternoons, when it's dark outside but you have a fire going in the fireplace and everything's warm and...cozy," he said.

"I suppose so. I've never been in the country in the winter," she confessed.

"Never?"

"Never."

They were at the front door as he spoke, and he reached into his pocket for a key. He would have a key to the house, of course, Jennifer reminded herself, and watched him turn it in the lock. He went ahead of her into the house to stop just inside the door, dealing with numbers on a small panel that was a duplicate of the one in the kitchen.

So, he'd activated his alarm system before they left the house. It occurred to Jennifer that he was a man who would miss very few tricks, who seldom slipped.

Already the rooms were losing the sunlight, and she said, "I hope Julia's remembered correctly where she's stashed all these papers. They're supposed to be in a flat metal file box on the closet shelf in her bedroom."

"I'll go up with you," Marc told her quickly, and she wondered if maybe he didn't trust her so completely after all. Nevertheless, she led the way up the stairs, deliberately slowing her pace a bit because of his bad leg.

He kept up with her though, and he followed her down the hall, seeming to move easily enough, with only a slightly off-beat tempo to the sound of his footsteps giving a clue to his disability. This was enough, though, to make her think about the experience he'd endured. He'd left out volumes in what he'd told her, she was sure of that. She could only guess at what his feelings had been when he'd discovered that he was permanently disabled, disabled enough to have to retire from the police department, his career shattered in midstream.

There must have been tremendous frustration involved in everything that had happened to him...and he'd been married as well. Had his divorce had anything to do with the accident's aftermath? Questions tumbled around in Jennifer's head.

Julia's room was in a front corner of the house, a spacious chamber furnished with beautiful antiques, complete to a four-poster with a frilled white canopy. Because the light was fading fast, Jennifer went directly to the big closet and looked in the corner of the second shelf, where Julia had assured her she'd find the metal file box. As she'd more than half suspected would be the case, it wasn't there, which was typical Julia. She had a way of moving things, especially important things, from one place to another, and then completely forgetting having done so.

Muttering impatiently, Jennifer scanned the full length of the second shelf, then the first shelf. Next she opened the built-in chest in the corner of the closet and went through all its four drawers. After that she examined the floor space under the clothes bags filling one side of the closet, and then delved into the bags themselves, just in case Julia had decided one of them would provide a good hiding space. The quest was fruitless.

She emerged from the closet to see Marc standing at the window, looking out over the front lawn to the beautiful stretch of pine woods beyond that extended up the hillside. His back to her, he was in silhouette, and for a small interval of time Jennifer just looked at him, and again she felt that spiraling corkscrew twist inside her. Crazy, she thought, but it was as if her life juices, long dormant, had started to flow again. She could sense a marvelous vitality tingling from her toes to her fingertips; she could feel herself growing warm with feelings toward this man, feelings she couldn't give credence to. She hadn't known him long enough to think about him like that, she chided herself, and their introduction to each other had been totally bizarre. Yet she continued to feast her eyes on him, admiring him, and shivering a little because of the unexpected, the very unexpected, reaction he was having upon her.

"Marc," she said, her voice pitched a little lower than it usually was because this unprecedented "something" seemed even to have invaded her throat.

He turned. "Yes?"

"I wondered...the light's not too great, but could you look on the top closet shelf. I can't see up that far."

Jennifer was tall, but he was considerably taller. She'd already noted that her head came just about to his chin.

"Sure," he said easily, and moved toward the closet.

Jennifer stood aside, letting him get through the door. Then she moved closer as she watched him exploring the top shelf, hoping as she watched that he'd suddenly produce the metal box. But he didn't.

He swung around, saying, "It's not there." But he hadn't realized Jennifer had edged so close and, trying to avoid her, he went off balance. Jennifer heard him swear softly as he came down on his bad leg. He clutched outward, trying to stave off a fall, inadvertently grabbing her shoulders as he did so.

He was a big man, and this nearly threw her off balance herself. But she quickly steadied, letting him hold on to her, her breath coming more rapidly, her pulse beginning to accelerate.

He was so close to her, his warmth seeped into her. His heartbeat thudded, pumping steadily through the opening in the red wool jacket. She smelled his woodsy scent, clean and fresh, mixed with soap and some of the pine that filled the air outdoors.

He lurched slightly, regaining his balance. Then he dropped his hands from her shoulders and said lightly, "I'm sorry. Sometimes the damned leg lets me down when I need it the most. I didn't hurt you, did I?"

"No," Jennifer said a bit hollowly. She was feeling deprived with his arms gone away from her. She wished that instead of dropping his hands from her shoulders he'd drawn her toward him, taken her into his embrace.

Are you going crazy, Jennifer Bentley? she asked herself.

Marc said, "We really need some light in here."

Do we? Jennifer posed the question silently, not at all sure she agreed with him.

"I have a pretty strong flashlight in the van. I'll get it," he suggested. "We can go over this room, then. If Mrs. Gray told you the file box is in here, I daresay we'll come across it somewhere."

"Somewhere," Jennifer said direly, "but not necessarily in here."

"Did you say you had a dinner date in Boston?" he asked her.

"Well...yes," she allowed. She'd completely forgotten about her engagement with Kenneth Trent.

"Maybe you'd better call your date," Marc told her. "It's almost five. There's no way you could make Boston before nine or nine-thirty even if you left right now. But maybe you favor late dinner hours?"

"Sometimes. But you're right. I should call Ken."

There was a phone on Julia's bedside table, and she moved toward it, conscious that Marc was leaving the room. She heard his uneven footsteps in the hall, then descending the stairs.

There was barely enough light left to see the dial, but she managed, hoping that she'd catch Ken at the publishing house. Often he left earlier than this, but as it happened, he was still working. At first he appeared to be delighted to hear from her, but when he asked where she was and she told him she was in the Berkshires she could hear the disapproval in his voice.

"The Berkshires, for God's sake," he protested. "What are you doing out there?"

"I came on an errand for Julia. I thought I'd be back in Boston by seven at the latest," she said. Their engagement was for eight. "Ken, I'm sorry."

"It's okay, Jen," he told her. "I have reservations at a new French place that's supposed to be fantastic, but we'll try it another time."

Ken sounded resigned, which was the way he usually sounded when things weren't going his way. But the resignation was a camouflage for an underlying anger that Jennifer had encountered before and hadn't especially liked. She enjoyed Ken's company, and he was her publisher. It was important in a business sense to be on good terms with him. But there were other publishers who handled the type of children's books—complete with watercolor illustrations—that she did. She'd told herself a couple of months ago that if Ken became too possessive, she'd have to think seriously about making a change. As it was, she was afraid she was going to learn the hard way that business and pleasure seldom mixed well.

She mollified him because it was easier than getting into an argument just now, and agreed to dine with him the following night. Only after she'd hung up did she stop to think that she'd planned to have dinner at the hospital with Julia tomorrow night. Julia had said she could arrange it, and Jennifer had no doubt at all that she could.

Finding the file box, on the other hand, was something that did have to be accomplished now if she was going to get back to Boston by midnight. As it was, she hated the thought of going back into the city by herself so late at night.

Though Marc's flashlight shone a powerful beam, Jennifer soon discovered it wasn't the most effective way of conducting a search. By the time they'd canvassed the room unsuccessfully, it was totally dark outside, and Jennifer shook her head in defeat.

"I don't know where to begin next," she admitted.

"Nowhere tonight, I'd say," Marc told her. "Look, let me take you over to my place. I'll get a fire going, I'll mix you a drink, and you can call Mrs. Gray from there.

Maybe she'll be able to remember where she moved the box...if she did move it, that is."

Jennifer glanced up at him quickly, trying to read his face in the aura cast by the flashlight. "You don't think someone broke in here and stole it, do you?" she demanded.

"With my alarm system activated?" He grinned. "No way," he assured her.

"Marc, the file box could have been stolen before you put the alarm in."

"I doubt that, unless it happened while Mrs. Gray and her friend were still in residence," he said.

Jennifer grimaced at his use of the word *friend*. He was speaking of Ricardo Castel, she knew without even asking, and he was not only a friend of Julia's he was, allegedly, her fiancé. Jennifer used the word *allegedly* to herself every time she thought of their relationship, as though this possible disclaimer could keep it from being true.

"You put in the alarm system immediately after Julia left?" she asked Marc.

"The following day," he said, "and when I came out here there was no evidence that there'd been any intruders. No, I think she moved the box, just as you say she has a habit of doing with things, Jennifer. No more than that. Probably she'll be able to tell you what she's done with it and then we can come back and get it. Come on," he urged.

He led the way down the stairs, shining the light back for her so that she wouldn't stumble. Outside the house he took her arm so she wouldn't falter walking across the uneven ground, since she was wearing high heels. This brought back the memory of the summers when she'd lived here in Julia's house. She'd always worn flats, and Roger had hated them.

"I think this time maybe we should take the van and leave your car here," Marc suggested. He opened the van door for her. "It's a high step," he warned. "Here, let me help you."

She felt his arms around her, hoisting her upward; inadvertently she let herself go limp, let him hold her. For a long moment their touching hovered between assistance and embrace. Then Jennifer asserted her own muscles, slid into place, and Marc clanged the door shut.

As he started up the motor she asked, "Where do you live?"

"On the outskirts of the village," he said. "I was lucky. I rented a house from Jack Thornton, a friend of mine who wanted to move closer to Pittsfield because he's a reporter on the *Berkshire Eagle* that's published there. It's he who got me to come up here in the first place. He thought they could use a company specializing in security and alarms around this area; there are so many summer places full of valuable things in these hills. For that matter, so many of the local people go south in the winter as well. I'm not without competition, of course, but I think I do offer a pretty good service. I've done well.

"Jack's a local," he added. "We went to college together...."

The words were out before she could halt them. "You went to college?"

"Yes," he said, and added dryly, "You'll find that many if not most of today's police officers are not entirely illiterate, Jennifer."

"Marc, I didn't mean—" She broke off and smiled at him ruefully. "Damn, but I do seem to have a way of putting my foot in my mouth with you," she admitted.

"Retaliation, because I nearly got you pinched by the Thrussington cops," he said smoothly, and what could have been a moment of tension passed.

Was he always that way? she wondered. Did he always bridge awkward situations so effortlessly? It was a knack she envied. She tended to flounder, to make things worse instead of better on such occasions. Marc's expertise, she decided, indicated that he'd been called upon to handle a lot of awkward situations with smoothness in his line of work.

There was a late harvest moon in the sky tonight, huge and golden. "Halloween," Jennifer said.

He glanced toward her. "Halloween?"

"Soon it'll be Halloween. The moon makes me think of it. It must be terrific around here at Halloween. Marvelously spooky."

He laughed. "Marvelously spooky?" he quoted. "Well, I suppose it is. I get a fair share of trick-or-treaters at my place."

"Fields full of pumpkins and dried cornstalks, ghosts, goblins, witches," Jennifer said.

"You paint word pictures," he accused.

She chuckled. "It's what I do," she told him.

"What do you mean?"

"I write children's books and I illustrate them myself," she said.

"Really? That's fantastic. I'll have to go to the bookstore in the village first thing in the morning and buy one of your books," he promised.

"Marc, they're mostly for seven- to ten-year-olds," she protested. "Anyway, I'll mail you one."

She liked the thought of doing this. It would keep a link between them once she went back to Boston.

The lights of the village twinkled in greeting. Marc drove down a tree-lined street and parked in front of a small house. "It's really a cottage," he said. "Here, let me go on ahead and get some lights on."

It was more cottage than house, and it was charming. Charming and old. Jennifer noted the wide floorboards and the wainscoting in the living room and tiny dining room, and the steep stairs that went up to the second level. There were handhewn beams across the living room ceiling, multipaned windows, a stone fireplace.

"I love it," she said enthusiastically.

"I'm glad you do," Marc told her. Then he added without any change of expression, "Because you'll probably be spending the night here."

Chapter Three

There was a big, comfortable couch in front of the fireplace. Jennifer had been about to sink down into it; now she straightened hastily.

"I think you'd better take me back to Julia's so I can get my car," she told Marc Bouchard, his incredible statement ringing in her ears.

"Whoa, there," he cautioned her. "You're jumping to conclusions, Jennifer."

"Am I?" she countered. She tried to inject a light touch. "I get the impression I'm being kidnapped," she said.

Kidnapped. The word had a bad association, forcing waves of memories to surge toward her. During her growing-up years in New York, Jennifer's parents had always feared that she might be kidnapped. She had been watched too much, protected too much. Finally, when she'd broken away from her family and gone off on her own, she'd changed her name. Not changed it, really, but eliminated a part of it. She'd dropped the Chatsworth-Graham that was so significant, and since then had used only her first and middle name. Jennifer Bentley. It wasn't much of a camouflage. It had never really been tested over the intervening years.

This man had been a detective in New York, she remembered. Could he possibly know that she was not merely Jennifer Bentley but Jennifer Bentley Chatsworth-Graham? An heiress. Her father, Hugh Chatsworth-Graham, was very, very rich and she was his only child.

Jennifer bit her lip, suddenly miserable. She didn't want Marc Bouchard to know who she was. Every relationship she'd ever had, no matter how casual, had been altered once people learned who her father was.

Marc said abruptly, "What's come over you, Jennifer? You look as if you're seeing some of those Halloween horrors you spoke about."

"No," she answered somewhat shakily. "Seriously, Marc," she added then, "I'd like you to take me back to Julia's."

"That's ridiculous," he told her gently. "Look, I didn't mean to cause you to push a panic button. It seems logical to me that you should spend the night in Thrussington, that's all. You'll have to be here in the morning to find Mrs. Gray's box."

He was right. Jennifer nodded slowly. "I agree," she told him, the memories still not entirely banished.

"Good," he said, and she became aware that he'd been almost as tense as she'd been. Relaxed, he added, "Make yourself comfortable. It'll only take a minute to get the fire going, then I'll fix us a drink."

"You needn't go to all that trouble," she protested. "Do you have a phone?" she added.

"Sure. It's in the kitchen. You want to call Mrs. Gray?"

"Yes, but first I want to find a place to stay. I'll need the directory. Or maybe you can recommend a motel?"

He grinned. "I could, but it wouldn't do you much good."

"Why not?"

"We're coming up on the Columbus Day weekend, Jennifer," Marc said patiently. "It's peak foliage time, and more of a holiday around here than the Fourth of July. People come from all over to see the autumn leaves, and I don't think there's a vacant room to be had for miles around."

Jennifer was just beginning to relax, but his statement unraveled her. "You must be mistaken," she insisted.

"I'm afraid not," he said cheerfully. "That's why I said I imagine you'll be spending the night here." He looked down into her astonished face and a wry smile twisted his lips. "I have a guest room upstairs that's not in use," he said. "It's all yours, with a private bath to boot. I think you'll be comfortable."

Comfortable? With this man sleeping in the same house as her? A tantalizing vision of Marc Bouchard lying in bed, a lock of that dark hair straggling over his forehead, taunted Jennifer and she swallowed hard. Being alone with him all night would be as dangerous as transforming oneself into a moth, then deciding to fly around a candle flame.

As if he could read her mind, he said levelly, "I'm offering you my hospitality, and nothing more. Does that satisfy you?"

The word stung, and Jennifer felt unaccustomed heat surge into her cheeks. Her throat went dry with embarrassment because he'd read her so accurately.

"If you don't mind," she said, gathering up the shreds of her dignity and draping them around her, trying to make whole cloth out of them, "I'll try the telephone."

"As you wish," he said, nodding. "The directory's right next to it."

There was a small stool next to the telephone, and Jennifer perched on it. She turned to the yellow pages in the directory and meticulously started calling motel after motel, inn after inn, lodging house after lodging house, with a total lack of success.

Finally she was convinced that unless she drove up and down the area streets ringing doorbells, there was not a bed to be had in the Thrussington area, or as far afield as Lenox and Lee and Stockbridge in one direction, and Pittsfield in the other.

By the time she'd reached this conclusion, Marc Bouchard had come into the kitchen and she heard him dropping ice cubes into glasses. After a moment he thrust a squat tumbler toward her and said, "Here. I hope you like bourbon—fixed up a bit."

Usually, Jennifer confined her drinking to wine, but she had no objection to having something stronger tonight. She sipped the drink, and found that he'd concocted a bourbon sour which, she suspected, was not half as innocuous as the taste would lead her to believe.

She gazed at him over the rim of her glass, defeated. "You're right," she conceded.

He smiled. "I won't say I told you so."

"Thanks," she said ruefully. "I guess this means I really will have to ask you to take me back to Julia's so I can get my car. I won't bother to call Julia from here," she added. "I'll stop by the hospital and see her in the morning instead."

"Okay," he agreed. "But why don't we enjoy our drink in front of the fire and then have some dinner before you do anything?"

She considered this. An extra hour really wouldn't make that much difference. She was going to be on the highway late anyway, getting into the city late. There was always a parking problem in the area where she lived, and she didn't look forward to wandering through the Back Bay streets to her town house alone. But there was no alternative.

"All right," she said not too graciously, thinking about the drive ahead.

She caught an expression in Marc Bouchard's eyes that caused her to hesitate. Disappointment? Was that what it was? Annoyance? Maybe a tinge of anger?

"I suppose I should be flattered, in a way, to think you evidently find the thought of spending a night in my house so perilous," he said evenly. "I don't suppose anything I could say will change your mind, but just for the record, I'd like to state that I don't make advances toward unwilling subjects. It's not my style."

Hurt? Was that what it was? The expression was still lingering in those very blue eyes, and suddenly Jennifer felt ashamed of herself. If she found the thought of staying in his house "perilous," as he'd put it, it was because of the reaction this man provoked in her, not because of any move on his part.

She managed a smile. "I wouldn't think it would need to be your style," she told him, which was true enough. No man as attractive as he was should have any difficulty in finding any number of willing "subjects."

He grinned. "I'll take that as a compliment," he said. "Now, are you going to waste the best fire I've ever made?"

Again he'd smoothed over a moment of tension. And as they sat together in front of the fire, Jennifer on the couch, Marc in a nearby armchair, he kept things between them on an easy, even keel.

They talked about Thrussington, and he told her what it was like to live in a small town after having spent all of one's life in one of the world's biggest cities.

"Are you a Bostonian?" he asked at one point. "You don't have the accent."

She stiffened. She didn't want to identify herself with his city, yet she also didn't want to lie to him. She had the feeling that if she were to utter even a harmless fib he'd somehow find her out.

She said carefully, "No, matter of fact I'm from New York too."

"The city?"

She nodded. "Yes."

"What part?"

She hesitated. "Manhattan." He'd already told her that he'd been born and brought up in Brooklyn. Flatbush.

"Where in Manhattan?" he persisted.

"Well..." She hesitated again, this time with a tight smile. "I was born in a midtown hospital."

"I'm asking where you lived," he retorted.

"In the East Sixties."

The East Sixties encompassed a lot of territory. Ethnic enclaves. A wide economic spectrum. It was a safe enough statement.

"Brothers and sisters?" he asked next.

"No. I was an only child."

"I was one of seven," he said. "About in the middle, age-wise. Growing up in our household was an experience. My father is French, very French. He was born in France. My mother was born here, but she's of French ex-

traction. Their families were friends, that's how they met."
He smiled. "My father was reasonably liberal with his
sons, but extremely strict with his daughters. As a result,
my three sisters were all little hellions."

She smiled at this. "Your parents are still living?"

He nodded. "They moved to Florida several years ago.
They live in a mobile home park down there and they seem
happy with their life-style." He added after a brief hesitation, "One of my older brothers was killed in Vietnam.
The rest of my siblings are married and scattered all over
the country, doing all sorts of things. I have a brother
who's a doctor in California, another who's an accoun-
tant in Chicago. One of my sisters is a teacher; she lives in
Michigan. My father was great for education. He'd never
had much formal education himself and like a lot of first-
generation people in this country, he wanted his kids to
have everything he hadn't had. He pushed us to both work
and study hard. He wanted me to go to law school. Both
he and my mother were upset when I went on the police
force after I got out of college."

"What about your wife?" Jennifer asked him.

He looked startled. "What about her?"

"Was she French too?"

"No. Helen was of Irish extraction. She lived on the
same block in Flatbush, we went through school together." He flashed Jennifer a rueful smile. "One of those
things," he said. "We married too soon, we were too
young, neither of us knew what we were doing."

"Children?"

"No, we didn't have any kids. It made it easier when we
broke up. What about you?"

"No, Roger and I didn't have any children," she told
him quietly.

"How did you meet Roger?"

"At a party some mutual friends gave. It was right after he'd published his book. *Rendezvous*. You may have read it. They made it into a movie."

"I read the book and saw the movie," Marc Bouchard told her. "I didn't especially like either."

She smiled at this. Neither had she, but she knew hers had been a minority opinion.

"So," he probed, "you met Roger Gray at the time when he'd just become a successful author, and you married him, and...?"

"He wasn't all that successful when I met him," she said. "The book had just come out, and it took a while for it to climb onto the best seller list. It was around Christmas when we met. You know how New York is at Christmas. Lots of lights, lots of excitement..."

"Yes."

"Roger walked me home that night after the party. We stopped at Rockefeller Plaza to watch the skaters. The Christmas tree was up, I suppose you could say there was magic in the air. It helped, all that atmosphere."

"Helped?" he queried.

"To make me think I was in love with him. To fall in love with him."

"There is a difference," Marc pointed out gravely.

"Yes, I know there is." Dealing with this subject was making her uncomfortable. "Anyway," she said, trying to reach a conclusion, "we also married too soon. We'd known each other only a few weeks...."

He let it go at that. After a moment he asked, "Are your parents still alive?"

Jennifer said carefully, "My mother died when I was twelve. My father remarried a couple of years later. He and my stepmother have an apartment in New York, where they live most of the time."

She was not about to tell him that the apartment in New York, a sumptuous Fifth Avenue penthouse, was just one of her father's residences. Or that he also had a yacht that could traverse the Atlantic and sometimes did. These days, he mostly preferred jet travel, then leasing a yacht when he got to Italy or Majorca or Greece or wherever he was going. He'd always had a great affinity for the sea.

"Do you see much of them?" Marc asked her.

"My father and my stepmother? No. Occasionally I visit them."

"Same with me," Marc told her. "I go down to Florida to see my parents when I can, but that's not too often. They don't have much room in their place, and they get insulted if I suggest putting up at a motel. Usually I wind up sleeping on a cot in the mobile home. It's remarkable, though, what my mother can manage to cook up for me in a kitchen that's about as big as most people's hall closet."

He stood. "Speaking of cooking..." he began.

"Marc, honestly," she protested at once. "You don't have to fix anything for me."

"Then suppose I cook for myself, and you share what I make?" he suggested. "I'm into Chinese food these days. Want to come see what I can do with a wok, or would you prefer to bask by the fireside?"

She preferred to watch him. She perched on a little stool in the kitchen as Marc surprised her yet again, this time with his culinary performance.

"I took an adult ed course in Chinese cooking at the regional high school last year," he confessed as he sliced celery and water chestnuts, bamboo sprouts, mushrooms, and an assortment of other vegetables on a wooden board. She watched him turn the vegetables into a wok in which oil was already sizzling, stirring them with a long pair of chopsticks which, he said, were designed especially for cooking. Then he added shrimp and chunks of fish, seasonings, and before she could quite believe he'd accomplished all this he was putting a steaming bowl of food before her.

It was so delicious that Jennifer, who'd not even been hungry, asked for seconds, and Marc smiled his pleasure. Afterward they both had a demitasse in front of the fireplace, and wafers filled with chocolate which, he admitted, were store bought.

Replete with marvelous-tasting food, mesmerized somewhat by the fire's orange glow and its warmth, Jennifer felt more thoroughly at peace than she had for a long time.

Marc veered away from personal reflection in their conversation now. They discussed things like music and art and movies and plays and discovered that they both liked Dustin Hoffman and Tennessee Williams's *Streetcar Named Desire*, Mozart, early rock and roll records, and that they also shared a fondness for the French Impressionists.

"I used to wonder whether if I saved a percentage of my salary each week I'd have enough to buy a genuine Renoir by the time I was eighty," Marc told her.

Jennifer was at one end of the couch at this point, and he was at the other, his legs propped up on a hassock which he'd first offered her, and which she'd declined. He looked comfortable and relaxed, and the firelight emphasized his features. Jennifer felt as if she could watch him forever, the play of expressions on his face when he talked were so varied; he was a person with many facets to his character. She felt that she could listen to his voice forever too; its deep sexiness washed over her and she shivered slightly. It was essential to keep her distance. Wisdom warned her of that, yet she yearned to slide closer to Marc and wondered what he'd do if she yielded to impulse.

She fought a brief battle with herself, then she said reluctantly, "We'd really better go get my car so I can be on my way, Marc."

He turned toward her, his eyes looking almost black in this light. "There's no way I'm going to stand for your driving back to Boston tonight, Jennifer," he said simply. "You might be safe enough on the highway, but it's stupid for a woman to wander around city streets by herself late at night. It would be bad enough if you had to, but you don't have to. You can take my word for that much, can't you?"

"Yes," she said reluctantly. "But—"

"No buts," he told her firmly. He stood up, and the sight of his tall, lean figure outlined by the firelight stirred Jennifer's poorly suppressed feelings again.

"It's too late to phone Mrs. Gray," he said. "You can call her in the morning, or we can go out to the house and take another look first, if you like. Right now I'm going to go upstairs and get some towels and turn the electric blanket on for you," he told her. "Just make yourself comfortable till I get back."

Comfortable? She nearly laughed aloud once he'd left her, because she was totally on edge, not with nerves or tension this time but with desire.

No one she'd ever met in her life had evoked so much so soon in her. It took an effort to remember that in so many ways she and Marc Bouchard were poles apart, their lifestyles entirely different. Tomorrow she'd find Julia's blasted metal box, then she'd go back to Boston with it, and that would be that. She'd send Marc a couple of her books, autographed, with a thank-you note. Probably he'd write a thank-you note in return. But that would be the end of this strange and wonderful encounter, and realizing this she felt a sharp sense of loss. Nevertheless, it would be folly to try to pursue it, to try to pursue him. It was almost certain to be a losing game, and she'd played too many losing games. Ultimately, Marc would find out that she was Hugh Chatsworth-Graham's daughter, and after that things would never be the same between them. She'd yet to meet a man who couldn't become blinded by the sight of dollars, lots of dollars, glittering before his eyes, she thought cynically.

No. Better to remember this single evening they'd shared. The Chinese dinner he'd cooked for her, the time talking in front of the fireplace, their mutual confidences, the closeness that made it seem impossible she'd known him for only a few hours.

Damn, Jennifer said, mouthing the word silently, aiming it at the flickering flames. Damn, damn, damn!

After Jennifer had gone to bed Marc went back into the living room and sat down in front of the fireplace, switching on a table lamp and picking up a book he'd been reading.

The book dealt with the French revolution, and it was interesting, but Marc began to wish he'd opted to read it in the original French. The translation wasn't especially good, and made the prose heavy going.

Probably, he conceded, it would have been impossible to concentrate on any book tonight. His mind wasn't in this room at all. It was upstairs, centered upon the maple bed in which Jennifer must now be lying, wearing the pajamas—his pajamas—that he'd set out for her.

She'd be lost in them, of course. He chuckled at the vision of Jennifer being lost in his pajamas, and then he felt a pang of longing for her so sharp he nearly gasped aloud.

Incredible, how much he wanted her! He'd never seen her in his life until this afternoon, but what a job she'd done on him! Physically, she appealed to him tremendously; it had been all he could do to keep his distance when they'd been sitting on this couch together. Once he'd nearly moved toward her, ready to take her in his arms, to pull her toward him, to feel her heartbeat as he'd felt it when he'd literally stumbled into her arms this afternoon in Julia Gray's closet, of all places.

Marc chuckled. For once, his bad leg had done him a favor. He'd legitimately gone off balance. If he hadn't grabbed Jennifer's shoulders, he would have fallen. But the awkwardness which he usually detested had given him the chance to hold her for just a minute, to feel the softness of her pale gold hair, to smell her sweet scent.

He imagined that he could still smell that elusive, haunting perfume that was faint yet permeating. She intrigued him; she mystified him almost as much as she attracted him physically. She was not an open book. She'd been reluctant in discussing her parents, and he'd sensed that she disliked talking about herself as much as he normally disliked talking about himself. He'd been unusually free in this respect with Jennifer; she'd even gotten him to speak about Helen.

She'd been vague in her answers to his questions though. The East Sixties. Most native New Yorkers were neighborhood-conscious, and they would have been more specific. He'd had the feeling that Jennifer, for some reason, had wanted to conceal the address where she'd lived, and it was impossible not to wonder why. It was impossible not to wonder a great many things about her.

He didn't have a great many facts about Jennifer. An only child who'd been born in a midtown Manhattan hospital, she'd lived in the East Sixties, and had married a writer she'd met at a party, who happened to be the son of one of the most famous artists in the country. Jennifer herself was both a writer and an artist. He reminded himself to go buy one of her books first thing in the morning, even though she'd said she'd mail him one. He wanted to see what sort of thing she did.

Her marriage had ended in divorce, yet she'd stayed on good terms with her mother-in-law, which was somewhat unusual. There seemed no doubt that Jennifer and Julia Gray were very close.

What else? There wasn't much else, Marc thought glumly, except that she lived in a Back Bay apartment in Boston. Alone, he hoped. Tonight she'd had a dinner date with someone named Ken. Was Ken important to her?

Stop chasing wild geese, Marc told himself irritably, and tried to get back to the French Revolution.

Jennifer fell asleep almost immediately. The bed was warm, comfortable, and she liked the feel of Marc's pajama top wrapped around her.

In no time at all, though, she was awake again. She'd heard something—an owl hooting, she thought. A country sound. Something she wasn't accustomed to. It had snapped her out of her slumber, and she lay staring into the darkness, all her senses alert.

Where was Marc? Where did he sleep? There was another room across the hall from her. Just two rooms, in this old Cape Cod-style cottage. But he'd said something about the other room being used for storage.

Was there a bedroom downstairs? Back of the living room perhaps?

Was he asleep? Jennifer wriggled, her body betraying her. It was a long time since she'd been with a man. Things had been good with Roger in that respect at the beginning of their marriage. At least, she supposed they'd been good. She didn't have much experience to judge by. But Roger had grown tired of her before very long. There was no other way to put it. She'd learned, eventually, that no woman could satisfy Roger for very long because he was always looking for something different. Something unattainable.

Had he found this unattainable something with Colleen O'Brien? Jennifer doubted it. She knew Roger too well. If he was staying married to Colleen, it probably was only because it was expedient, for the sake of both their careers. And whether Roger stayed married to his second wife or not wasn't important to her. She'd lost any feeling she'd had for Roger a long time ago, but the hurt, she had to admit, had lingered. A bruise not easily healed. She still flinched when she thought of his rejection at the end of their marriage. He had made her seem so undesirable. Maybe that's why she still avoided deeper relationships with men. Between Roger's effect on her and the strain being her father's daughter had always imposed on her, she inevitably drew back from the thought of getting too close to a man emotionally. At a certain point she always reneged. Before long she was going to renege with Ken. She knew it.

Would she renege with Marc, if she had a chance with him at all?

This was an impossible question to answer, Jennifer told herself sharply and, irritated by her own foolishness, she swung her legs over the edge of the bed and stood up.

Marc's pajama top came to her knees. He'd left the bottoms for her to use, too, and now she slipped them on, pulling in the string around the waistline, then stooping to roll up several inches of pantleg. Only then did she venture forth, moving carefully toward the steep staircase.

There was no way she could get back to sleep tonight without help. Help in the form of a cup of hot milk, and a magazine or book to read until her eyes began to get heavy.

She moved carefully down the stairs, having no idea that Marc might still be awake, and she was about to pass the door that led into the living room when she heard his voice.

"Jennifer?" He spoke out of the darkness, for he'd turned off the lamp and only the firelight's glow, ebbing now, illuminated the room. He repeated her name. "Jennifer?"

He switched on the lamp at his side as he spoke, and Jennifer, in the doorway, could only imagine what a ludicrous picture she must make in his flopping pajamas. She saw his smile, but he only inquired quietly, "Is something the matter?"

"Something woke me up," she confessed. "I—I think it was an owl."

Marc had gotten to his feet and Jennifer moved toward him, narrowing the space between them, not even conscious of what she was doing.

"I thought...I thought maybe if I got some hot milk..." she began. But Mark didn't pick up what she was saying.

She saw that he was devouring her with his eyes, and the longing that had been stirring inside her all evening became insatiable. She was hungry for this man; she wanted him. Nothing else seemed important.

"God," he said, rasping the words as if they were being torn out of him, "you're so beautiful."

"In this?" she choked out, gesturing toward the baggy pajamas.

"In anything. In nothing." He was coming toward her as he spoke, and she met him halfway. He stretched his arms out, and she went into them. He pulled her close to him, lowering his head, his mouth brushing her forehead, her nose, then moving on to claim her lips. His kiss became an invasion, an act of piracy, an invitation that branded Jennifer with its heat and urgency.

His tongue spiraled within her mouth and she clutched at him, her hands beginning to move feverishly across the nape of his neck. Her fingers lost themselves in the thickness of his hair and her body twisted toward him, edging closer, closer, closer. As close as she could get.

His words were almost a moan. "Jennifer, Jennifer...do you know what you're doing?"

She tilted her head back to look up into his eyes. There was one thing she had to be sure of. And when she saw desire that reflected her desire, she knew that this was right. This man wanted her as much as she wanted him. He wanted her for herself alone. He was finding her as irresistible as she was finding him. His expression, the expectancy, the yearning, told her that and more.

"Yes," Jennifer said, "yes, oh, yes, oh, yes. I know exactly what I'm doing, Marc."

"If we start this," he said huskily, "I'll have to have you. You understand that?"

For an answer she tugged at the buttons on the plaid shirt he was wearing, pulling off one of them in the process. She heard it clatter as it hit the hearthstone, and Mark's exultant chuckle followed in its wake.

She felt his hands clasp her waist, untying the pajama string. The baggy pants fell to the floor. She helped him pull the top up over her head. She felt the last of the dying fire warm against her bare skin; she felt herself heated through, as if the glowing embers had invaded her body, imbuing her with passion for the tall man who stood before her, guiding her trembling fingers toward his body, letting her help him divest himself of his clothes. Then he drew her toward him, flesh touching flesh, and Jennifer went out of control. Never before had there been anything like this for her. Never before.

She felt him drawing her toward the couch and she let him guide her. As she sank with him into its softness, she knew she was plunging into ecstasy.

Chapter Four

The fire went out, but neither Marc nor Jennifer noticed. Wrapped in each other's arms, their mutual passion kept them warm.

Marc was a tender and considerate lover. Jennifer was aware that he was ready to match his pace to hers, but there was no need for such a display of patience. Her response to him came from the very wellspring of her being. They meshed as if they had been made for each other. As if they had been fashioned expertly by nature to blend, one with the other, in order to gain the ultimate of all that was masculine and all that was feminine as they touched and caressed and explored and made love in a way that was totally transcendental.

It was only when they were lying quietly on the couch, Jennifer nestled in the secure circle of Marc's arms, that she shivered slightly.

He said quickly, "You're cold."

"No, no," she protested. The shiver had been inadvert-ent, of course, but she wasn't cold. At least, not in a way that counted. Marc was keeping her warm. Physically cold or not, she didn't want to move. She never wanted to move. She wanted to stay here on this couch with Marc for ever and ever and ever.

He was prodding her gently, forcing her to sit up. "Come on," he said. "We'll go upstairs."

The little bedroom under the eaves acquired a new di-mension for Jennifer when Marc occupied it with her. They snuggled together in the darkness, drawing up the old-fashioned quilt until it touched their chins. They talked softly, whispering small confidences.

"I never had a teddy bear," Jennifer said. Astonish-ingly, this was true. Jennifer had always had enough toys, enough for a dozen children. But she'd never had a teddy bear.

"I had a teddy bear," Marc answered promptly. "I wouldn't be surprised if he's still around someplace. Probably with the stuff my parents took with them when they moved to Florida. They never throw anything out."

He was smoothing her hair back from her forehead as he spoke and Jennifer stirred, loving the way he touched her. He asked, "What did you have that was special to eat at Christmas when you were a kid?"

"Oh, I don't know," she said vaguely. There had been every possible delicacy to eat in her home at Christmas during her childhood. She remembered canapes of Beluga caviar, champagne in tulip-shaped glasses, a flaming des-sert with marrons and fruit and spun sugar....

"My mother used to make a *bûche de Noël*," Marc confided. "It looked like a log covered with chocolate, all decorated with candied cherries and leaves made out of frosting. Quite a work of art, but we kids didn't have much

respect for that. We wanted to get our grubby fingers into
the icing and my mother used to try to protect her *bûche*
like it was the crown jewels. She'd bring it out when the
family was all assembled on Christmas, and we kids had
to wait till all the grown-ups had been served before we got
a slice."

"Will you go to Florida to have Christmas with your
parents?" Jennifer asked him.

"I doubt it. I feel I should stick around here that time
of the year. Unfortunately, the holidays bring with them
an urge to rip off unoccupied houses, even occupied
houses," Marc said. "Will you visit your father and his
wife at Christmas?"

"No," Jennifer said a bit too abruptly. "This year I
imagine I'll spend Christmas with Julia."

"What about your ex-husband? Isn't he apt to fly east
for Christmas with his mother?"

"I imagine Roger will have enough on his holiday plate
in Beverly Hills," Jennifer said dryly. "Anyway, Ricardo
may be back by then, and he and Roger are not overly fond
of each other."

"Ricardo?"

"Ricardo Castel."

"The concert pianist?"

"Yes."

"By chance, was he the friend who was visiting here
when Mrs. Gray consulted me about the alarm system?"

"Yes," Jennifer said reluctantly. "He and Julia are engaged. Practically engaged, anyway. Right now he's on a
concert tour that's taking him through several European
countries. Julia was in Athens with him when she had her
accident."

"You don't sound as if you like him."

"I don't dislike him. It's not that. He's younger than Julia, though, and quite an international figure in his own right. And...oh, I don't know," she concluded.

Marc switched the subject. "It's beautiful here at Christmas," he said reflectively. "We've had a white Christmas, each year I've been here. Every place you go, it's like looking at another Christmas-card scene."

"That must be lovely," Jennifer said rather wistfully. "Snow and jingle bells and skaters...do you skate, Marc?"

There was a crystal quality to the small silence that fell between them, but it wasn't until he said, a shade too casually, "No," that Jennifer realized she'd made a gaffe.

"I forgot about your leg," she admitted frankly.

His mouth twisted. "I'll take that as a compliment," he replied ruefully. "I never did learn to skate or ski though. Brooklyn isn't renowned for its winter sports. What about you?"

"I used to do some skiing," she hedged. She didn't tell him that during holidays as a teenager she had skied in Switzerland and Aspen and, one winter, in the Italian Alps.

"I'd like to see you soaring down a slope," Marc said softly. "Poetry in motion."

She laughed. "I don't exactly soar down slopes, Marc."

His face was very close to hers. Jennifer looked deep into his eyes and wondered how she could possibly feel so in tune with this man in such a short time. Somehow, they had leaped a lot of boundaries.

He said huskily, "I want you again, Jennifer. Am I too greedy?"

She caught her breath, jolted by her physical response to his question, astonished at the scope of her desire for him.

"No," she whispered. "No, you're no greedier than I am."

It was cold in the little room, but under the bedcovers it was warm. Again Marc and Jennifer found each other, again they gloried in each other, and again they lost themselves to each other.

Jennifer awakened slowly, and sniffed. Delicious smells were emanating from downstairs. She wasted no time in slipping into her clothes and tracking them to their source.

Marc was in the kitchen, frying sausages. "Pour yourself a cup of coffee and sit down," he invited.

He was wearing a shirt that was the deep blue of his eyes, and he looked terrific, she mused. She obeyed his instruction, more than willing to sit at the kitchen table and sip coffee as she watched him work. He was glowing with health and vitality and brimming with a kind of masculinity she found irresistible.

He brought her a plate of sausages and fluffy scrambled eggs and apple muffins. She smiled her thanks, and asked, "Do you do this for all your guests?"

She posed the question lightly, but there was nothing light about his answer. "You are the first guest I've ever had," he said.

"Here?"

"Anywhere."

He had turned back to get his own breakfast as he said this, so she couldn't see his face, and decided it was as well he couldn't see hers either. There was a bleakness to his single-word answer that was very revealing. Far more revealing than Marc had intended it to be, Jennifer felt sure.

What kind of a life must he and his wife have led together if they'd never had a guest in their house? Even she and Roger had entertained, both in the apartment they'd shared in Boston after their marriage and at Julia's, where they'd spent their two wedded summers.

Marc, obviously, had not had an easy life. He spoke of his childhood fondly, despite the fact he'd mentioned his father had been very strict. But once past childhood—she imagined this was a threshold he had crossed at a fairly early age—she suspected that there had been little joy for him. His work had been grim. His marriage appeared to have been equally so.

She felt a surge of compassion toward him, but knew this was something she must hide. Marc was the kind of man who would hate pity, especially so because of the disability that had caused him to become sidelined from his career at an early age.

Well, she didn't feel sorry for him in the conventional sense. He was much too strong a person, and far too attractive, to elicit that brand of feelings. Rather, she wished that his life could have been better in that period between childhood and yesterday.

She smiled at this. Her own life hadn't been that great! Different entirely from Marc's, she was very aware of that. But equally lacking, she would wager. And she didn't have a childhood she could look back on with all that much fond nostalgia.

Her life, too, had tended to be bleak...until yesterday.

Yesterday. She was giving yesterday a lot of stress, maybe too much. Marc had come on her scene so unexpectedly, and in such a bizarre way. But, because of him, even the autumn leaves visible through the kitchen window looked brighter, the sunlight had never been so golden, or the sky so blue.

He had altered her perspective, and in one short night he had taught her the meaning of sharing, in the most intimate of ways. They had shared each other, their bodies, their passion. It had been a mutual coming together, leaving her with a lesson deeply ingrained.

Jennifer knew that she would never again be quite the same.

Marc was watching Jennifer narrowly as he carried his coffee and his plate of food over to the table and sat down across from her. He'd caught the sympathy in her lovely gray eyes, and it made him uncomfortable.

It had been stupid to say that he'd never entertained a guest before, though it was essentially the truth. In his childhood home his parents had limited their visitors to family members as much as possible. Later, once he was married, he had worked nights for the most part, and Helen had worked days. Weekends, Helen always wanted to clean the apartment and do the laundry. To attend, in short, to a number of details that he found mundane, boring, even though he knew they were things that had to be done. He would have been willing to handle a lot of them in afternoons before he went to work and before she got home from work, but Helen had her own way of doing things and didn't like his. She had worked in a small factory, putting together electronic components. Hers was a well-paying job, but more than once Marc had urged her to try for something else, something with more challenge to it, more of a future. Helen had been more interested in the hourly wage she was getting.

Helen had spent every cent she made and most of what he'd made as well, and he sometimes wondered what the money had gone for. They'd had the biggest and best color TV, and a lot of expensive kitchen equipment they seldom used. Helen's wardrobe would have enabled her to plunge into the maelstrom of New York's social life if she'd had the chance to do so, although Marc had personally deplored her taste. This woman sitting opposite him was the complete opposite of Helen—understated in her dress and makeup but with a quiet elegance, an air about her, an assurance, a certain way.

She's out of my league, Marc warned himself. He knew he was issuing the warning too late. He'd taken a giant step last night with Jennifer Bentley.

He wanted to beg, *Please don't start feeling sorry for me. I've been getting along fine. I'll get along fine.* But instead he said, "Hey, you're letting your sausages get cold."

She smiled, the smile lighting a face Marc had decided was patrician in its loveliness. She said, "I'm not used to eating so much breakfast."

"You work off food in this climate," he told her. "Just breathing the cold air burns up calories."

She laughed at that. "Winter's not quite with us yet," she reminded him.

"No," he agreed.

He was thinking ahead toward winter and wishing that she'd be here to share the living Christmas-card scenes he'd spoken to her about. A foolish wish, he told himself, because there was no way it possibly could be granted.

He asked, "More coffee?"

"No, thanks."

"Another muffin?"

"Marc, I couldn't possibly," she protested.

"Well," he said reluctantly, "I suppose pretty soon we'd better be getting back to your mother-in-law's house so we can see if we can find that metal box."

"Yes," Jennifer said slowly. "Yes, I suppose so."

Their eyes met and held, and it was with an effort that Marc kept himself from blurting out the question that was raging in his mind. Was he going to see her again after today? When was he going to see her again? Where was he going to see her again? Did she want to see *him* again?

He stood and picked up her plate and his and took them over to the sink. He seemed intensely conscious of his limp. He'd told Jennifer the truth when he'd said that he'd adjusted to his handicap and wasn't sensitive about it. But there were times when his leg was quite painful physically, and other times when it was even more painful psychologically. Right now he was hurting psychologically, Jennifer realized.

He ran cold water on their dishes so the eggs wouldn't stick, and with the water running he didn't hear Jennifer come up beside him. Turning, he almost bumped into her, then was so startled by the impact of her nearness that he froze.

She was carrying their coffee cups, and she put them under the running water, then stacked them together. He noted that her hands were trembling slightly, and knew she was every bit as unnerved as he was.

He summoned up training acquired over a period of years and forced himself to smile at her as if he didn't have a care in the world.

"Well," he suggested, "shall we be on our way?"

It was a glorious morning, but it was considerably colder than it had been the day before.

"Are you sure you're going to be warm enough with just that jacket?" Marc asked Jennifer. "I could give you something heavier to wear."

"I'll be fine," she assured him.

This time she climbed into the van without his assistance. There had been a subtle change in his manner as they'd stood by the sink together, and it perturbed her. A slight chill still lingered between them.

She pondered about what she might have done or said that had caused this and couldn't come up with anything.

One minute Marc had been looking at her as if he'd like to take her back upstairs with him. The next minute he'd been as polite as ever, but he'd somehow carved a small chasm between them.

On the way to Julia's house Jennifer commented occasionally on the scenery. It was so breathtakingly beautiful that she couldn't keep her reactions entirely to herself.

Marc added a few similiar comments of his own, but on the whole they said very little to each other.

At the house she waited for him to punch out the numbers that would disengage the security system. Marc stood back, letting her precede him.

"Where would you suggest we begin to look?" he asked politely.

Jennifer shrugged. "Your guess is as good as mine. The library, I suppose, would be as logical a place to start as any."

The library was in a small ell that had been added at the far side of the house. It was a comfortable room, and the books filling the many shelves that lined the wall looked as if they'd been used, as if they'd been well-read and loved.

Marc fingered some of them, reading off titles, asking Jennifer if she'd read this one or that one. She was meticulously searching the drawers in an old maple desk as she spoke and, finished, she sat back with a sigh. "Nothing here," she reported.

Marc put aside the book he'd been holding and scanned the shelves with an expert eye. "Unless one of these volumes has been cut out to make a secret safe of sorts, I'd say there's nothing here either," he allowed.

"Julia said the papers are in a metal file box," Jennifer reminded him.

"Okay." He moved to the single closet in the room, and examined it quickly. "No luck," he said, turning back.

"The box could be out in a kitchen cabinet," Jennifer told him. "Julia isn't always organized in the way most people are."

Marc grinned. "I'm beginning to wish I knew her better," he said. "I had only one brief meeting with her when we mapped out the alarm system."

They were moving toward the kitchen, and Jennifer was so aware of Marc, virtually at her elbow, that it was all she could do to walk steadily.

The kitchen refused to yield up a tin box. So did the living room, the dining room, and the lone downstairs bedroom. They went upstairs, giving Julia's room a repeat search, with results just as unsatisfactory as they had been the previous night. They explored the other three bedrooms, now used as guest rooms.

Jennifer flinched only slightly when they came to the corner room she'd occupied with Roger during their summers here. The room had been stripped of personal possessions. If Roger had left anything behind him, his mother must have packed it and stored it away in her attic or elsewhere, Jennifer guessed.

Finally, they went back to the kitchen.

"I wish I could offer you a cup of coffee," Jennifer told Marc apologetically. "I don't think I've ever appreciated having running water until now."

He smiled. "Spoken like a true city girl," he said.

"I think we've covered everything." Jennifer was frowning as she said this.

"We have the garage to go," Marc reminded her. "Also that separate building out back that I believe your mother-in-law uses as an art studio."

"The studio." She stared at Marc as if he'd stumbled upon a miraculous revelation. "The file box has to be in the studio," she stated positively.

At her side the wall telephone rang.

Marc reached for it instinctively, out of habit, then caught himself short. "You take it," he told Jennifer.

She gave him a curious look, but then she plucked the receiver off its hook and said her hello into the mouthpiece.

A moment later she was cupping the mouthpiece to report to Marc, "It's Julia."

She watched him wander over to the window as she spoke to her mother-in-law. In Jennifer's mind there was nothing "ex" about her relationship with Julia.

Again she liked what she saw, admiring his silhouette as she had yesterday when he'd stood at the bedroom window upstairs, looking out. Sunlight glinted off his black hair, bringing out those bluish tints she'd noted with her first glimpse of him. He looked strong and dependable and he'd already proved to her that he was capable of being both loving and caring. It came to Jennifer that Marc was, essentially, everything a woman could ever want in a man.

In her ear Julia was murmuring profuse apologies, and Jennifer could not repress a smile. Julia was being so totally Julia.

"It's all right, dear," she said into the telephone mouthpiece. "Look, I enjoyed coming out here. It's so absolutely beautiful this time of year." A significance that would elude Julia but shouldn't fail to register with the tall man standing at the window crept into her voice. "I wouldn't have missed coming out here for anything," she said.

A few minutes later, after Julia had finally run out of apologies, Jennifer hung up the receiver and spoke across the room to Marc.

"You won't believe this," she told him.

He turned. "Won't believe what?" he asked her, and she had the feeling that his thoughts had been far away.

"Julia's remembered that she took the metal box back to Boston with her when she left here just before Labor Day. She says it's out at her house in Chestnut Hill. She stored it in a wall safe there for safekeeping."

"Behind a portrait?" Marc teased.

"Or maybe one of Julia's own paintings," Jennifer suggested.

Suddenly there was a forced quality to Marc's smile, and no levity at all in his deep blue eyes. "So," he said, "I guess that's that."

"Yes, I guess it is," Jennifer agreed uncomfortably.

"Speaking of her paintings," Marc said as if he had something important in mind, "that's why she installed the alarm system, or did I mention that to you yesterday? Late in the summer she decided to move many of her paintings out to this place. I guess not all of them have been hung yet. But when we were going around here, I was looking at those that have been. She's very good, isn't she?"

"Very, very good." Jennifer nodded.

"What about you?"

"What do you mean?"

"I told you I wanted to get into town to buy one of your books, but there hasn't been a chance so far," Marc reminded her.

She laughed. "If you're asking me if I'm an artist in the same league with Julia, the answer's a resounding no," she assured him.

Marc was glancing around the kitchen as if to make sure nothing was out of place. Jennifer said heavily, "Well, I suppose we'd better get along. Will you set the alarm?"

He nodded. "I'll show you the combination if you like," he offered. "I'm sure Mrs. Gray would have no objection. Then if you want to come out here again for any reason, you'll be able to let yourself in without any more incidents.''

Jennifer shook her head. "No," she said, "I'd only forget it. I'm terrible with numbers.'' She marched resolutely down the hall and out the door, wondering how she was possibly going to say good-bye and wrench herself away from him.

She dug her car keys out of her handbag and Marc said, "You'd better let your car warm up for a while, it's been sitting so long. I'll follow you along to the village to be sure you don't stall out."

Suddenly Jennifer prayed that the car wouldn't start at all. Or that she'd get a flat tire as she drove out of the driveway. Or that she'd run out of gas. Anything, anything at all that would delay her departure.

She said tightly, "You don't need to follow me. I'll be all right. There's no point in your going out of your way."

"It isn't out of my way," he returned evenly. "I'm supposed to stop by at the Berkshire-Hudson Bank and Trust Company. They want to talk to me about installing a new alarm system in the bank."

Jennifer sensed that he was waiting for her to do something, so she opened her car door and slid behind the wheel. She turned the key in the ignition switch, and to her distress the engine immediately purred into action.

"Let it warm up for a while anyway," Marc advised.

She nodded.

"Drive carefully on the way back," he said.

He was standing by the car door, which was still open. Now he reached out and closed it with a firmness that Jennifer found very disconcerting. Automatically she rolled the window down so she could speak to him. She felt shy as a schoolgirl as she said, "Thank you."

He looked surprised. "For what?" he asked her.

"For cooking dinner for me, for cooking breakfast for me, for..." She stumbled, suddenly embarrassed. Then she smiled. "For keeping me out of jail," she told him.

"I'm the one who nearly put you in jail, remember?"

"But you rescued me in time," she pointed out. She looked up at him, her eyes dove-gray. "You spoke about my coming out here without any further incidents if I knew how to work the alarm system," she said. "I'm not sure I'd want to do that." She drew a deep breath. "Having that alarm go off yesterday was probably the most wonderful thing that ever happened to me," she said simply.

Marc's eyes darkened and for a moment he looked as if she'd shocked him. Then, impulsively, he bent to lean through the car window, his mouth finding hers unerringly. He touched her only with his lips, but there was an eloquence to his kiss; it spoke a language that came straight from the heart and had a meaning, a poignancy, that bridged all barriers.

Slowly he drew back. "I'll see you," he promised huskily.

I'll see you. The three words were all Marc could manage and as he watched Jennifer drive onto the dirt lane that would start her on her way back to Boston, Marc cursed himself for having suddenly become tongue-tied.

At the very last minute he'd wanted to rush after her and to beg her to come back. He'd wanted to ask her to stay with him, to beg her to stay with him. Now she was gone, and he felt like a fool. He'd had his chance, and he'd blown it.

He slowly climbed into his van, then sat at the wheel staring out at the glorious autumn foliage Jennifer loved so much.

In all fairness, he had some justification for his behavior, he reminded himself. Six years ago Helen had come to his hospital bed to tell him that she wanted to be free. He'd faced a very uncertain future then, not even knowing if he'd ever walk again. Helen's request had driven a wedge of self-doubt deep into him, and with it a distrust of women. Since then he'd been wary. Instinctively he was still wary.

He wasn't so blind as to think that all women would respond as Helen did in the same situation. Roughly he reminded himself of that too. It had been over between Helen and himself long before he'd been shot. They'd both realized their mistake early. He'd stayed with the marriage primarily because of some admittedly old-fashioned convictions, convictions he still held. He suspected that Helen had stayed with it mainly because it was expedient to do so.

During the long months of recuperation there had been no place for a woman in his life. Since then, he'd made the move to Thrussington, established his own business, and while he had dated occasionally, he had kept his relationships with women on a very superficial level.

Then yesterday a lovely blonde had come from her world in Boston to knock the props out from under him. Marc felt in a state of shock, and he suspected that this was a feeling Jennifer was sharing with him.

He smiled a genuine smile as he thought of her saying that her experience with a mechanical banshee yesterday probably had been the most wonderful thing that had ever happened to her.

He should have picked her up on that.

Suddenly Marc snapped out of his reverie. He'd told Jennifer that he would follow her into the village to see if her car was performing satisfactorily, and yet he was simply sitting in the driveway bogged down in his own thoughts.

He drove down the lane as quickly as the potholes would allow, then turned toward the village, searching ahead for Jennifer's car, but it was not in sight.

As he drove, he kept hoping that she'd had some car trouble and he'd find her parked at the side of the road, waiting for him. It was a vain hope. By the time he reached the village Marc was forced to realize that Jennifer must be on the Massachusetts Turnpike by now.

He was tight-lipped and impatient with himself as he parked in front of the Berkshire-Hudson Bank. But at least he'd come to a definite conclusion.

Though he'd lost Jennifer for the moment, Marc was determined to find her again.

Chapter Five

Jennifer drove directly to her Back Bay town house when she reached Boston. Miraculously she found a parking space without difficulty. Usually this area was cluttered with parked cars.

She'd bought the house a few months after her divorce from Roger had become final, and she loved it. It was a narrow, three-story brick, facing an equally narrow street illuminated by old-fashioned gas lamps. At night Jennifer felt as if she were living in the London of Charles Dickens.

She had decorated the house room by room, furnished it piece by piece. Now, for the first time in her life, she had something that was entirely her own, reflecting her taste and her personality.

The living room occupied most of the first floor. Jennifer had done it in soft shades of green and gray. The upholstered furniture was contemporary, the occasional pieces antique. The two styles blended well.

She'd always found it relaxing just to step into this room, ever since she'd had the house. But on that October afternoon Jennifer's subdued decor did nothing to soothe her. She'd been stirred so thoroughly by Marc Bouchard that it was impossible to settle back into her comfortable, well-padded rut.

She winced at her silent word choice. She'd never thought of herself as being in a rut, even a well-padded one, until now. As a matter of fact, she'd organized her life exactly as she liked it since her divorce. She enjoyed her home, her work, her friends. She was becoming increasingly successful in her chosen career, and this was a satisfaction.

My God, but you sound smug!

Jennifer spoke the words aloud into a silence that suddenly rang around her ears.

I don't even have his telephone number. This thought came next, followed by the logical, *but he has to be in the book*.

What was happening to her?

She shrugged off her coat. Then, forcing herself to fit back into her usual habits, she turned on the answering machine she kept on a corner table to see if there had been any phone calls in her absence.

There had been several. Three of the messages were from Kenneth Trent, and he'd displayed an audible mounting irritation each time he'd called.

Jennifer tried to remember whether she'd told Ken she'd definitely have dinner with him tonight, or whether it had been a tentative promise.

She wasn't necessarily trying to stall Ken. At best, she knew she could hope to put him off only briefly. Ken was much too accustomed to having things his own way.

Tonight, though, she wanted to see Julia. She wanted to talk to Julia, maybe even to tell her about the alarm going off and meeting Marc Bouchard.

Would that be wise? Julia was a very perceptive person. Jennifer knew she could not hope to discuss Marc with Julia without her becoming aware that the interest shown in the owner of Bouchard's security and alarm systems was more than superficial.

Jennifer had skipped lunch, having eaten far more for breakfast than she usually did...thanks to Marc. She still wasn't hungry, but she brewed herself a cup of tea and took it up to her studio with her.

Her studio occupied the third floor of the house. Her bedroom, a bath, and a guest bedroom filled up the second floor. On the ground floor there was the living room, a small dining room, and a compact kitchen.

As far as Jennifer was concerned, the space arrangement was perfectly suited to her needs.

As she climbed the stairs she found herself imagining Marc in this setting. Hers was a town house, his was a cottage, but they were equally intriguing in their different ways. Marc would like her house; she felt sure of it. The strong wish that he could be here with her, sharing the moment with her, swept over her with such intensity that she paused, her hand gripping the stairwell.

Why hadn't he suggested that they meet again? He'd let her go with no word about a future meeting. Yet theirs had not been the type of single encounter a door could be closed upon. To be able to do that would mean that the time they'd shared together had been a mere casual encounter. Nothing could be further from the truth as far as Jennifer was concerned, and she was deeply sure that Marc's feelings would match hers.

Jennifer stepped into her studio, the room where she spent so much of her time both painting and writing, and she was jolted by the impression that struck her, right on the threshold.

Sterile. Barren. The room was much too uncluttered for an artist's working space. Everything was stacked neatly, put away precisely. There was no verve to the surroundings, no excitement, no mess.

Last night was the first time in my life I ever really let myself go.

This realization was jolting too. Jennifer sat down at her desk and stared at the blank screen of the computer she'd purchased a year ago to facilitate getting her books down on paper. She felt as blank as the screen.

It was a shock to know how dormant she'd been until she'd met Marc.

Rallying, she knew she couldn't possibly face Kenneth Trent tonight. He wasn't the last person in the world she wanted to see, but was close to it.

Without giving the matter any more thought, Jennifer went back downstairs, put her coat on again, and headed for the New England Medical Center.

Julia was full of news. She was sitting in an armchair by the window, her leg, in its cast, propped up on a hassock, and she was glowing with excitement.

"I think they're going to let me out of here in just a few more weeks," she proclaimed as soon as she saw Jennifer. Then she added, "Darling, I'm sorry I sent you off on such a wild goose chase. I really must try not to be so forgetful about little details."

Jennifer smiled. Julia looked at life in broad strokes, so a great many things fell into the little-detail category with her.

Jennifer pulled up a straight-backed chair and sat down. She said, still smiling slightly, "I enjoyed the wild goose chase, Julia."

"Well, I must say that you persevered," Julia rejoined. "Did you stay over at the house last night?"

"No. There's neither water nor electricity on. Just the telephone."

"Of course," Julia said, impatient with herself. "I left the phone on because of the security system I had installed." She paused, frowning. "Did I tell you about the security system, Jen?"

Jennifer's eyes danced with merriment. "No," she said, "you didn't tell me about it. I walked right into it."

"You mean it went off?"

"Yes, it went off right in my ears. My hearing may never be the same."

"Oh, Jennifer, how terrible." Julia could not have been more contrite. "I'm so sorry. What did you do?"

Jennifer was enjoying this. She detailed her experiences to Julia, right to the moment when Marc Bouchard had appeared in the driveway in the van and had prevented her from being carted off to the police station. She embellished her account with considerable drama, and Julia hung on her every word. Watching her mother-in-law's reaction to her performance, Jennifer decided that she was going to have to transfer some of this kind of storytelling into her books for children. In comparison to what she was telling Julia, her plots were very dull.

She was disconcerted when Julia said, "Handsome, isn't he."

It was more of a statement than a question, yet it required an answer.

"Marc Bouchard?" Jennifer stalled.

"Yes. I met him only once, but he made quite an impact."

Jennifer's face gave her away, and Julia laughed. "I'd say it's too soon to have fallen in love with him, but he's certainly done something to you, darling," Julia opined.

Jennifer's cheeks flamed.

"He came to see me about installing the alarm system, that's the only time we met," Julia volunteered. "But I do think he's one of the best-looking men I've seen in a long while. Too bad he's lame. How did it happen, do you know?"

"He had a very special job with the New York City Police Department," Jennifer said. "He was shot in the line of duty. They retired him early. When he was well enough again, he moved to the Berkshires. He opened his business in Thrussington four years ago."

"Is he married?"

"No. He has been though."

"Children?"

"No."

"Does he like modern jazz?"

"He likes all kinds of music. He—" Jennifer paused and looked at her mother-in-law reproachfully. "Julia," she protested.

Julia laughed. "Well, my dear, you do seem to have learned a lot about Mr. Bouchard in one encounter. I gather you buried the initial hatchet?"

"Yes."

"Did he help you search the house?"

"Yes."

Julia leaned back against her chair cushions and surveyed Jennifer. Then she said, her tone serious, "I don't think I've ever seen you look like this before, Jen. If Marc Bouchard was able to effect this transformation, more power to him. I've the feeling that you've come alive. There's a sparkle in your eyes, a glow to your skin. Are you planning to see him again?''

Jennifer stared down at the tips of her smooth black pumps. "We didn't get into that," she said.

"Would you like to see him again?"

"Yes..." Jennifer nodded after a moment. "Yes, I would."

"Then," Julia said triumphantly, "you're going to love what I'm about to tell you."

They were interrupted by a nurse arriving with medication for Julia. After that, her orthopedic specialist stopped by. He was in a sociable mood, and they chatted a while. After that, a phone call came through from Ricardo, who was in London, where it was nine o'clock, and he was calling during his concert intermission.

Meantime, Jennifer's impatience mounted. She knew her mother-in-law. She knew only too well that there was no telling what Julia had in mind. Julia was capable of thinking up a scheme at an instant's notice. She'd probably plotted out something as she was questioning Jennifer about Marc Bouchard, and it would undoubtedly be much too wild in concept to put into execution.

How could Julia possibly suggest anything logical that would involve future meetings with Marc Bouchard?

Finally they were alone again. Some of Julia's exuberance had faded. Jennifer thought she looked tired.

"Where were we?" Julia asked vaguely, as if to confirm this.

Jennifer had no problem in recalling their conversation. "You were about to tell me something you said I'd love to hear," she reminded Julia.

"Yes." Julia brightened. "As I started to tell you, they're going to let me out of this place sooner than I thought they might."

"Yes, so you said, and that's wonderful!" Jennifer's delight was genuine.

"With a little bit of luck I'll be able to lose this cast in another ten days or so," Julia went on, glancing ruefully at her plaster-swathed leg. "I'll be given a removable cast, and I'll be on crutches, but I can leave."

"So you'll be going back to Chestnut Hill to convalesce?"

"No," Julia said firmly. "The doctors think it would be advisable for me to get away from the city entirely. There would be too many people coming around in Chestnut Hill. They think I'd be inclined to—I think *overextend* was the word they used. Also, I'll be needing therapy, and I'll have to do my own share of home exercises. The therapy sessions can be arranged at the Berkshire Medical Center in Pittsfield, which isn't all that far from Thrussington."

Jennifer sat bolt upright. "What?" she demanded.

Julia chuckled. "You heard me, darling. I discussed it with my doctors this morning, and they think Thrussington would be the perfect spot for my convalescence. The doctors at the Berkshire Medical Center can relay progress reports to my doctors here. I called Trina this morning and asked her how she'd like to spend Thanksgiving and Christmas in the Berkshires, and she can't wait."

Jennifer smiled inwardly at this. Trina Moreno had been Julia's housekeeper for years, and Jennifer knew she would have agreed enthusiastically to almost any course of action Julia suggested.

"So," Julia persisted, "there's only one more hurdle to get over."

Jennifer fell into the trap. "What's that?" she asked innocently.

"You," Julia told her blandly. "I've thought it out; I've spent all day thinking it out. If you hadn't shown up, I was going to phone you to beg you to come over so we could talk. I want you to come to Thrussington with me, Jen. Ricardo's going to be on tour in this country after he gets back from Europe. He'll come to the Berkshires when he can, but I can't expect him to be around most of the time. Though I want to be out there in Thrussington—in fact, I'm surprised at how much I love the thought of being there—I don't want to be alone."

Julia paused, waiting for her words to sink in.

After a moment Jennifer, frowning, queried, "Are you asking me what I think you're asking me, Julia? Are you asking me to move to Thrussington with you?"

"I think it would be a good move for both of us," Julia said frankly. "I need to get away from Boston for a while, and I think you do too. There's been something very...abstract about you, Jen, for a long time. I know you're going to say you lead a full life, that you're busy every minute, and I'm sure that's true. But in my opinion, there's been something lacking. That's why I detected something new in you so quickly when you came in here this afternoon. A sparkle, a—" Julia spread her hands wide. "You know what I'm saying."

"Yes," Jennifer said slowly. "Yes, I know what you're saying. I..."

Words failed her as she thought of yesterday, of her meeting with Marc, of last night, of the loss she'd felt when she'd left him this morning.

Julia was offering her the opportunity to move right into his backyard. But the offer was coming so quickly on the heels of what had happened between Marc and herself that she wasn't ready for it. She wasn't ready to handle it; she wasn't ready to make a decision.

Into the silence Julia said, "My studio is heated."

Jennifer looked at her blankly. "What?"

"I said my studio is heated," Julia repeated patiently. "You could work out there. It's a fabulous place to work in, Jennifer. I always felt it gave me new vision. I think you'd love working there. We can move in a desk and a typewriter. You'd have the studio entirely to yourself." Julia smiled. "There wouldn't be anyone to interrupt you."

The offer astonished Jennifer. Julia, so generous about almost everything else, had always guarded the security of her studio in Thrussington. It had been off limits, even to Jennifer herself when she'd lived in the Thrussington house those two summers.

Julia said perceptively, "I didn't know you as well when you were living in the house as I do now, Jen. We've both come a long way since then. I'd like you to use the studio...and I don't know of another person in the world I could say that to and be honest. It's a very special place to me. I've done my best work there, as I hope to again. But I'm not going to attempt painting for the next few months. I'm used to standing up to paint. I suppose I could manage to work sitting down, but I'd rather wait until my ankle is really strong again. I did quite a job on it," she conceded ruefully, "and I'm not as young as I used to be. At my age, it takes longer for bones to knit properly."

In Jennifer's opinion, her mother-in-law was ageless. Age wasn't something even to be thought of in connection with Julia. Still, physical facts were physical facts. She supposed it would take a definite amount of time before Julia could expect to get around again in her usual spry fashion.

She looked across at Julia, noting her fine complexion, the masses of beautiful hair that had turned silver when Julia was still in her twenties and, actually, gave her a strangely youthful look. She scanned the cameo features and large hazel eyes that added up to form one of the loveliest faces Jennifer had ever seen.

She said a bit huskily, "You'll never be old, Julia. Not if you live to be a thousand, as I hope you will."

Touched, Julia said, "Thank you, dear. But none of us can defeat time entirely. The doctors promise I'll be as good as new come spring...if I behave myself meantime. So I seriously want to behave myself for once in my life." Julia paused. "You haven't told me what you think of my plan for us, Jen," she pointed out.

Jennifer squirmed uncomfortably, still not ready to deal with this, certainly not ready to make any promises, not even tentative ones.

She knew Julia was watching her closely. Her discomfort increased when Julia said, "You're not really committed to anything here in Boston, are you? I mean, maybe you could take your work with you."

"There is the house," Jennifer began.

"Of course there is the house," Julia agreed. "You could close it up for a while though. Or maybe find someone you trust to stay in it for the next few months."

The next few months. The thought of living in the Berkshires for the next few months, in close proximity to Marc Bouchard, was unnerving. It was also exciting...provocative...delightful....

"Julia," she said, "I can't give you an immediate answer about this. It wouldn't be fair to either of us."

"Sleep on it," Julia advised.

"I don't think just sleeping on it is going to be enough," Jennifer said. "I need some time."

"Not too much time," Julia disagreed. "Darling, sometimes when you think too much about something it can be as bad as thinking too little about it. If the only thing that's worrying you is your house, certainly that can be handled. I'm going to be closing up my house in Chestnut Hill, after all. And I've never lived in the country in the winter in my life."

Every place you look, it's like seeing different Christmas-card scenes. Maybe that wasn't exactly what Marc had said, but it was close enough. Jennifer felt as if she were hearing his deep, wonderfully melodious voice telling her all over again about what winter was like around Thrussington.

Temptation dangled enticingly; Jennifer resisted it.

Faced with the opportunity of moving right into his territory, she found herself apprehensive about encountering Marc Bouchard again.

Suppose, on second sight, he wasn't as he'd appeared to be on first sight. Suppose the whole unusual scene surrounding their meeting had set its own mood, and the next time she saw him it wouldn't be like that. They wouldn't feel the same response toward each other, the magic wouldn't be there.

Everything between them had happened so quickly. Had it been the spell of a beautiful golden autumn day mixed with excitement and a heady mutual dose of chemical attraction? Had it been something that had happened once, but wouldn't happen again?

Jennifer was afraid to find out.

"I'm sorry," Julia said suddenly.

Jennifer looked up, snapped out of her introspection and taken aback by Julia's statement.

"Why should you be sorry?" she demanded.

"I've upset you. No, don't deny it, Jen, I can see it written all over your face. I don't quite understand why I've upset you, but then you know the way I am. I tend to get overly excited when something strikes me. Logically, though, there's no real reason why I need to go to Thrussington for the winter. I can do my exercises in Chestnut Hill and simply tell Trina to handle telephone calls and uninvited guests. I can have my therapy sessions right here at the medical center. Probably, that would make a lot more sense."

Jennifer stared at her mother-in-law, appalled. "That's the most ridiculous thing I've ever heard," she blurted out. "Are you saying that if I don't go to the Berkshires, you won't go at all?"

"Yes," Julia admitted. "Childish of me, isn't it? I adore Trina, but she's happy to go to bed at nine o'clock at night and to watch her soap operas every afternoon before she starts getting dinner ready. If she goes to church on Sunday, that's her outing for the week. I won't be doing much gallivanting myself, that's for certain, but I'd like to have someone around who could play a game of cribbage or backgammon once in a while or...or talk about the ridiculous assortment of things that interest me.

"No," Julia amended, "that isn't what I'd like at all. I'd like to have you around, specifically. I feel very close to you, Jen, and I guess I've also been feeling rather self-indulgent. I've no right to lean on you because of my affection for you." Julia paused. "I'm saying this very badly," she decided.

"No," Jennifer said slowly, "no, you're not saying it badly at all. It's funny. As I was driving back to Boston from Thrussington, I was wondering how I could possibly arrange to get to the Berkshires again without being painfully obvious about it. Now you've given me the perfect reason. I don't know myself why I'm not grabbing it.''

"Marc Bouchard?'' Julia guessed.

Jennifer nodded.

"So much so soon?''

"Yes.''

"And you're afraid maybe you were blowing bubbles, is that it?'' Julia asked. "Lovely, iridescent bubbles that glistened like rainbows but were gossamer-fragile.''

"You should have been a writer,'' Jennifer said wryly.

"No. I paint my pictures. But I know what you mean. I understand what you mean. But if you don't see him again,'' Julia concluded wisely, "you'll always wonder, won't you?''

Jennifer stopped at a convenience store on her way home and bought herself a frozen TV dinner.

She slipped it into the oven, poured herself a glass of wine, then went into the living room and sank down in the most comfortable chair, kicking off her pumps and wriggling her toes.

She sipped the wine slowly and tried to relax. Her mind was still whirling.

The telephone rang, and she got up reluctantly to answer it. It was certain to be Kenneth Trent and she didn't want to cope with his irritation right now.

But it wasn't Kenneth.

"Jennifer?'' Only one man in the world spoke her name that way.

She choked. It became impossible to answer him, and he asked again, "Jennifer?''

"Yes,'' she croaked.

"What's the matter?'' Marc demanded. She could picture him frowning as he spoke. "Have you come down with a cold? I told you you should have worn something heavier when we went out to the Gray house this morning.''

This morning? Could it possibly have been only twelve hours or so since she'd gone to Julia's house with Marc?

"I'm fine. I swallowed the wrong way,'' she temporized. Then, puzzled, she asked, ''How did you get my phone number?'' Her number was unlisted.

He chuckled. ''I used to be a detective, remember?''

''Seriously, Marc...''

''Seriously, I have my methods.'' He paused. ''Okay, I called Mrs. Gray at the medical center.''

''You called Julia and she gave you my phone number?''

''Yes. Shouldn't she have?''

''No. Yes.''

''Which is it, Jennifer?''

''Of course she should have given you my number.'' Jennifer had taken only two sips of her wine before the phone had rung, but suddenly she felt giddy, light-headed, as if she'd drunk the whole bottle.

Marc continued. ''I have to drive into Boston tomorrow to get some supplies. I know it's short notice, but I was wondering if maybe you'd be free to have a drink or something.''

''I—I think I might be.''

''For lunch? Or a drink? Or dinner?''

''For a drink,'' she said. She was certain she wouldn't be able to eat a bite if he were sitting across the table from her. She hesitated. ''Would you like to come here and have a drink?'' she asked him.

''Your house?''

''Yes.'' As soon as she'd said this Jennifer thought about the implications of having him at her house for a drink...or anything else. Her memory of the previous night washed over her with the force of a tidal wave. Weak with the thought of being alone with him like that again, she nearly said that maybe it would be better if they met somewhere. But before she could form the words, he spoke.

"Your house would be fine," he said. "What time?"

"Five or so?" Jennifer suggested, and wondered if her voice sounded as weak as she felt.

"Five it is. I'll see you then."

She sensed he was about to hang up, and she said quickly, "Wait. Let me give you my address."

Marc chuckled. "No need," he told her. "I already have it."

Chapter Six

By four o'clock the next afternoon Jennifer had developed a strong empathy toward all the caged lions and tigers in all the zoos in the world.

It was with an effort that she refrained from physically pacing her living room floor.

Then, exactly as the grandfather clock in her tiny foyer struck five, the doorbell rang. Jennifer suffered an acute attack of stage fright. Her pulse began to pound and her hands became clammy.

She stretched out a hand to turn the door handle, but that hand seemed to freeze in space. The doorbell pealed again, and her action was an involuntary response to the sound. She opened the door and found Marc standing close to her on the flat cement stoop. She instinctively took a step backward.

He was wearing a thick, gray wool car coat, the collar pulled up around his neck to ward off the cold. He was bareheaded, but even on this gray afternoon Jennifer fancied that she could see the bluish streaks against the smooth blackness of his hair. She met his eyes, and saw a guarded look to them. It came to her that he was as much on edge about this meeting as she was.

"Come in," she invited.

She took his coat from him and led him into the living room. She glanced at him apprehensively, waiting for his initial reaction to her house. It was important to her; she was surprised at just how important.

He looked around and said simply, "This is beautiful."

Jennifer's breath caught in her throat. "Thank you," she murmured softly.

"I've never been in this part of Boston before," he confessed. "Have you lived here long?"

"I bought the house over three years ago."

He was standing in the center of the floor, looking around, his eyes sweeping over everything. It occurred to Jennifer that he had been trained in the art of acute observation. He was registering each detail, but she could tell nothing from his expression. Then again, he'd been trained in that respect too.

He asked, "You live here alone?"

"Yes," she answered.

He nodded, but made no comment.

Jennifer, nervous, said, "Sit down, won't you? What would you like to drink?"

He turned toward her, a wry smile tugging at the corner of his mouth. "Can't I help you make the drinks?" he asked her.

Jennifer had been responding to her training too. There'd been a consistent formality to the way in which she'd been brought up. She'd been treating Marc like a guest and he was a guest, of course. But so much more.

She relaxed, her tension lightening. "You can mix the drinks for both of us," she told him.

He followed her out to her tiny kitchen and she showed him the cabinet where she kept her liquor supply. When he decided to make whiskey sours she got out the mixings and the glasses, but she let him do the work.

They took their drinks back into the living room. Jennifer usually kept a supply of pressed logs for her fireplace, and she'd lit one at a quarter to five. Now it was flaming, and because these logs were specially treated, the flames darted tongues of blue and green as well as red and orange up the worn chimney bricks.

She and Marc settled down on the couch in front of the fire, keeping a wide distance between them. Jennifer asked Marc how the drive had been from the Berkshires into Boston and he answered that there had been a fair amount of traffic on the Massachusetts Turnpike. After that, a dull silence fell between them, and Jennifer began to feel sick at heart.

Could it be possible that they really had nothing to say to each other?

She wondered if Julia had mentioned the possible move to Thrussington when Marc had spoken to her on the phone. She wondered what he would think of the idea of her living in Thrussington. She wondered what he really thought of her, but there was no way of telling. Marc's face, as he stared toward the fireplace, was absolutely inscrutable.

Marc had learned, early in his career, how to keep himself from revealing emotions when it was wiser not to. As he watched the multicolored flames, he was warning himself that he was going to have to keep a tight grip on his feelings.

Jennifer was out of his league. Completely out of his league. He'd been afraid of that from the very beginning. Now that he'd seen her house, he knew it.

He could imagine what a town house in a Boston neighborhood like this would cost. He couldn't imagine having enough money to pay such a tariff. Also, everything in the house was exquisite. Though Marc had never been able to afford such things himself, he had always appreciated them.

In addition, Jennifer had the quiet assurance that spoke of having come from a moneyed background. He could imagine what the soft, beige wool dress she was wearing had cost. It was cut with a simplicity that only a master designer could accomplish. She was wearing a few single gold chains but they were gold, not facsimiles thereof, and her square-cut emerald ring was equally genuine. Everything about Jennifer was genuine and expensive and Marc knew there was no possible way he could afford her, in any sense of the word.

An involuntary sigh escaped him because it was a long time since he'd felt so discouraged about anything. He told himself that it would have been much wiser if he'd yielded to common sense and had shut off the impulse to call her up and ask her if he could see her again.

Jennifer heard the sigh, and turned toward him curiously. At that exact instant he glanced at her, and she was surprised at the intensity of the emotion revealed in his deep blue eyes.

"What is it?" she asked him quickly.

She saw his mouth tighten but he didn't answer her. More urgently, she asked, "Marc, what is it? What's the matter?"

He smiled, that twisted smile that tore at her heart. "It would be stupid to say nothing, wouldn't it?" he told her.

She nodded. "Yes. Yes, it would be."

"I guess I'm...kind of out of sorts," he said, his evasion obvious.

"About what?" she persisted.

He drained his drink instead of answering her. Then he said, "Would it be gauche to inquire if I could make us a refill?"

"Gauche?" Jennifer surveyed him. "That's a funny way to put it," she observed. "I can't imagine your ever doing anything gauche."

She saw him draw a long breath and expel it. Then he said quietly, "Thank you."

She became impatient with him. "What's come over you?" she demanded.

The bittersweet smile tugged at his lips again. "I guess I have to say that I feel like a fish out of water," he admitted.

"What?" This was the last thing she had expected.

He waved his hand vaguely at nothing in particular. "This," he said. "Your house is so perfect, Jennifer," he said. "Everything about it."

Jennifer had the impression that there were all sorts of hidden meanings in his words, and this made her uncomfortable. She decided to ignore the hidden meanings and to concentrate on the words themselves. "You've seen only my living room and my kitchen," she reminded him. "Would you like to see the rest of the house?"

He hesitated. Then he said, "Yes, I would. Very much."

"Do you want to make us another drink and we'll take it along with us?"

"All right," he agreed.

Jennifer stayed in the living room while Marc left to make the drinks. She needed a little time and space from him. There was a current flowing between them that bothered her. She knew now that the problem wasn't that they had nothing to say to each other. It was that Marc, for reasons she couldn't understand, had evidently stumbled upon some sort of obstacle. She suspected it was going to be up to her to find out what it was and to clear it from their path.

He returned, carrying their drinks carefully as he limped toward her. She saw that it was a slight struggle for him to walk evenly enough so the drinks wouldn't spill.

She deliberately set a slow pace as they started up the stairs.

"Let's go up to the studio first," she suggested.

"Okay."

She paused for a moment at the bottom of the second flight, then started up it. At the top, she flicked on the wall light that illuminated the studio, and she wondered if Marc would find the room as sterile as she'd found it when she'd come back from Thrussington.

He stood, looking around. "This is where you work?" It was a superficial question, and Jennifer merely nodded.

"Are you working on a book currently, Jennifer?"

"Yes." She led him over to her easel, where the latest watercolor she'd done was propped up.

"This is to be a children's story set on Cape Cod, hence the beach scene," she explained.

His eyes softened as he looked at the picture she'd painted of two tow-headed children playing in the sand. They had just struck the edge, with their shovels, of what was plainly going to be a treasure chest, and were gazing at their discovery, enraptured.

He said, "You've really captured their feelings in the expressions on their faces. Funny, that's a dream I used to have when I was a kid. Going to the beach somewhere and finding buried treasure. I suppose it's something every kid dreams about."

He looked across at her. "Did you used to dream about it?" he asked her.

"No," she said slowly. This was true. Buried treasure had never held any enchantment for Jennifer, perhaps because, in so many ways, she'd been surrounded with real treasure. She'd had other dreams.

"I used to dream about being a world-famous ballerina," she confessed. "I think I wore a different colored tutu in each dream. I used up the whole rainbow of colors, many times over."

He laughed. "Did you take ballet?"

"Yes, and I danced like I had two left feet," she said ruefully.

"I don't believe that."

"It's true. I'm all right at ballroom dancing, and the simpler things, but ballet defeated me. I don't think my toes were made right." She smiled at him. "What about you? Did you used to go out to beaches and try to find hidden treasure?"

"No," he said. "We used to go to Coney Island or Jones Beach once in a while, but I remember both places mostly as great big mob scenes. You couldn't see the sand for the people. And when I was a little kid, the roller coaster at Coney Island scared the hell out of me."

"I've never been on a roller coaster," Jennifer admitted. "Just looking at most of the rides in amusement parks scares me."

He grinned. "A couple of chicken people," he teased. Again, the tension between them began to ease.

"I bought a couple of your books," he told her.

"Marc, you shouldn't have. I planned to send you some copies," she answered quickly.

"I couldn't wait. I wanted to see what you're doing, and even though I'm a bit past the age of your readership, I thought the books were terrific."

He was looking around the studio as he spoke. "Do you keep regular working hours?" he asked.

"Pretty much so. I usually work for about four or five hours in the morning. That seems to be enough. I tend to wear out after that point."

She turned. "Come on," she suggested.

On the middle floor she showed Marc her bedroom and the guest room, conscious of the fact that her bedroom was so different from the one she'd shared with him in Thrussington.

She'd done her room in a stark contemporary style. There was a great deal of white, navy blue, and slashes of a brighter blue. For the first time, she realized how cold the room was.

Downstairs, she showed him her small dining room, and the little study off the living room where she kept the TV and a desk at which she usually wrote her letters and handled bill payments and such.

"That's it," she said then, turning toward him with a smile. "The grand tour's finished."

He nodded and glanced at his wristwatch. "It's after six," he observed. "I guess I'd better be off."

Jennifer had turned to her stereo just before he said this, flicking on the switch. Soft music filled the air in the wake of his words. It was an old Sinatra record she'd put on; she'd remembered him saying he liked Sinatra, and now the words and the music filled the room. They stared at each other, the music an aphrodisiac. Involuntarily Jennifer closed her eyes as her yearning for this man standing so close to her mounted. Her eyes were still closed when she felt his warmth as his arms stole around her.

He kissed her so deeply that she lost all sense of time and all sense of balance. The kiss ended, and he continued to hold her, pressing her so close to him that she could hear his heart thumping through the tightly woven fabric of his tweed jacket. He held her like that for a long time, his chin pressed against her forehead—he was that much taller than she was.

The record ended. Into the resulting silence reality crept.

Marc released her slowly, and he said just as slowly, "I didn't mean to do that."

This hurt. Jennifer was just beginning to get her breath back and his words made her gasp slightly, the hurt plunging deep.

There was a calculated blankness to his eyes when she looked at him. She felt as if he'd put on his professional suit of armor, and she was afraid that there was going to be no way to penetrate it.

Marc said as if he'd rehearsed the short speech, "Thanks very much for the drink. Thanks very much for...everything."

He drew a deep breath. "I don't think it would be wise for us to see each other again," he told her flatly.

The sudden and unexpected statement shocked her. Jennifer stared at him, feeling the tips of her fingers go icy, just as they had when she'd heard the doorbell ring earlier.

What could she say? The obvious thing would be to ask him why, but she couldn't bring herself to phrase the question.

He said gently, "I'm sorry, Jennifer."

She'd put his coat in the little closet off the foyer. Marc got it out himself and shrugged into it. He moved toward the door, telegraphing his anxiety to leave.

Baffled, it was beyond Jennifer to ask him to stay.

With one hand on the doorknob, Marc turned to say, "Thank you again. And," he added, his voice breaking slightly, "God go with you, Jenny."

She heard the door thud and stared at its blank surface helplessly.

It was quite a while before she rallied enough to feel relieved because she hadn't told him there was a chance she'd be moving to Thrussington.

That chance, she told herself dully, no longer existed.

By the end of the next two weeks Jennifer had decided that Julia was probably the most stubborn woman in the world.

"I'm sorry, Jen," Julia said on a chilly Thursday afternoon when Jennifer came to the hospital to visit her. "I can leave here next Tuesday, if all goes well, but I have definitely given up on the idea of going to Thrussington, since you won't go with me."

Julia brought forth a brave smile that Jennifer didn't quite trust. She knew Julia's high sense of drama.

"I'll be fine in Chestnut Hill," Julia promised.

This was true enough. Julia's home in Chestnut Hill was actually more luxurious than her Berkshire estate. Also, her privacy could be guarded by Trina and others. But Julia loved people, she loved to have them around her when she wasn't working. The Chestnut Hill house would become a center of social activity once Julia was in residence, Jennifer felt sure of that.

Probably, there was no reason why Julia shouldn't plunge into a social whirl, provided she kept off her feet most of the time while doing so. Yet the fact that Julia had wanted to go to Thrussington so much in the first place said something.

Julia, too, needed a change of space, a change of place and life tempo.

Too.

The word was significant.

I need this kind of change just as much as Julia does, Jennifer admitted to herself frankly. *I need to climb out of that well-padded rut of mine before I sink into it permanently.*

If only going away with Julia didn't involve Thrussington!

"What happened between you and Marc Bouchard?" Julia asked abruptly.

It was a completely unexpected question. Julia hadn't mentioned Marc Bouchard since the first time they'd discussed him. She'd never said that she'd given him Jennifer's phone number, and Jennifer hadn't brought this up either. Jennifer had been trying to shut Marc out of her thoughts in every way, and had been consistently unsuccessful in her efforts. His memory was far too invasive.

Jennifer bit her lip as she stared at Julia, wondering how to answer her question. She settled for honesty, in a general sense.

"Nothing happened," she reported.

"When he phoned me to ask for your number he told me he hoped to be seeing you the next day," Julia observed. "Did he?"

"Yes."

"Had the bubble burst so quickly?"

"Yes. No. Oh, I don't know," Jennifer said miserably.

Her eyes were dull as she shrugged slightly, as if in defeat, then said flatly, "He told me when he left that he didn't want to see me again, Julia."

"That's exactly what he said?"

Jennifer considered this. It wasn't exactly what Marc had said; he'd said he didn't think they should see each other again. But it seemed to her that this added up to the same difference.

She reported the correct words and her conclusion about them to Julia, and Julia surveyed her with slightly upraised eyebrows.

"I think he's fallen in love with you," Julia decided.

Jennifer's patience snapped. "That's ridiculous," she blurted out. "For one thing, we don't know each other well enough for falling in love to even enter into it. For another thing, it seems obvious that after he had time to think things over he decided he didn't want to get involved with me any further."

As she spoke, the words stung, the hurt returned.

"Then why did he make a trip to Boston to see you?" Julia demanded.

"He was coming to Boston anyway."

"Was he?"

"He said he had to get some supplies," Jennifer reminded her mother-in-law.

"Are you sure he couldn't have gotten those supplies in Pittsfield?" Julia asked. "I don't know that, of course, but from the way he sounded on the phone I suspect that Marc drove here purely to see you, Jen. Did the two of you quarrel?"

"No, we didn't quarrel," Jennifer retorted. "We didn't...anything," she concluded dismally.

As she said this she remembered Marc's kiss just before his final statement. A wave of sensation swept through her with the memory; it was as if she could taste his kiss, as if she could still feel the warmth of his lips on hers.

"I really don't know why he feels as he does about our meeting again," she added frankly. "Something very powerful developed between us very quickly. There's no denying that."

"You indicated that Marc was burned by his first marriage," Julia pointed out.

"Did I? I don't know that he was burned by it. I guess I just got that impression. He didn't say much about his first wife."

"Regardless," Julia said. "Jen, for these past two weeks you've been moping around looking pale and wan and miserable. You're an entirely different person from the one you were that afternoon when you came in here straight from Thrussington. Am I wrong in surmising that Marc's behind the change in both cases?"

"No," Jennifer admitted, after a moment. "No, you're not wrong."

"It occurs to me," Julia said, "that there could be some very simple reasons for his decision not to see you again."

"Oh?"

Julia smiled. "Sometimes even I forget how rich you are," she admitted.

Jennifer flinched at this. It was true that she was wealthy in her own right. She had inherited a liberal amount of money from her grandmother. Eventually she would be her father's only heir, at which time she would become one of the richest women in the country. This was something she seldom thought about. She hated to think about it. To her, money always had been far more of a drawback than an asset. Now the idea that maybe this was the obstacle between Marc and herself was close to unbearable.

But, she asked herself, how could it be? Marc didn't even know her full name. He knew her only as Jennifer Bentley. Certainly he had no idea that she was Hugh Chatsworth-Graham's daughter.

Julia was watching Jennifer closely. "Your house gives you away, Jen, and I presume that's where you saw Marc when he was here?"

Jennifer nodded slowly.

"Well, your house is exquisite, and anyone with any perception at all would know that it cost a great deal of money, not so much to buy it, but to furnish it as perfectly as you've done. And that's just one manifestation. You look expensive, darling."

Jennifer flinched again. "Even so," she said, "what does that have to do with Marc?"

"A lot, probably. He may feel, perhaps justifiably so, that he can't measure up to you."

Resentment flared. "That's absurd!" Jennifer sputtered.

"Is it?"

"Yes, I think so." Jennifer looked as confused as she felt, despite this statement. She sighed. "I really don't know what his problem is," she confessed.

Julia played her trump card. "Then why don't you change your mind and come to Thrussington with me and find out?" she asked sweetly.

Marc had been at the Berkshire-Hudson Bank all afternoon, conferring with Brock LaFollette, its president, about the merits of installing a new alarm system. This was the biggest job that had come Marc's way thus far, and he was eager to get the contract for it.

He had just walked in his front door when he heard the phone ringing. He sighed impatiently. He wanted nothing so much as to pour himself a good drink and to settle down with it in front of the television.

There was a strong November wind blowing outside, creating a chill factor that placed the relative temperature below zero. Marc was cold to the bone, and his leg ached fiercely as he yanked the telephone receiver off the hook and barked, "Hello?"

"Mr. Bouchard?" He didn't immediately recognize the woman's voice.

"Yes."

"This is Julia Gray," he was told, and immediately he had a vision not of Julia, but of Jennifer.

It was two weeks since he had seen her, and he could not get her off his mind.

"How are you, Mrs. Gray?" he asked automatically.

"Better than might be expected," Julia responded with a chuckle. "They're going to let me out of the hospital next Tuesday."

"That's great," Marc said, and he was sincere about this. He knew what it could mean to be let out of a hospital after a long period of confinement.

"I plan to move to Thrussington for the balance of the fall and winter," Julia announced to his surprise. "As a matter of fact, I'll be going directly from the hospital to Thrussington, and I wondered if you would do me a couple of favors."

Marc's mind began to race. If Julia Gray was going to move to Thrussington, did this mean that Jennifer would be coming here to visit her from time to time?

His throat went dry at the thought.

"I'd be glad to do anything I can, Mrs. Gray," he managed after a moment.

"I thought I should call you rather than phoning the people involved directly, because of the alarm system,"

Julia said. "In other words, if you could possibly arrange to let them into the house, I would really appreciate it. The water needs to be turned on, so does the electricity, and I need to know that the furnace and the plumbing are working properly. I don't expect you to handle all this personally, but perhaps you have someone who could be at the house to let these people in to do what they have to do?" Again, Julia chuckled. "Even if we were to furnish the men with keys, I wouldn't want the alarm going off in their ears the way it did when my daughter-in-law went out there last month," she told him.

So Jennifer had told Julia Gray about their first encounter.

Marc tried to assess the significance of this, and couldn't.

"My housekeeper—Trina Moreno—will be driving up on Monday to get things ready," Julia said now. "I'd like to have everything working before she gets there, and the house warm. I haven't been outdoors myself for quite a while, but I understand it's pretty cold."

"Yes, it is," Marc conceded. "But don't worry. I'm sure there'll be no problem in having everything in working order before your housekeeper gets here."

"That's wonderful," Julia said. "Another favor..."

"Yes."

"Would you come out Tuesday evening and show me how the alarm works?" Julia asked. "I don't want to have the police rushing out there because I've goofed with it. Which reminds me. Perhaps you'd better shut it off so that Trina will be able to get in the house without being blasted."

"Why don't you ask your housekeeper to stop by my office on her way into town," Marc suggested. "Then I can go out to your house with her and show her how the system works. I'll also be glad to come out Tuesday evening so that you'll feel comfortable with it."

"You're very kind," Julia said. "I'll see you then."

They terminated their conversation, and Marc was frowning as he hung up the receiver. There had been a note of merriment in Julia Gray's voice laced with something that sounded like triumph.

Chapter Seven

Moving Julia and everything she felt necessary to take with her to Thrussington provided a challenging exercise in logistics. By the time they finally set off for the Berkshires, Jennifer had begun to think that life would have been a lot simpler if her mother-in-law had decided to convalesce in her Chestnut Hill home.

Julia had insisted on taking an assortment of her favorite books, photographs, records, several new pieces of needlepoint to work on, and a potpourri of address books, letters to be answered, and miscellaneous trivia. Several boxes packed to the brim were dispatched with Trina Moreno on Monday. The remainder were put into the back of Julia's comfortable sedan when she and Jennifer left Boston Tuesday morning.

Julia was so happy to be out of the hospital and in such high spirits that it was impossible to remain annoyed at her because she'd been so determined about lugging along so many superfluous things. Jennifer felt privately that Julia would never look at half the things she'd insisted on taking along, and a number of them had been difficult to extricate from their hiding places at the Chestnut Hill mansion. But that no longer seemed to matter.

Also, finding what Julia wanted had kept Jennifer busy enough so that she hadn't had time to brood about her impending move. Now, as she swung the car onto the Massachusetts Turnpike and headed west, she began to fight a new bout with apprehension. Had she been an idiot to let Julia talk her into making this move?

She still wasn't sure.

It was a cold November day, but at least the sun was shining. Nevertheless, there was a bleakness to the landscape that found a reflection inside Jennifer. Lingering amber leaves still clung to some of the oaks, but most of the deciduous trees were bare. The pines seemed especially dark green and sharp in contrast, but when they passed an occasional lake nestled in a valley, the water was slate-blue rather than summer's sapphire. Winter was on the way.

Jennifer was concentrating her vision and her attention on her driving, but a part of her mind wandered. She knew she would be approaching spending the winter in the Berkshires in an entirely different way had she not had that interim meeting with Marc. Had they not met again, she could have gone back to Thrussington in a spirit of anticipation, hopeful, at least, that he would be glad to see her again.

Now she didn't know what to expect.

Julia's property was several miles outside the town proper. Nevertheless, the whole Thrussington area was a small one. Jennifer knew that there was little doubt she and Marc would run into each other in the village occasionally, unless she decided to remain housebound and not go into town at all.

Obviously that would be impossible. She'd then be putting the burden of doing all the shopping and just about everything else on Trina Moreno. She'd already decided that this was one area in which she could be of considerable help.

She glanced at Julia, ensconced in the front seat with her leg, in its removable cast, propped in front of her. They'd slid the passenger's portion of the front seat as far back as possible so that Julia and her leg would fit into the car comfortably. Even so, Jennifer was hoping that Julia wasn't being jarred too much.

"Are you okay?" she asked.

"I've never been better," Julia reported happily. "You can't imagine what it means to be free again. Now I know how people who've been in prison for years feel when they're released."

Jennifer smiled sympathetically. She'd been fortunate never to have had the experience of a long stay in the hospital, but she could imagine how wonderful it must feel to emerge from such a restricted environment into the wide world.

Inevitably she thought of Marc. He'd done his time in hospitals. She found herself wishing that she'd been with him to help him bear his long ordeal.

A little hand-holding? Would Marc have wanted hand-holding from her?

Julia said suddenly, "I'm glad you said yes to this, Jen. I don't know when I've wanted something so much. I don't even know *why* I want it so much," she admitted, "but I do."

She added reflectively, "I need to think out a few things. And experience has taught me that my house in Chestnut Hill isn't the place for reflection."

"You think Thrussington will be?"

"Yes, I think so."

Jennifer slanted a glance at her mother-in-law. "Am I right in suspecting that your 'thinking out' involves Ricardo?" she asked bluntly.

"Yes," Julia nodded. "He wants to marry me, Jen. I just don't know."

Jennifer's lips tightened, but she refrained from saying anything. Ricardo Castel was darkly handsome, tremendously talented, world-famous...and she didn't trust him. She wondered if maybe it was his somewhat saturnine good looks that went against him, with her. In the dark evening clothes he wore for concerts, with a starched white shirt and a black bow tie to complete his costume, he was impressive, she had to give him that, and he had the manners to go with his looks. Smooth, very continental. It was easy to understand why Julia had been attracted to him, and equally easy to see how he might break Julia's heart before they were through with each other.

Julia said slowly, "Ricardo is several years younger than I am, and although he insists it doesn't matter to him, it sometimes does to me. I suppose I picture us ten years down the road. I'll be an old lady," she said ruefully, "and he'll still be in his prime."

Jennifer laughed. "You'll never be an old lady," she assured Julia. "It seems to me I've told you that a number of times before."

As she spoke, she suddenly pictured Marc and herself ten years down the road. She could imagine that Marc's black hair would be sprinkled with silver by then, but this would only make him handsomer than ever.

A shard of longing for him pierced her, sweet and hurtful all at once.

Marc had had a bad day. He'd been more tired when he awakened that morning than he had been when he'd gone to bed the night before. During the hours between midnight and dawn he'd been jolted out of his sleep three times by alarm systems going off in houses he serviced. Two of the houses were unoccupied, and he promptly called the police. In the third house, the family cat had gotten in the way of one of the infrared beams that set off the alarm. When Marc had dialed that number, the man of the house had sheepishly confessed what had happened.

The police had checked back with him later to tell him that one of the vacant house alarms had been a false one. In the other case, though, someone actually had been trying to gain entrance and they'd caught him fleeing down a back road.

This gave Marc some definite satisfaction, but the additional calls from the police had also caused him to lose further sleep.

When he fixed himself breakfast he burned the toast and the coffee tasted bitter. He nicked himself while he was shaving, and then his van refused to start promptly, as it usually did. It was a cold morning; nevertheless, he wasn't ready to cope with a sluggish engine. He was swearing by the time he'd revved the motor.

A series of small mishaps continued to mar his day. Little things, he forgot most of them as soon as he'd dealt with them, but by the time he got home late that afternoon he'd had it.

Then he remembered that he had promised to go out to Julia Gray's house early in the evening to explain her alarm system to her.

He'd just poured some Scotch on the rocks when he remembered this, and he swore softly.

He wasn't in the mood for any more encounters with anyone until he'd had a decent night's sleep. Nevertheless, he didn't feel that he could put Mrs. Gray off. He'd taken her housekeeper, a pleasant, middle-aged woman, out to the house the day before and had gone over the system with her. He couldn't see why she couldn't relay what he'd said to Julia Gray. But Mrs. Gray had asked that he do this personally, and Marc's credo from the time he'd started his business had been to please his customers in every way he could.

If Julia Gray wanted his personal attention, he'd have to give it to her.

He showered, put on some charcoal wool slacks in lieu of the flannel-lined jeans that had become his winter working costume, and a heavy gray and white Icelandic sweater. He heated up a can of hash for his supper, rinsed it down with a cup of the reheated coffee which tasted more bitter than ever, and hoped that his business with Julia Gray wasn't going to take too long.

The house was in order when Jennifer and Julia arrived in Thrussington, and it had never looked lovelier. Trina had divided her day between cleaning and laying in supplies. Everything shone, and there were special touches, like the clusters of multicolored Indian corn ornamenting the front door, and the bowls of bittersweet in the downstairs rooms.

They had a late lunch, and then Julia gratefully yielded to the suggestion that she take a nap before dinner. Trina had fixed the downstairs bedroom for her, including all of the books and photographs and other personal things that she had brought with her, and Julia was asleep by the time her head touched the pillow.

Looking closely at Jennifer, Trina said, "You could do with some rest yourself, Jen. Why don't you go along upstairs?"

"Maybe," Jennifer hedged. She usually wasn't much for daytime sleeping.

She did go upstairs, though, with the intention of unpacking some of her belongings. She'd asked Trina to put her up in the corner room they called the Yellow Room, this at the far end of the house from the space she'd once shared with Roger.

Trina, she noted, had already unpacked quite a few of her things for her. And suddenly the big bed, with its white candlewick spread and yellow quilt, looked very inviting.

Jennifer put off her nap by taking a fragrant bubble bath. Then she put on a thick terry robe and curled up on the bed, pulled the quilt up over her, and blanked out.

It was dark when she awakened. She stirred slowly, so comfortable that she hated to move. Then the luminous dial on the bedside clock told her it was seven-thirty, which seemed unbelievable.

As she got up Jennifer had to admit she'd needed the rest. She'd been more tired than she'd realized.

She decided to stay comfortable and casual tonight. She slipped on an emerald green velvet lounging robe, thrust her feet into gold kid flats, and gave her light blond hair a brushing that brought out the shine. A touch of green eyeshadow, a hint of lip gloss, and a splash of perfume completed her "dressing up for dinner."

As she was going down the stairs the doorbell rang. Jennifer called over her shoulder, "I'll get it, Trina," and went to answer it.

Marc Bouchard stood on the threshold.

The shock of seeing each other made them both mute. Marc's eyes widened. They were an incredible, intense shade of blue. Beautiful eyes. It was with an effort that Jennifer managed to look away from them, but then her gaze fell to his mouth and her emotions began to swirl, treacherous as a sandstorm.

He spoke first, saying harshly, "I didn't know you'd be here."

She managed the faintest of smiles. "I didn't know you were coming here."

"Mrs. Gray asked me to meet with her tonight. Didn't she tell you?"

"No."

Marc ran a hand through his hair, something Jennifer had never seen him do before, and it gave her a clue to his agitation. He asked abruptly, "Where is Mrs. Gray?"

"I don't know," Jennifer admitted. "Still in her room, I imagine. We both took naps after lunch and...I guess we both overslept."

"You mean you haven't had dinner yet?"

"No."

He frowned, biting his lip. "I seem to have come at a bad time," he said then. "It might be better if I come back tomorrow."

He was like a powerful animal on a leash. Jennifer saw that he couldn't wait to break free, to get away from her. The hurt was reflected on her face, and it stopped him short.

"Look," he said awkwardly, "if you want to find out if she wants to see me now, it's okay. I'll stay."

Jennifer nodded and sped away from him. She needed the chance to breathe normally, the chance to regroup.

She found Julia in her room, still propped up on her pillows, sipping a cup of tea Trina had brought her.

"I must get up," Julia said ruefully, "but I keep putting it off. It's such a production."

Julia had taken her cast off while she was resting. Jennifer said hastily, "Let me help you get the cast on again." She added almost under her breath, "Marc Bouchard is here. He says you sent for him."

"Yes," Julia acknowledged calmly. "I didn't intend to crash as I did." Her gaze swept over Jennifer perceptively. "You too?"

"Yes."

"I guess we both needed the rest," Julia said. "Look, dear, send Trina in. She can help me with the cast. Tell Mr. Bouchard I'll be out to see him as soon as I can navigate. I'd suggest he come talk to me in here, but I really need to see the various boxes, and such, associated with the alarm system if I'm going to understand it."

Julia added, "Why don't you fix him a drink while he's waiting, and have one yourself."

Jennifer stared at Julia helplessly. She was about to suggest that she help Julia with the cast and let Trina make a drink for Marc, but she knew this wouldn't go over. She shrugged and gritted her teeth. Whether he liked it or not, Marc was going to have to tolerate her company for the next hour or so.

She found him in the living room, standing in front of one of Julia's paintings. He'd tilted his head back slightly as he assayed it, and Jennifer stood stock-still just inside the doorway, watching him. Her kid slippers had soft soles; he hadn't heard her come into the room. He was absorbed in the painting, and she let herself take advantage of the opportunity to watch him.

The gray sweater and slacks he was wearing were a perfect foil for his dramatic coloring. He was handsome as ever, Jennifer thought wryly, even more handsome, but he did look tired. There was a tight line to his mouth that revealed tension.

It was all she could do not to throw her arms around him and nestle her head against his broad, powerful shoulder. She wanted his nearness; she wanted to feel him right next to her. She wanted him.

Bleakly she wondered why it was that he'd decided they shouldn't meet again. She accepted, finally, that there was only one way she could find out.

Sooner or later she was going to have to ask him.

"Marc," she said softly, and he whirled around so quickly that once again his bad leg played a trick on him. She saw him go off balance and fought the impulse to rush to him. Slowly he steadied himself, but she saw his mouth twitch and recognized his frustration.

"Julia will be with us as soon as she can get up and around," she reported. "It takes her a while. Meantime, she's suggested you and I have a drink. Would you like Scotch?"

She could see that his refusal was at the tip of his tongue, but then he reconsidered.

"Thank you, yes," he said.

"Would you...would you like to fix the drinks yourself?" she suggested haltingly.

He looked startled. "Here?"

"Why not here?"

He didn't answer this, but he did follow Jennifer as she started toward the dining room cabinet where Julia kept her liquor.

Trina had already set out a bucketful of ice and glasses. Surveying this, Marc asked, "What will you have?"

"I think I'd like a glass of sherry. There is some, isn't there?"

He glanced over the assorted bottles. "Yes," he said shortly.

He poured a glass of sherry and handed it to her, then fixed Scotch on the rocks for himself. The silence between them deepened as they went back to the living room, and with the depth came a darkness. Jennifer felt an increasing sense of hopelessness as she sat sipping her sherry, trying not to look at him. Then she nearly gave up. Maybe this was the moment to ask him why he'd made the statement that had halted their relationship. Maybe she should simply plunge right into it.

She wasn't given time to do so. Julia walked into the living room slowly, hobbling on her crutches with difficulty. Trina hovered anxiously just behind her.

The atmosphere changed. It lightened, for Julia and Marc at least. As the two of them chatted with each other, Jennifer began to feel very much left out.

Marc and Julia, for one thing, encountered common ground. Watching her progress with the crutches, which was extremely halting at best, Marc finally said, "I've had a lot of practice with those things, and there are a few tricks that make it easier."

"Tell me," Julia implored, and the ice was broken.

By the time they'd gone over the alarm system, Julia also had learned how to handle the crutches, how to better balance herself on them, and how to use them to maximum advantage so that they would work with her rather than against her. When she sank into an armchair and started sipping the extra dry martini Marc had made for her, she expelled a sigh of satisfaction.

"Well," she said, bestowing a radiant smile on Marc, "you've taught me two lessons tonight. Navigation, and how to cope with an alarm system."

Marc's smile was genuine, and heartstopping, as far as Jennifer was concerned. "My pleasure," he said. He had fixed himself another Scotch at Julia's request, and he seemed relaxed, or almost relaxed. Occasionally when he glanced toward Jennifer he stiffened. She noticed it every time he did it, and each little incident became a stab.

"Trina's fixed a late supper for us tonight rather than a real dinner," Julia said after a time. By then Marc had been persuaded to set a fire in the fireplace, and the living room could not have looked warmer or cozier. But there was a core of ice at the center of Jennifer's heart that refused to melt.

"We're just going to have cheese omelets and a salad and some dessert," Julia elaborated. "You'll join us, won't you?"

"Thank you, but I had dinner before I came out here," Marc said.

"Dinner?" There was an archness to Julia's smile. "Care to reveal the menu?" she dared him.

He grinned. "Canned hash," he confessed.

"Then certainly you'll join us," Julia decided. She turned to Jennifer. "Tell Trina, will you, dear?" she asked.

Jennifer was glad to get out of the room. She lingered in the kitchen, urging Trina to give her something to do to help, but Trina, as usual, had everything under control.

Jennifer felt as brittle as a matchstick when she returned to the living room. Marc and Julia were deep in conversation, and she felt totally apart from whatever it was they were talking about. She was tempted to pick up a magazine and start reading, and wondered if they'd even notice if she did.

Marc and Julia continued to do virtually all the talking during dinner, and there was no lag in their conversation. By the time Trina had brought in chocolate ice cream laced with Kahlua for dessert, Jennifer felt she'd become totally superfluous.

Trina suggested she serve their coffee in the living room, and Julia nodded agreement. But before Julia could be established in her large armchair, Trina announced that she was wanted on the phone. Overseas.

Ricardo, Jennifer thought dully.

"We'll have to have some more phone jacks put in," Julia decided as she made her way out of the room to the phone in the library.

With Julia gone, the room closed in, and Jennifer felt a sudden desire to rush outside, to breathe in great gulps of the cold November air.

She knew Marc was watching her. She could feel his eyes on her. Finally she couldn't keep herself from meeting his intent blue eyes.

He said softly, "You've been thrown a curve, haven't you?"

"What do you mean?"

"You came here for Julia's sake, but certainly you didn't want to come. You knew it would mean seeing me. I'm sorry about that, Jennifer."

She found her voice. "Why?" she asked him.

He blinked, and she knew that briefly, at least, she'd thrown him a curve with such a direct question. He rallied, and said, "Well, we agreed it was wiser not to see any more of each other."

"No," Jennifer corrected him. "We didn't agree to anything at all. That was your edict."

His dark eyebrows arched interrogatively. "Are you saying you didn't think so too?" he asked her.

"Yes, I'm saying I didn't think so too," she told him defiantly. "I don't know what came over you that day at my house, and certainly you weren't about to explain it."

Her resentment had all been simmering deep within her for a long time and it began to surge to the surface. "As far as I'm concerned, you were pretty damned unfair!" she blurted.

She'd never seen anyone look quite so disbelieving. Then he asked slowly, "Jenny...Jenny, are you telling me you wanted to keep on seeing me?"

"Oh, come on, come on," she chided, her impatience with him mounting. "Why wouldn't I have wanted to go on seeing you? I thought a small miracle had happened between us. But evidently you—"

She stopped when she saw the expression on his face. He looked dazed, and he shook his head slightly, as if he weren't sure of what he was hearing.

He said very slowly, his voice husky, "I, too, thought a small miracle had happened between us. But I guess I've never really believed in miracles and I was afraid this one wouldn't last. I guess I was afraid that to try to prolong it would only cause us both to wake up and...and see our own folly."

"Our own folly?" she echoed.

He nodded gravely. "We're worlds apart, you and I," he stated flatly. "I don't especially like putting it that way, but it's true."

"Aren't you being a snob, Marc?" she accused him.

He laughed shortly. "Me, a snob? I can assure you I have nothing to be snobbish about, Jenny. That's the problem. I haven't very much of anything."

"Do I detect an incipient inferiority complex?" she asked him coolly.

She saw him wince, but he said, "No. I'm a realist, that's all. I've never had much money, or much in the way of material possessions. When I moved up here I put everything I had in the world in a suitcase and two cartons. I'm doing better financially than I've ever done before, but I don't imagine I could pay the monthly fuel bill for your Boston town house." He managed a laugh. "You may not be filthy rich," he said, trying to make light of it, "but you're plainly endowed with a lot more of this world's goods than I am, lady. I guess I took a long look and thought to myself, I have nothing to offer you."

Jennifer nearly lost the last part of this because the words *filthy rich* had echoed loudly in her mind. The problem was that she was filthy rich, and destined to be so forever. He had no idea how filthy rich her potential was, and the last thing in the world she wanted was for him to find out.

She'd have to talk to Julia about this.

"Are you hearing me?" Marc asked suddenly, and she forced her attention back to him.

She said evenly, "I think you're looking only at surface things. I felt personally that there was—"

Her voice broke on this, and she had to stop.

Marc was looking at her as if his entire world hung on her next sentence. "Go on," he urged her.

"Well, I felt personally that there was something so...so terrific between us. I don't know about you but I—I'd never done anything like that before in my life. I mean, I'd just met you and..."

"I know what you mean, sweetheart," he said gently.

She looked up at this, and met his intense gaze. Marc covered the distance between them, and Jennifer went into his arms.

"I've counted the hours," he said. "I've counted each hour since the last time I saw you and considered it wasted. I've gone through hell, wondering how I could undo what I did and get you back again. But that doesn't mean that it's right, Jenny. That's something you've got to understand. I have to level with you about this, it wouldn't be fair otherwise. There can't be any real future for us. You've got to understand that.''

Was he telling her that he knew he could never see his way clear to marrying her? Was that what was bothering him? Was that what he was trying to say?

Jennifer didn't know, and just then she didn't care. Neither the past nor the future even existed for her—just the present, a present to be shared with this man who'd staked a claim on her heart she could never imagine being freed from.

Trina, peering through the doorway to see if more coffee was required, saw Jennifer in Marc's arms, saw them kiss. She backed off, smiling to herself as she went to tell Julia to stay out of the living room for a while.

Chapter Eight

Jennifer stood in the middle of Julia's studio, looking around. The studio occupied a single-storied building a hundred feet from the main house. It consisted of one enormous room with a high, vaulted ceiling and a huge skylight.

The November sun was streaming through the skylight, but it wasn't enough to dispel the chill. The studio had a separate heating system and men would be arriving shortly to reactivate it. Meanwhile, Jennifer shivered, even though she was wearing a heavy sweater and a thick jacket.

Regardless of her temporary discomfort, the studio intrigued her so much that she didn't want to leave it. There was a calculated disorder to Julia's paraphernalia. Jennifer was sure Julia could immediately lay her hand on any tube of paint or size canvas she wanted. Julia undoubtedly had her own kind of filing system. But to the uninitiated, the place was a fantastic mélange. Even more

You know the thrill of escaping to a world where

Love, Romance, and Happiness reach out to one and all . . .

Escape again...with 4 FREE novels and

Get more great Silhouette Special Edition novels —for a 15-day FREE examination— delivered to your door every month!

*S*ilhouette Special Edition novels are written especially for you, someone who knows the allure, the enchantment and the power of romance. Romance *is* alive, and flourishing in these moving love stories that let you escape to exotic places with sensitive heroines and captivating men.

Written by such popular authors as Janet Dailey, Donna Vitek, Diana Dixon, and others, Silhouette Special Edition novels help you reach that special world—month after month. They'll take you to that world you have always imagined, where you will live and breathe the emotions of love and the satisfaction of romance triumphant.

FREE BOOKS

Start today by taking advantage of this special offer— 4 new Silhouette Special Edition romances (a $10.00 Value) *absolutely FREE,* along with a Cameo Tote Bag. Just fill out and mail the attached postage-paid order card.

AT-HOME PREVIEWS, FREE DELIVERY

After you receive your 4 free books and Tote Bag, every month you'll have the opportunity to preview 6 more Silhouette Special Edition romances— *as soon as they're published!* When you decide to keep them, you'll pay just $11.70, (a $15.00 value), *with never an additional charge of any kind and no risk!* You can cancel your subscription at any time simply by dropping us a note. In any case, the first 4 books, and Cameo Tote Bag are yours to keep.

EXTRA BONUS

When you take advantage of this offer, we'll also send you the Silhouette Books Newsletter free with each shipment. Every informative issue features news about upcoming titles, interviews with your favorite authors, and even their favorite recipes.

Get a Free Tote Bag, too!

EVERY BOOK YOU RECEIVE WILL BE A BRAND-NEW FULL-LENGTH NOVEL!

Escape with 4 Silhouette Special Edition novels (a $10.00 Value) and get a FREE Tote Bag, too!

Silhouette Special Edition ®

Silhouette Books, 120 Brighton Rd., P.O. Box 5084, Clifton, NJ 07015-9956

Yes, please send me FREE and without obligation, 4 new Silhouette Special Edition novels along with my Cameo Tote Bag. Unless you hear from me after I receive my 4 FREE books, please send me 6 new Silhouette Special Edition novels for a free 15-day examination each month as soon as they are published. I understand that you will bill me a total of just $11.70 (a $15.00 value), with no additional charges of any kind. There is no minimum number of books that I must buy, and I can cancel at any time. The first 4 books and Tote Bag are mine to keep, even if I never take a single additional book.

NAME _____
                    (please print)

ADDRESS _____

CITY _____ STATE _____ ZIP _____

Terms and prices subject to change. Your enrollment is subject to acceptance by Silhouette Books.

SILHOUETTE SPECIAL EDITION is a registered trademark.

CCS425

important, it fairly burst with the exuberance and color that was such a part of Julia's personality.

Jennifer smiled. This would be a good place to work. These surroundings should be enough to give anyone inspiration.

She browsed, checking out supplies, only to come to the conclusion that she would start work immediately, as soon as the studio was warmer, and she wouldn't need a thing for ages to come. Julia believed in stocking up and then stocking up again.

Colorful paintings, mostly by friends of Julia's, adorned the bare wood walls. There was a motley collection of furniture, all of it comfortable. The old day bed in one corner looked as if it had been well used. Jennifer could imagine Julia taking naps there, when she'd been working hours on end, and resolved that maybe she'd try the same thing.

She was beginning to feel more optimistic about herself and her work. And Marc? Certainly their evening had ended a lot better than it had begun. He'd left fairly early. She'd walked to the door with him. On the threshold he'd leaned over and kissed her deeply and tenderly. Involuntarily her arms had stolen around his neck. Raising herself on tiptoes, she'd returned his kiss, savoring the warmth of his lips, their pliability.

"Take care," he'd said very softly, and she'd nodded.

Yes, she'd take care. She'd take great care with this relationship between Marc and herself because she wanted—wanted very much—to establish something so firm between them that it wouldn't be shaken easily. Then, maybe, if one day he found out more about her, he wouldn't be so rocked by the revelation. In the meantime, for the first time in her life, a man would have come to know her for herself alone.

She could only hope that she'd stand up to the test.

As for her work, she felt more confident of standing up to the test careerwise than she ever had before. She was doing what she loved to do, and she knew at this point that she was capable of doing it well.

She had a February first deadline on her next book and she'd been worrying because time was slipping by and the book was only half done. Now she felt convinced that she could plunge in and finish it with time to spare.

Jennifer left the studio, carefully locking the door behind her. She turned toward the house, and the cup of happiness that was filling up within her threatened to overflow.

Marc's van was careening into the driveway.

Jennifer watched him park, then climb out and reach up to tug something down after him. Apples. Marc crossed to her, carrying the better part of a bushel of shining, rosy apples.

She grinned. "Have you gone into the orchard business?" she asked him.

He grinned back. His eyes were an unbelievable shade of blue. Jennifer felt as if she could look at them all day. A glorious color, she thought abstractedly.

"I put in an alarm system last month for a man who owns an orchard," he confessed. "He loaded me down with apples. He says they'll keep if you wrap each piece of fruit in newspaper and store it in a cool place. I'd rather see them used up though. I thought maybe Trina could make something with these."

"Like a hundred apple pies?" Jennifer teased. "Come on," she invited. "Let's take them into the kitchen."

Trina was at the kitchen sink, busy polishing a copper bowl. Jennifer noted that the housekeeper's eyes lingered approvingly on Marc.

"I think maybe I'll make some pies and freeze them," Trina decided. "And maybe some apple butter.

"Right now," the housekeeper added, "I'm going to finish up my polishing and then make a fresh pot of coffee. Miss Julia's therapist was here, she's done her exercises, and she's in the study watching TV. Why don't you two join her and I'll bring in some coffee for all of you."

Trina turned back to her task, so confident that her suggestion would be accepted that she didn't pause to notice the reaction it had incurred.

Marc, all of a sudden, looked very doubtful. So doubtful that Jennifer reached out to grab his hand and tugged at it.

"Come on," she said. "It's time for a coffee break."

He followed her out of the kitchen, but once they were beyond Trina's hearing he said, "Look, I didn't intend to butt in."

Jennifer turned, to see conflicting expressions cross his handsome face. Quietly she asked him, "What is it, Marc?"

She saw his lips tighten, then he frowned. "It was just a crazy impulse, bringing those apples out here this morning," he said after a moment. "Last night when I got home I had a talk with myself."

"Oh?"

"Jenny..."

Very briefly Jennifer saw stark longing in his eyes, an expression so intense that it jolted her. Her breath caught in her throat, and she stared at him, wondering if her eyes were mirroring her emotions as his just had.

She, too, was reacting intensely to him. Yet an inner sense of timing prompted her to recognize that this was not the time to be too serious. Not on this sunny November morning, when her world was just beginning to be brighter than it had been for a long time.

She forced a smile that was successful. It warmed her gray eyes and curved her lips. She said lightly, "Just having a cup of coffee isn't that much of a commitment, Marc."

Reluctantly at first, he returned the smile. He said almost grudgingly, "I suppose you're right. I—"

She reached out a slim finger and placed it over his lips. She could feel his lips moving beneath her finger, and it had an oddly erotic effect. It was with an effort that she managed, "Let's just relax and go have some coffee with Julia, okay? I'm sure she's lonely, and equally sure that she'd be delighted to see you."

Marc looked startled by this. "Me?" he demanded.

"You," Jennifer said. "You've made quite an impression on her."

Before he could answer she turned and started for the study.

After a moment, in which Jennifer suspected he was indulging in a small mental wrestling match, Marc followed.

Julia, as Jennifer had predicted, was delighted to see Marc. Her smile shone with approval on both Marc and her former daughter-in-law. She insisted that they turn off the television set. "If I watch much more daytime TV, I'll need to take a sanity test," she said.

"That bad?" Marc asked.

"I suppose it depends what you're looking for," Julia admitted.

Soon she was leading Marc into talking about his business, and Jennifer marveled at Julia's aptitude when it came to drawing people out.

Marc confessed that the going had been very slow at first, but over the past four years he'd steadily built up a list of clients who depended on him.

Now, if he was retained by the bank to install an up-to-date alarm system, his place in the business community would really be secure.

"Brock LaFollette, the president, is in favor of me getting the job. But Paul Freyton—he's LaFollette's son-in-law and a vice-president—is against making a change. He refuses to believe that their present system is antiquated."

Marc continued. "The final decision will be up to the bank's board of directors, and they'll be meeting the first of the month." He added, "It will mean a lot to me to pull this off. Also I'm beginning to develop clients throughout a large sector of the Berkshire region, which is great. My going this far afield involves considerable cooperation with local police departments in the various towns. But, to date, they've been very supportive."

"Perhaps because you were once involved in police work yourself?" Julia suggested.

Marc glanced at Jennifer before he answered this, and she could feel warm color flooding her cheeks. He must have realized that this was something Julia had learned from her.

"Perhaps," he said casually. "I suppose the fact I was once with the New York City Police Department has gotten around, though I haven't exactly advertised it, Mrs. Gray."

"Last night it was Julia," she reminded him.

Marc shifted his position. He reminded Jennifer of an uncomfortable schoolboy. "Yes," he said, "Julia." He paused, and then smiled, a smile so disarming that Jennifer caught her breath.

"That takes some getting used to," he admitted.

"You find me so formidable?" Julia asked archly.

The smile widened. "No, that's just it," Marc said. "I don't find you formidable at all."

"But you expected to?" Julia persisted.

"Yes, I suppose so. You were more than pleasant at our first meeting, it isn't that. But—"

Julia said gently, "External facts are not always complete unto themselves, Marc. What I'm trying to say, I guess, is that you shouldn't always think that the cover of the book necessarily reflects the contents." Julia had leaned forward as she spoke; now she relaxed against the pillows again. "I have a nerve," she said frankly. "I'm preaching at you."

Yes, Julia had been preaching, Jennifer allowed silently. But why?

Julia had a motive; of that Jennifer was sure. It occurred to her that Julia was laying groundwork so that if at a later date Marc found out that Jennifer was not merely Jennifer Bentley, but Jennifer Bentley Chatsworth-Graham, he'd be able to take the shock in stride.

At least that's what Julia was hoping.

More power to her if her little plan works, Jennifer thought wryly.

Thus far in her life, nothing had ever diminished the impact to people that learning she was her father's daughter had made on them.

"I think I know what you're saying, Julia," Marc said. "Would you call it reverse snobbery?" he asked.

The question was such an astute one that Jennifer caught her breath, wondering how Julia would deal with this.

Julia handled it with a touch of humor. "I think I might call it exactly that," she informed Marc, returning his smile.

Julia's smile had its own devastating effect. Jennifer calculated that if her mother-in-law hadn't already befriended Marc, she would have done so at that moment. She could feel the rapport growing between the two of them, and she felt a pang of envy.

Trina appeared with coffee and a tray of fragrant, warm cinnamon buns. As they enjoyed this mid-morning repast, Julia skillfully led Jennifer into the conversation until Jennifer was talking about her work and confessed that she'd been worried about meeting her next deadline but wasn't any longer.

Her face glowed with enthusiasm as she said, "Your studio is terrific, Julia. I'm going to love working in it."

"I always have," Julia agreed. "Marc, do you think you should extend the alarm system to the studio? I know I told you originally I didn't think it necessary, but now I wonder. Some of the paintings done by old friends of mine have assumed considerable value. And Jennifer will have her work in progress out there...."

Jennifer laughed. "No one's about to steal anything I'm doing," she assured Julia.

"You underestimate yourself," Julia said. "But then, you've always tended to do that, darling." She turned to Marc. "She's actually quite good," she confided.

He nodded. "I know. I've bought all her books. I've been intrigued by the stories and delighted by the illustrations."

Jennifer stared at him, her eyes wide and her lips parted. What he was saying indicated quite plainly that he'd bought more of her books during that terrible intermission when he'd decreed they shouldn't see each other again.

A shot of pure exultation penetrated an area close to her heart, then ricocheted throughout her.

Fortunately Julia continued to lead the conversation, and Marc went along with the dialogue easily. Jennifer, on the other hand, was tongue-tied. Maybe she was attaching too much importance to his interim purchase of her books, but she liked the kind of significance this action on his part had for her.

He hadn't been able to forget her any more than she'd been able to forget him.

The coffee finished, Marc rose reluctantly. "I'm afraid I have to get back to work," he confessed.

"I've really enjoyed this," Julia told him.

"So have I." Marc's gaze shifted to Jennifer as he spoke.

"Marc," Julia added, "stop by when you get a chance, will you, and take a look at the studio? Tell me what you think we should do insofar as security is concerned. It was foolish of me not to have you do the whole thing as a package, now that I think of it. I was interested primarily in protecting the contents of the house, but that was shortsighted of me."

"No problem," Marc said easily. "I'm sure we can take care of it. I'll get back to you in a couple of days."

He and Julia bade each other a friendly good-bye, and Jennifer said swiftly, "I'll see you to the door."

She and Marc were silent as they walked through the house. She stood with him at the front door. The sun had retreated, and there was a gray tinge to the clouds.

"If it were a few degrees colder," Marc said, "I'd say we're in for some snow."

Jennifer shivered. "Does it have to be colder than this to snow?" she asked him. "I wouldn't think so."

He smiled. "A shade so," he said. "You're going to have to learn to dress warmer if you're going to winter up in these hills," he advised. "Layering is the name of the game. You put on layer after layer of clothing, then if you go in someplace where it's overly warm, you can start peeling off.''

He paused, staring down at her. A vivid memory came back to sear Jennifer's mental vision, and she suspected it was searing his with equal force.

There had been a moment when they had both "peeled down." She remembered their reaching out and finding each other, snuggled under the quilt in the old maple bed in his guest room. She remembered what it had been like to have Marc become a part of her, in the ultimate of physical senses.

She wanted him so much that it hurt, and she shuddered.

He said softly, "Jenny..."

Involuntarily she had closed her eyes, her lashes fanning her cheeks, her lids tight. Now she opened them, to find him very close to her, his face echoing everything she was feeling. It was like looking into a mirror to see a masculine image revealed, whereas until now she'd seen only her own face reflected.

Two nights later Julia's studio was robbed. Jennifer discovered the door to the studio unlocked when she went out shortly after breakfast, having determined that she'd work that morning with the aid of a space heater to keep her warm. The people scheduled to reactivate the heating system had been delayed because of a series of emergencies, and wouldn't be around for at least two or three more days.

Jennifer had no sense of premonition as she turned the door handle and stepped into the huge studio room. Later, she thought she should have had. Later, the memory was much clearer of having locked the door the previous afternoon, after taking a number of her own things out to the studio and also trying out the typewriter that had been rented from a business machines agency in the village.

That morning, though, it had begun to sleet as Jennifer left the house, and she traversed a miserable hundred feet to the studio door. So she was intent only on getting inside.

She switched on the overhead light, and the gloom was instantly dispelled by the clever and effective lighting system that made Julia's studio a perfect place to work even on the darkest of days.

Then Jennifer gasped and involuntarily pressed the back of her hand to her mouth as if to stifle an incipient scream.

The walls were virtually bare. Only a few of the relatively unimportant paintings still hung against the plain wood surface. Stacks of canvasses had been overturned; the place was in a shambles. Yet a quick initial examination showed Jennifer—admittedly not an expert in this sort of thing—that this had not been a case of vandalism but, rather, had involved pure theft.

The extension phone had been hooked up in the studio. Jennifer went to it, wondering if the wires had been cut. Didn't thieves usually cut phone wires?

She lifted the receiver and heard the hum of the dial tone.

She scanned the slender Thrussington area phone book quickly. Then she dialed Marc Bouchard's number, praying that he wouldn't have gone out yet on this dismal November morning.

He hadn't; he answered the phone on the second ring.

Jennifer's words tumbled over one another as she told him what she'd just discovered, horror tightening her throat by the time she'd finished speaking.

Marc swore. Then he said abruptly, "I'll be right out."

Jennifer sank down onto the nearest chair. She was trembling, beginning to shake uncontrollably. The realization was hitting her that at some point during the night someone—one person or two people or more—had trespassed onto Julia's property and come in here and made off with God knows how much.

People, evil, wicked people, had crept in under the cover of darkness.

Hot tears began to fill Jennifer's eyes and spill down her cheeks.

She had composed herself to an extent by the time Marc arrived, but the traces of tears still remained, and she was still unsteady.

He glanced at her swiftly, but it was a glance so needle-sharp and thoroughly appraising that it made her flinch. Marc, indeed, had been well trained!

"Any idea when this happened?" he asked.

"It must have been last night," Jennifer said weakly. "Late last night, I'd think. Julia and I watched a movie on TV. Trina went to bed before we did. So I set the alarm before I went upstairs. We have a rule that the last person to go to bed—Trina or myself, that is—sets the alarm. Once Julia has settled into her room for the night she stays there. Were she to come out of her room, she'd deactivate her own panel, of course."

Marc nodded impatiently.

"I locked up when I left here yesterday afternoon," Jennifer said. "I'm sure of it." She was sure of it, now. She'd reviewed her actions of the previous day one by one, memory returning with a clarity that made her certain she'd turned the key in the door when she'd left.

"What time was that?" Marc asked her.

"About four. I just brought a few things out and tried the typewriter I'd rented."

Her glance swept the table where the typewriter had been. It was gone.

"Oh, God," she said miserably.

"What is it, Jennifer?" Marc asked sharply. Not Jenny, not now. Jennifer.

"They took the typewriter too." Shock kept her voice to a whisper.

"Have you told Julia about this?"

She shook her head. "No one. I—I called you. I—I just thought of calling you first."

As he heard Jennifer admit that she'd instinctively turned toward him first, an expression that was highly unprofessional flickered across Marc's face.

He couldn't help himself. He reached out to her. "Sweetheart," he said huskily. "I know how you must be feeling. It's a hell of a thing to have your space violated like this. A lot more of a jolt than people who've never had the experience realize. Very personal, very unnerving."

At the question he read in her expression he added gently, "No, it has never happened to me. But I've seen it happen so often to others, I've seen the reactions...."

He didn't add that he'd never owned anything worth stealing himself. Not, at least, till he'd come to Thrussington. He'd developed an interest in nice old things since he'd been here, and for the first time in his life had had a little spare change with which to buy something, occasionally, that he didn't really need. As a result, he had several pieces of furniture and some old pottery and a few other odds and ends stashed among the other furnishings in Jack Thornton's house.

Jack also had some good pieces, inherited from his family who had lived around the Berkshire region for years. It occurred to Marc that it wouldn't be a bad idea for him to put an alarm system in his present place of abode. Thus far, he supposed he'd been lucky.

He sighed. When Jack Thornton had first suggested to him that he move to Thrussington and start a security and alarm business, he had been amused. Amused, he thought with irony, and stupid enough to think that crime was on holiday outside big cities.

He'd learned differently, to his regret.

He felt outraged, bitter, and frustrated as he looked around Julia Gray's studio. He had no way of knowing what had been taken, since he didn't know what had been in there in the first place.

"Were any of Julia's paintings in here?" he asked Jennifer. He'd been holding her, holding her tenderly, smoothing her beautiful pale blond hair with a hand that suddenly seemed to him too rough for this task. She'd had her face nuzzled against his jacket. Now she stepped back to look up at him.

"I don't know," she said. "Most of the paintings hanging in here, if not all of them, were by friends of Julia's. Remember, she mentioned the last time you were at the house that she imagined some of them had attained quite a value. A lot of Julia's friends have become famous over the years, just as she has. Not as famous, but even so..."

Jennifer's eyes were moving around the studio as she spoke. Marc could tell that she was trying to assess things. "I think that most of Julia's paintings have been hung in the house," she said. "At least I hope so." She shrugged helplessly. "I really don't know."

"I'll have to call the local cops," Marc told her. "They'll probably call in the Staties on anything this big. They don't have the facilities in places like Thrussington to deal with something of this magnitude on their own."

His face was grim. "First let's talk to Julia," he suggested, "and find out where we stand."

Julia handled the news of the theft as she handled most things.

She always keeps her cool, Jennifer thought admiringly. *Would that I could be more like her.*

She watched Julia reach for her crutches and struggle to her feet. At once Marc was at her side, giving her some instructions in low tones, these aimed at making the chore of dealing with the crutches easier.

"I have to go out and see for myself," she said, and Marc nodded. But he stayed close to Julia, occasionally reaching out a steadying hand, and he kept telling her that the going would be easier if she balanced this way or that way, and how to handle obstacles like the front steps.

The hundred-foot trek from the house to the studio seemed like a marathon course to Jennifer by the time they arrived at the studio door. Then she forgot about Julia's slow and difficult progress once they'd all stepped inside the studio.

She heard Julia gasp, even as she herself had gasped earlier. After a moment Julia said wryly, "Well, I guess they knew what to take and what to leave behind."

Marc pulled out a chair for her, and Julia sat down carefully. "What about your own work?" he asked her.

"We'll have to go through the canvasses...and the crates," she said. "I stayed at the Chestnut Hill house when my paintings were being shipped out here, Marc. Ricardo came out and handled things for me at this end. As you know from being in the house, quite a number of my paintings are hung there. But," she added reluctantly, "quite a number of them were stacked here waiting to be framed, and others that had been framed still hadn't been uncrated. Time became of the essence; we were getting ready to leave for Greece—"

Julia broke off. "The paintings old friends gave to me matter more than my own work," she admitted after a moment.

"I can understand that," Marc said gently. "Nevertheless, when we're dealing with values, it's your paintings that will bring the biggest prices in some underground art market." He paused, staring at the blank spots on the walls. "Before we get into this, I'd better call the cops," he decided.

The two Thrussington police officers who had responded to his call the morning Jennifer had set off the alarm system came to the house again this time. As Marc had predicted, they called in the state police. Two troopers came, to be followed after a short time by a detective lieutenant assigned to the Berkshire County district attorney's office. It was he who would be in charge of the investigation.

It was a very long day. Trina brought sandwiches and coffee out to the studio, where it was still cold though two space heaters had now been turned on. Julia and Jennifer and Marc and whichever of the police officers were on the premises at the moment munched the sandwiches and sipped coffee while they made a painstaking inventory of the studio's contents.

The missing pictures that had hung on the walls were listed first. Then the typewriter, and a few other portable items, these including a radio and an intercom linking the studio and the house. Then they started going through the crates and the stacks of canvasses.

It was difficult, and when they'd finished a preliminary inventory it became necessary to go into the house to list those paintings of Julia's that had already been hung there.

Marc and Jennifer attended to this task. By the time they'd finished, Julia had returned from the studio, and was being assisted solicitously by State Police Detective Lieutenant Brent Cranston into the most comfortable chair in the living room.

The list of the paintings hanging in the house and those that Julia was sure had been shipped on from Boston was compared, and Julia, finishing her perusal of it, glanced up with a sigh.

"Fourteen missing," she said. "I'll try to describe them for you, Brent."

The state police lieutenant was looking at her anxiously. "We can get to that tomorrow morning," he decided. "Meantime, we'll be sending out men from our lab to dust for prints and go through all the rest of the physical evidence routine. But I'm not too optimistic about coming up with anything that will be helpful," he admitted.

The state police lieutenant was a nice-looking man, tall and lean with a shock of reddish hair and eyes that were almost as blue as Marc's. Almost, but not quite.

He said reluctantly, "The thieves got in a back window that was unlocked, Mrs. Gray. Maybe we'll get some identifiable prints but, as I said, I'm not counting on it."

"I should have had an alarm system in the studio as well as in the house," she admitted. She turned to Marc. "I'd like to go ahead as soon as you can on a system for the studio, Marc. Even though we may be locking the barn door after the horse has been stolen," she concluded wryly.

"I blame myself for this," Marc said tersely. "We spoke about a system for the studio the other night. I should have been out here the following morning," he finished bitterly.

"Stop blaming yourself," Julia commanded. "I marvel I had an alarm installed in the house, to tell you the

truth. It was Ricardo's idea, and he had to sell me on it."
She smiled sadly. "I imagined that Thrussington was still
a kind of paradise in which there was no crime."

"I'm afraid there are no more places like that," Lieutenant Cranston pointed out softly.

"Yes, more's the pity," Julia said. "But it's a nasty lesson to learn."

Shortly after that Lieutenant Cranston left. A few minutes later Marc announced that he was going to have to
leave too.

"History's not going to repeat itself," he told Julia and
Jennifer. "So don't worry. I'll get back here first thing in
the morning."

He was standing near Julia's chair, and he leaned down
to squeeze her hand. "Take it easy," he cautioned.

He turned to Jennifer. "See you tomorrow," he said,
and she had the odd feeling that once again something intangible had happened to drive a small wedge between
Marc and herself.

This was confirmed when he left the room without
waiting for her to say she'd walk him to the door.

Chapter Nine

The evening passed slowly. Neither Jennifer nor Julia had any appetite for the excellent casserole Trina had prepared for their dinner. Neither of them could concentrate on the fare television offered that night.

At around eight o'clock Trina appeared to say that there was a phone call for Jennifer. She went to answer the summons, hoping that it would be Marc calling her. But it wasn't.

She heard Kenneth Trent's imperious tones, and she wished she had asked Trina to screen her calls. She wasn't prepared to talk to Ken. She knew he was annoyed with her. He'd put a firm stamp of disapproval on her move to the Berkshires, and he wasn't a person who would easily change his mind about any situation.

After they had exchanged perfunctory greetings, he said, "We need to talk, Jennifer. Do you want to come in to Boston, or would you prefer that I drive out there?"

Jennifer sighed. It was an audible sigh. "I'd rather we postpone any business discussions for the moment," she told him. She was taking it for granted that he would realize she was not about to enter into any personal discussions.

"Jennifer, I need to have some sort of commitment from you," Ken said patiently. "You have a February deadline on your present book. Do you realize you've given me no indication at all of what you plan to do for us after that?"

"Yes," she answered, trying to match his patience.

"You know how far ahead we schedule," Ken reminded her. "You and I need to sit down and make a few plans. I want a couple of proposals from you. As a matter of fact, I would like more than that. I would like to know what we can expect from you over the next two or three years. We're planning an extensive advertising budget, I want your books to be a featured part of it. We can't promote your books, Jennifer, if we don't know what you're going to write for us."

Jennifer closed her eyes tightly and silently counted to ten. There was validity in what Ken was saying to her, she was willing to concede that. But he could not have chosen a worse moment in which to raise the issue of her future writing plans.

She reminded herself that in fairness he couldn't be blamed for his bad timing. He knew nothing of yesterday's theft. He knew nothing about Marc. And she had no desire to enlighten him in either case.

"I can't possibly go into Boston just now," she said, and realized too late that she'd left the door wide open for him.

"Then I'll drive out to the Berkshires." There was an air of resignation in Ken's tone. "The weekend will be best for me. Saturday, shall we say? I'll plan to stay overnight. Can you put me up, or shall I book a motel?''

''We can put you up,'' Jennifer told him.

She relayed the word to Julia that they were going to have a weekend guest, and Julia brightened. Julia always loved to have company.

The night passed. Marc arrived shortly before eight o'clock the following morning, ready to start work on the alarm system in the studio.

He was persuaded by Trina to have a cup of coffee in the kitchen, and it was while he was sitting at the kitchen table chatting with the housekeeper that Jennifer walked in.

She hadn't known he was there, and she was not ready to face him. She was wearing an old wool housecoat, and she'd combed her hair and washed her face. But she still felt weary and in somewhat of a state of shock because of the robbery.

Trina poured out another cup of coffee and plunked it on the kitchen table before Jennifer could stop her. There became nothing to do except to sit down and drink it.

Marc had been laughing as she entered the kitchen. Now Jennifer was painfully aware that he'd fallen silent, and when she stole a glance at him she saw that there was no smile on his face.

She'd been plagued by bad dreams during the night, and she was still disturbed at the thought of having Kenneth Trent as a weekend guest. She also was discouraged and puzzled because Marc was acting so oddly, and she didn't know what to do about it.

Fortunately Trina stepped into the gap to say, ''I heard the weather forecast earlier. They say we're in for some snow.''

Good, Jennifer thought. *Maybe we'll have a blizzard and then Ken won't be able to come.*

"I wouldn't be surprised," Marc said. "It smells like snow out."

Jennifer raised her eyes. "How does snow smell?" she asked him.

"It's hard to define," he admitted. "A certain quality in the air. A kind of coldness. Not really cold but different. A freshness."

"Mmm," Jennifer said doubtfully.

"I guess that's not a very great explanation, is it?" he admitted.

"If you mean do I now know how snow smells, the answer is that I don't," she answered a bit more shortly than she'd intended.

She saw his expression alter subtly, but then he smiled at her. His smile had the kind of effect it invariably had on her. It dazzled her. Caught up in its magic, her face became a mirror of the emotions playing within her. Their eyes met, held, and—not for the first time—she knew that Marc was experiencing those same emotions.

Trina's presence became inhibitive, and the moment passed. Marc went out to the studio to meet the members of his crew who would be working with him to install the alarm system. Jennifer sought out Julia, who was still propped up in bed and had just finished her breakfast. But it was impossible to keep her thoughts away from Marc. It was very difficult to know that he was so near physically, yet far away.

Julia said, "Ricardo called a little while ago."

"At this hour of the morning?"

"You forget, darling, that there's a several-hour time difference," Julia reminded Jennifer. "Anyway, Ricardo is coming back to the States, he'll be with us for Thanksgiving. Isn't that marvelous?"

Jennifer nodded, trying to summon enthusiasm. Then she stiffened as Julia added, "I thought we might ask Marc to join us for Thanksgiving dinner."

Julia's eyes narrowed when Jennifer didn't respond. "Do you object?" she asked.

"Object? Oh, no," Jennifer said quickly. "Of course, I'm not sure he'd come...."

"I would think he might," Julia said serenely. "He has no family as far as I can ascertain."

"He has brothers and sisters," Jennifer corrected her. "But they're scattered all over the place."

"So?"

"You'll have to ask him and see what he says," Jennifer told Julia rather shortly.

Julia's eyebrows rose. "Have the two of you quarreled?"

"Quarreled?" Jennifer shook her head. "No. Nothing so definitive." She hesitated, not really wanting to talk about this. But Julia was so perceptive, it was ridiculous to think she could be left in the dark.

"Marc...turns on and off," she told Julia frankly. "Sometimes I feel very close to him. Then he shuts me out. I seldom can fathom the reason for the change, and I find the changes very disconcerting."

Julia considered this. Then she said, "Marc has a few complexes."

Jennifer had been staring at her hands, folded in her lap. Now her head jerked upward in surprise. "Complexes?" she demanded incredulously.

"Yes. I think he's said a bit more to me about his handicap than he has to you. In a way we're fellow sufferers. The difference is that I will get over my present incapacity; the doctors say that my ankle will be good as new. I

won't even have a limp to remind me of this whole difficult time.

"Marc, on the other hand," Julia continued, "has a
permanent disability. He will always be saddled with a bad
leg and a limp, and although he pretends to be blithe about
it, this goes very deep with him. Also, he comes from a
background that's very different from yours, and he's
aware of that too. You and I have discussed that before.
Then, the failure of his marriage didn't help either. I gather
that his wife came to him when he was still in the hospital
and didn't know whether he'd ever walk again or not, and
she told him she wanted out. I think all of these things add
up to a staggering total, as far as Marc is concerned."

Julia's analysis was disconcertingly correct.

Jennifer tried to laugh. She tried to quip by saying,
"You should have been a psychiatrist." But both the laugh
and the quip fell flat.

Julia asked quietly, "By chance have you fallen in love
with him, darling?"

The question rocked Jennifer. She hadn't let herself be
so specific, but now her heart gave her the answer to Julia's query, and she pressed her hand against her chest as
if trying to suppress it.

Julia smiled. "Don't say anything," she cautioned.
"Your eyes give you away. And do you know something,
Jennifer?"

Julia paused, to give her announcement dramatic em-
phasis. "I think he's right for you," she stated firmly.
Then she chuckled. "You've just got to convince him of
that," she told Jennifer.

In the middle of the morning Jennifer sauntered out to
the studio to see how the alarm installation was progress-

ing. Marc was working with two other men, but he broke away when he saw her.

He led her to a corner of the studio where they couldn't be overheard, then said, "I was wondering if there might be a chance of your having dinner with me tonight. Would Julia mind being left alone?"

"Not at all," Jennifer replied promptly. "I'd love to have dinner with you tonight." She added, "Speaking of dinners, Julia's fiancé is coming back from Europe for Thanksgiving, and she was saying a while ago that she'd like to have you join us. Would you?"

She held her breath, waiting for his answer. She saw his lips tighten, saw his hesitation, then he asked, "Are you sure?"

"Sure? About what?"

"Thanksgiving," he said briefly. "I mean, it's a day when people usually want people around who are close to them."

"I'd like to have you around," she told him softly.

His eyes darkened as he gritted out, "When you look at me like that it's all I can do not to go over the edge. Jenny, Jenny—" Marc broke off, then said hastily, "I'd better get back to work."

"Yes." Jennifer nodded in agreement. But as she left him her heart was singing.

The day passed. Jennifer played backgammon with Julia after lunch, watched the news with her on television, and then went up to her room and dressed carefully for her dinner date with Marc. She wore a wool dress in a cranberry shade that was a perfect compliment for her fair coloring, and she took special pains with her hair and makeup.

When Marc called for her at seven, she saw that he had dressed carefully tonight too. He was wearing trim gray slacks and a tweed jacket, and obviously had just shaved. The scent of his after-shave assailed Jennifer's nostrils, and the effect was much too tantalizing.

Marc was driving a compact car in lieu of the van tonight. Jennifer, snuggled in the front seat beside him, felt a rare contentment and a heightened sense of anticipation. This was the first time they truly had been alone in what seemed to her a very long while. She stole a glance at his profile, loving the strong line of it. As if he'd caught her eyes on him, he turned to smile at her, and her love for him overflowed.

Yes, she loved him. She'd been forced to admit it to herself in the wake of Julia's question that morning. Since then she'd let the knowledge of her love for Marc fill her, and once it had, nothing else seemed very important.

Julia was right though. Jennifer knew it was going to be up to her to convince Marc that they were suited to each other.

Marc's question interrupted her thoughts. "Like good Italian food?" he asked. "I mean really good Italian food."

"I love it," Jennifer told him. "I'm a pasta freak," she confessed.

He grinned. "So am I. As it happens, there's a little place at the other edge of town that's run by an Italian family straight from the old country. I think you'll enjoy it."

Jennifer enjoyed it thoroughly. The Barbini family had set up their restaurant in an old white frame house that was unprepossessing on the outside. Inside, they'd decorated it with a mass of artificial grapevines through which Christmas lights twinkled, a choice of decor that could have been tawdry but wasn't. The atmosphere created by the hanging bunches of inedible grapes, the lights, the marvelous aromas emanating from the kitchen, and the warmth of the Barbinis themselves made the place a delight.

The whole family was in on the act, from the grandmother, who presided at the cash register, to the youngest daughter, who was still in grade school but did her bit by setting the tables and handing out the menus. They all knew Marc, and welcomed him as if he were an old friend. Very soon Jennifer felt as if she'd been accepted into the fold too.

They strolled back to Marc's car, replete with espresso and homemade cannoli, which Jennifer had protested she couldn't possibly eat after the rest of the food she'd stowed away, and then had devoured to the last crumb. She sighed contentedly. "That was absolutely superb. And so are the Barbinis," she said.

"I'm glad you share my enthusiasm for the Barbinis and their food," Marc told her. They were holding hands, and he pressed her fingers as he spoke.

"I think there are many, many things I'd share your enthusiasm for," Jennifer said quietly. "Every time we've talked I've discovered that we like so many of the same things."

"Do you think you'd like what I'd like right now?" Marc asked her.

"Yes," she said. She was not about to pretend she didn't understand what he was saying.

"My house?" His voice was so low, she had to strain to hear it.

She nodded. "Yes."

Marc stopped short. It was a beautiful night, crisp and cold, the stars and the moon silver against a very black sky. It was cold enough so that Marc's breath came out in small white smoke puffs as he spoke. But the snow he and Trina had spoken about earlier had failed to materialize.

"I know," he said, spacing the words so that Jennifer knew he was choosing them with particular care, "that we're going to be making a certain...commitment if we are together again. This is something I can't be casual about. Nor, I'm sure, can you."

He drew a deep breath. "I guess what I'm saying is that if we're together tonight, I'm not going to be able to let you go again, Jenny." He laughed wryly. "I don't have that much fortitude where you're concerned," he confessed. He stared down into her eyes, his look as dark as the ebony sky.

"I want you so much," he said simply.

Never before had words been spoken that Jennifer wanted so much to hear.

It was very late when Marc took Jennifer home that night. Parting had never been as difficult for her as it was when he kissed her good night just inside the door of Julia's house.

"Sure you don't want a nightcap, or some coffee?" she asked. He was still holding her. She leaned back so that she could look up into his beloved face as she spoke.

He shook his head. "I'll never be able to leave you if I stay much longer," he admitted. "As it is, you're going to hear the ripping sound when I tear myself away. Jenny..."

Jennifer overflowed with love for him. "Oh, my darling," she murmured softly.

They had gone up into the little bedroom where she'd spent that first night at his house, and she had given herself to Marc so completely that there could have been no doubt about her offering. He had returned her gift by giving her one of his own—himself. And there were no reservations.

Love had fused with passion, and the resulting blend was all-encompassing in its scope. Jennifer had felt herself lifted onto a series of emotional planes as she and Marc culminated the thrusting force between them. In the aftermath of fulfillment, she had realized that never until then had she truly known the meaning of sublime.

Later, much later, Marc had said regretfully, "I suppose I'd better take you home."

"I suppose so," she had agreed, her regret matching his. "Julia certainly wouldn't wonder, but she might worry if I weren't around first thing in the morning. We're both early risers—she, especially so, these days. She says her leg doesn't like to let her sleep."

" I know the feeling," Marc commented ruefully.

It was seldom that he referred to his handicap, and Jennifer let this pass. But it wasn't so easy to disregard what Julia had discovered was a touchy subject with him when, as he was dressing, she clearly saw his scars for the first time. Before, they'd been in dim light or darkness. Now there was a lamp lit on the bedside table.

The scars on his leg were ugly and extensive, and inadvertently Jennifer flinched. Immediately she caught the expression in Marc's eyes, and was angry at herself for not having managed to be more of a stoic. He looked as if she had hit him.

"Repulsive, aren't they?" he queried levelly.

"I can only think of the pain tney must have caused you," Jennifer said shakily. And this was true.

"Life deals out a share of pain for all of us," he retorted abruptly.

He turned away, and she bit her lip. His pattern was becoming too predictable. She knew he was about to shut her out again, and this time she wasn't going to put up with it.

She said sharply, "Don't!"

He turned toward her, his blue eyes curious. "Don't what?"

"Don't draw away from me," she said. A shy smile curved her lips. Very softly she said, "I love you, you know. Scars and all."

The moment became electric. Sparks flew crazily between them, currents pulsed. Into the highly fused atmosphere Marc inserted a laugh. Amazingly it was a genuine laugh.

"How the hell do you think I can bring myself to take you home?" he teased her.

"You can take me home a little later," Jennifer suggested.

"Oh, no," he contradicted her. "I'm going to take you home right now, or there's no way I'll be taking you home tonight at all."

And so that is what he had done.

With him gone, Jennifer leaned against the door, her heart and her mind filled with Marc, just as he had filled her body earlier.

For the first time, she felt confident about their relationship. They had come a long way tonight. She couldn't have defined the obstacles they'd hurdled. But they'd managed to get past a few of them.

Kenneth Trent arrived in Thrussington that Saturday afternoon. By then Jennifer had set up her things in Julia's studio, and had put in a morning of work. But she left the studio well in advance of Kenneth's projected arrival hour, having decided that she would confine her time with him to the house. In the studio they'd be alone. In the house they wouldn't be. The choice of alternatives was clear cut to her.

Ken drove a black Porsche, and Jennifer was standing at the living room window as he pulled up in Julia's driveway. She watched him get out of the car and start toward the house, a sleek leather attaché case in hand. He was a handsome man of forty-two with silvery, prematurely gray hair, and an excellent physique. Ken took very good care of himself, exercised regularly in a Boston health club, and still ran an occasional marathon. He was literate, well-informed about almost everything, wealthy in his own right, charming, and had considerable influence in the publishing world which, after all, was her career field. Jennifer considered all these things and knew that it would be impossible for her to ever respond to the kind of feeling she was afraid he expected from her.

They had cocktails with Julia, and then she left them alone for an hour to discuss business.

"I really need a commitment from you," Ken said after a while, exasperation creeping into his voice.

The word *commitment* reminded Jennifer of Marc. He'd been right. Last night had been a commitment for both of them.

She remembered now that she'd forgotten to tell him Ken would be visiting for the weekend.

"Jennifer," Ken said peremptorily.

Jennifer turned toward him, still distracted by thoughts of Marc. "Yes?" she asked vaguely.

"Are you going to come up with a couple of proposals for us so we'll have some idea of what you plan to do?" he asked sharply.

"I'd rather wait till I finish my present book," Jennifer hedged.

This plainly wasn't what he had wanted to hear. "I can't go along with that," he told her flatly. "I'd like to schedule a second book six months after this one comes out," he added. "That means that I need a proposal from you *now*, Jennifer." He paused. "You're not losing interest in what you're doing, are you?" he asked her.

"No." This, at least, she could say definitely. "I like what I'm doing; I want to continue doing it. But," she added, with just a shade of defiance, "I don't want to be pressured."

"I didn't think I was pressuring you," Ken said coldly. "Most authors would be pleased to have a publisher pressuring them in such a way. All I'm asking for is more of your work."

Ken finished a second martini. "All right," he said after a moment. "All right, if you don't want to talk about it, we won't talk about it. How do you like living out here in the woods?"

Jennifer smiled. "I love it."

Ken frowned, and she knew this wasn't what he had wanted to hear either. It was a relief when Julia joined them.

Trina, again, had cooked a delicious dinner. Afterward, Julia, Ken, and Jennifer played Trivial Pursuit. By the time they'd finished two games, Jennifer could hardly keep her eyes open. She'd had a late night last night. Now she needed to curl up and go to sleep.

She escaped gracefully, leaving Julia to entertain Ken for the balance of the evening.

They were at breakfast Sunday morning when Marc arrived unexpectedly.

When he loomed in the dining room doorway, Jennifer's heart leaped.

Marc, after being introduced to Ken, said apologetically, "I wanted to test the studio alarm system, Julia. But it can wait for another time."

"No, no, go ahead and test," Julia said quickly. "Then join us for a cup of coffee."

Jennifer noted that Ken was staggered at the thought of Julia inviting someone who had obviously been hired to do work for her to join them at breakfast. Marc merely nodded, and said, "I'll just give it one short blast."

A moment later a sound that was much too familiar to Jennifer tore through the air. But Marc quickly suppressed the alarm and soon was back in the house again.

Julia laughed as she suggested that he pull out a chair at the foot of the table. "That probably woke up all the owls in the woods," she observed.

"I hope it woke up all the thieves in the woods," Marc said, and his expression sobered. "There have been a rash of robberies since yours," he told Julia. "Two last night. They're pretty much at random. No pattern, in other words. All in places where I haven't installed a system, which is gratifying. But the local police have never had so much on their plate."

"Have they called you in for consultation?" Julia asked him.

He grinned. "You might say so. Unofficially of course."

Julia explained to Ken, "Marc used to be with the New York City police."

Ken nodded politely. "I see."

Ken lapsed into silence, and Jennifer was equally silent. Julia and Marc seemed content to do the talking, and while he was talking with Julia, Marc drank two cups of coffee and ate three croissants, liberally spread with butter and jam. But despite his outward calm, Jennifer could see the questioning expression in his eyes every time he looked at Ken.

Marc left shortly after breakfast. Ken suggested that he and Jennifer go for a walk. They chose a woodland path, and she became so occupied avoiding branches and keeping briars out of her clothing that there was no chance for Ken to engage her in talk about much of anything.

By the time they got back to the house Trina had lunch ready. After lunch Julia said she was going to take a nap. Finally the way was paved for Ken to get into a discussion with Jennifer about her books, and he took full advantage of it.

By the time he left for Boston, at about four that afternoon, she had promised him that she'd get two story proposals to him before the first of the year.

"Sooner, if possible," Ken warned as Jennifer walked out to his car with him.

"I'll try," she said.

Ken bent and kissed her lightly on the lips. "I'll be glad when you come back to town," he informed her.

Jennifer sidestepped an answer to this. She knew that sooner or later she'd be going back to Boston. But that was something she didn't want to think about now.

Chapter Ten

Ricardo Castel arrived in Thrussington two days before Thanksgiving. Julia began to glow when she saw him, and it was a glow that lingered.

He seemed as glad to see Julia as she was to see him. Watching them together, Jennifer began to soften somewhat toward Ricardo. He evidently was genuinely happy to have his European concert tour behind him, and to be in the Berkshires with Julia.

"I'm almost beginning to believe he's really in love with Julia," Jennifer confided to Marc as they were driving back to Julia's house from the movies in Thrussington the night before Thanksgiving.

It had snowed that afternoon and a white mantle lay over the countryside. The roads, though, had been cleared so efficiently that driving was no problem at all, except on the dirt lane leading to Julia's house. In bad weather that was apt to be somewhat slippery. Because of this Marc had driven his van, since it had better traction than his small compact car.

Jennifer felt safe and secure with Marc driving. She watched his hands on the wheel. They were strong, competent hands. She scanned his face, etched by the lights from the dashboard, and decided he was the handsomest man in the world.

He said, in answer to her comment about Ricardo and Julia, "You're such a skeptic, Jenny. Personally I can't see why Ricardo Castel, or any other man, would find it difficult to fall in love with Julia. She's a delight."

"Mmmm," Jennifer protested. "Much as I adore Julia, you're making me jealous."

He laughed. "Jealousy is something you'll never need to be concerned about in connection with me," he told her.

Jennifer caught her breath at this. It was quite a statement, coming from Marc. He seldom was specific about any of the emotional equivalents that involved them; he had yet to come right out and tell her he loved her.

On the other hand, Jennifer had spoken to him of her love more than once. Her words had had a profound effect on him each time, and yet he hadn't responded in kind. Still, she knew that he loved her. She knew it.

She also knew that despite everything she'd said to him, Marc was still running scared. Scared? She questioned her own word choice. She doubted if Marc were really "scared" of anything. But Julia was right about him. His accident and the subsequent failure of his marriage had left deep emotional scars. These were far more difficult to deal with than his physical scars, Jennifer thought wryly. Again, she knew that she was going to need to build up Marc's confidence in himself, as well as his faith not merely in a woman's capacity to love but specifically in her, if they were going to achieve any kind of lasting relationship.

He'd questioned her about Kenneth Trent. He'd asked if there ever had been anything between them, and Jennifer had bristled at that. But when she'd answered with a swift negative, Marc had only said, "That's not because he hasn't wanted it."

Then, while she was digesting this, he had changed the subject.

Now, in the wake of telling her that she'd never need to be jealous where he was concerned, he changed the subject again.

"Two more robberies in the past couple of days," he told her, "again with no pattern." She saw that he was frowning. "There's something odd about it," he stated.

"In what way?" Jennifer asked him.

"I can't put my finger on it," he admitted. "The thefts don't make sense to me, that's all."

"Do thefts usually make sense, Marc?"

"In their own way, they do," he answered. "Most crooks set a certain pattern, usually a definite one. Setting a pattern—a routine method of operation—seems to go along with the criminal mentality. Most crooks are predictable, at least to an extent. They even go after the same sort of stuff when they rob. That hasn't happened here. These thieves have taken everything from the paintings to food processors. Actually, some of the stuff they've taken hasn't been worth stealing from what I can put together. Other things like the paintings, of course, are extremely valuable, but not exactly what you'd call negotiable property."

He concentrated on driving over a patch of snow at the turnoff into Julia's private road, then said, "After the studio was robbed, I assumed that these were art thieves.

They'd sell to underground collectors. That's not uncommon. Some collectors are content merely to possess a certain piece, regardless of whether or not they are ever able to display it openly. But a lot of the stuff that's been taken subsequently...well, it would bring little or nothing on the second-hand market."

"Why do you think they've taken it then? Evidently you think there's more than one person doing this?" she queried.

"Yes, I do. The weight of some of the stuff that's been stolen implies that, to say nothing of the quantity. Why do I think they've taken it?" Marc repeated her question. "It's a funny way to put it, but I'd say they've stolen it just to steal something in a lot of the cases. And that doesn't make much sense, does it?"

She thought about this. "No, it doesn't," she agreed. She pondered further. "Haven't the police found any clues at all?" she asked.

"Nothing of any significance," Marc said. "That's another thing that's puzzling. So many thieves virtually leave a calling card."

Julia's house loomed in front of them. With the windows lighted and the snow on the ground, it looked especially beautiful.

"At Christmas we'll put colored lights everywhere," Jennifer said, her eyes brilliant with anticipation. "Remember when you told me everything around here looks like Christmas-card scenes at the holiday season? I never thought I'd be seeing that for myself." She smiled across at him. "I can hardly wait."

"I wish I hadn't brought you back here tonight," Marc said suddenly. "I wish we'd gone to my place." He grinned ruefully. "Hell," he admitted, "I wish a lot of things."

He didn't elaborate, and Jennifer knew he wasn't going to. After a moment she suggested, "Come on in and have a nightcap."

He shook his head. "No, thanks. It's late. I'd better be getting straight back."

"You have someone covering the alarm system, haven't you?"

Marc nodded. He employed several people to cover the alarm system for him when he was unable to do so personally. He had worked out a small network of employees whose prime qualifications were alertness, and the ability to wake up swiftly and then to function immediately in an efficient way.

"I've been able to hire three people who are confined to wheelchairs, and they do fine for me. I also have a couple of men who are over sixty-five and collecting social security, but they want to augment their income."

There had been a quiet satisfaction in his voice as he had told Jennifer this. "I'm always especially glad to hire handicapped people who are housebound," he had added. "Perhaps because I came close to finishing up in that category myself.

"Also," he had said, "perhaps because they're especially eager to prove themselves, they do a very good job."

Jennifer suspected that Marc also had been "especially eager" to prove himself when he'd come to Thrussington and started his business. Well, he'd done it. He'd worked hard, and he deserved the success, and some time for relaxation and a little fun as well.

She said now, "It isn't late. At least, everyone's up, that's for sure. I think every light in the house is on. Julia asked me to bring you in. She suggested we make hot buttered rum, so how about it?"

Marc said reluctantly, "Look, you and Julia and Castel will have things to talk about...."

Marc had met Ricardo Castel briefly when he'd come to take Jennifer to the movies.

She looked across at him, vexed by his attitude. "I can't think of a thing we might have to say to each other that couldn't include you," she told him bluntly.

"Jennifer..."

Not Jenny—Jennifer. His use of her name was like a barometer, she decided, a barometer of his moods.

"Marc," she mimicked, using the same tone, an overly patient tone. "Look, if you don't want to come in for hot buttered rum, say so. On the other hand, if it's because of some misguided inferiority complex on your part..."

In the space of time that followed, Jennifer was reminded of an old saying.

You could hear a pin drop.

Just then, a pin would have sounded like a cannon exploding.

Then, surprisingly, Marc chuckled. "You land your punches right on the chin, don't you?" he commented. "Well, I suppose I had that one coming. Lead the way, lovely lady. I don't think I've ever had a hot buttered rum, but I can't wait to try one."

Julia and Ricardo were ensconced in front of the fireplace. It soon was quite evident that Ricardo had no more idea of how to make hot buttered rum than Marc did. Jennifer was called upon to do the honors, with Marc assisting her. But Julia added the proviso that they use her time-proven recipe.

Accordingly, Jennifer heated cider, laced it with whole cloves, stick cinnamon, and a dash of powdered nutmeg, and into this stirred rum, and pure maple syrup for sweetening. She poured the concoction into preheated mugs, and then added to each mug a small square of butter, which promptly melted into golden richness.

Contentment reigned as the four of them sipped the warm drinks and talked about a surprising variety of things, a conversation, Jennifer noted, in which Marc was more than able to hold his own.

Thanksgiving Day was equally pleasant—more than pleasant. As it progressed Jennifer decided that everyone should have this kind of Thanksgiving in their lives at least once.

Somehow Marc had prevailed upon the local florist to deliver flowers on Thanksgiving morning. A glorious centerpiece arrived to adorn the holiday table.

The gift card read, "To the two loveliest ladies anyone could ever know."

As she read the card, telltale tears stole into Julia's eyes. "He's a very dear person," she said, and looked across at Jennifer almost accusingly. "I hope you appreciate him," she added.

"I do," Jennifer responded fervently.

She did. When Marc arrived she met him at the door and, standing on tiptoe, kissed him squarely on the mouth. "That was nice," she said.

He shrugged off his coat and let her hang it in the hall closet for him. "What was nice?" he asked innocently.

"Sending the centerpiece. You've won Julia over completely. Not that you hadn't already."

"What about you?" Marc asked, and Jennifer was surprised to hear the husky note in his voice. "Have I won you over?"

She wanted to be clever, she wanted to say something terribly original, but words in that category failed her.

She looked him right in the eye. "I think you know the answer to that," she said softly.

He reached out to her. "Jenny..."

She walked into his arms. Their kiss was composed of passion and suppressed desire, of love and longing, all of these things laced with intangibles that made it a very heavy potion.

Jennifer broke away first, albeit reluctantly. She said, "Julia knows it was you ringing the doorbell. I looked out the window and saw your van. So..."

"So," Marc said, grinning. He added, "Julia's a very understanding woman."

Nevertheless, they went into the living room to join Ricardo and Julia, and to indulge in a glass of champagne with which they drank a toast.

Ricardo proposed the toast. "To us," he said. "Maybe that sounds selfish, but I think if I could be granted just one wish, it would be that history repeats itself, and that we all are together here in another year."

Sincerity rang in his voice and Jennifer looked at him, surprised. She caught him gazing at Julia, his heart in his eyes, and she thought, *My God, he really does love her.*

They entered the dining room where Marc's centerpiece adorned the table, which was set with a deep brown linen cloth that was an heirloom, and matching napkins. Trina had outdone herself in the preparation of their Thanksgiving dinner. They feasted, and when Trina asked for preferences in regard to pumpkin or mince pie, they groaned.

Dessert was postponed until later by a unanimous vote.

Julia lured Marc and Ricardo into playing Trivial Pursuit, and when Marc won the first game Jennifer felt a small surge of triumph for him. She was convinced that he tended to underestimate himself in so many ways.

It was late when Marc left, and again Jennifer walked to the door with him. When she took his coat out of the closet she also reached for her warm quilted one and slipped into it.

He looked at her inquiringly. "Going somewhere?"

"I wish I were," she said shamelessly.

"So do I," he told her softly. "It gets rougher to leave you each time we part, Jenny...."

He let the words trail off, and Jennifer could feel her pulse pounding in their wake. She knew that if he asked her to come with him right now, she wouldn't hesitate for an instant. She'd slip back in and tell Julia. Julia, of all people, would understand.

But Marc didn't ask her. After a moment she said, "I thought I'd walk out with you and get a breath of fresh air."

She could hear the dejection in her voice, and wondered if he heard it too. If so, he didn't respond to it.

The front steps were slippery. Marc held Jennifer's arm, steadying her as she went down them. "Better get hold of some rock salt tomorrow and sprinkle it around," he suggested. "You don't want anyone falling down."

She nodded, only half listening to him.

There was a huge silver moon in the winter sky tonight, the snow, glistening in its light, looked as if it were made of millions of tiny diamonds. The moonlight gave Marc's face a mysterious quality. But it also revealed the gravity of his expression.

He was staring down at Jennifer with a seriousness that invoked a strange feeling in her. It was as if he were weighing all sorts of things in the balance.

She could see his inner struggle, and there was nothing she could do but watch him helplessly, and to hope with a fervency that tore at her that he'd come to the kind of conclusion she wanted him to reach.

She saw his mouth twist; she saw him force a smile. He said, "This was a wonderful day. I'll never forget it."

Jennifer's throat tightened so that she couldn't respond. This wasn't what she had wanted him to say at all. Was he ever going to tell her he loved her?

The Berkshire-Hudson Bank and Trust Company's board of directors met in early December, and Marc called Jennifer to announce jubilantly that he'd been given the job of installing the new alarm system.

"Despite Freyton, they're going all-out on this," he said. "It will be a highly sophisticated system, the most challenging thing I've ever tackled."

"When will you be putting it in?" she asked him.

"Sometime this month," he said vaguely. "LaFollette wants it installed and working by the first of the year. The timing will have to be right. The old system will need to remain on until the last minute. We'll have to switch over to the new one during a period when the bank is closed.

"I'm happy about this, Jenny," Marc continued. "If the bank is satisfied with my work, it will be a real stepping-stone. It should mean an increasing number of business accounts, and they're profitable. Many of the old established businesses around here are operating with alarm systems as obsolete as the bank's. Brock LaFollette is very active in the community. I've the feeling that if he likes what I do for him, he'll spread the word."

"That's terrific, Marc," she told him.

"So, how about you?" he asked, again diverting the subject away from himself, as he usually did. "How's the book coming?"

She hesitated. She was having difficulties with the book. She'd finished the illustrations, but she was still struggling with the text. The problem wasn't with the writing—

she had her story line well in hand, and she'd developed a definite technique in writing for children. Rather, the problem was every time she sat down at the typewriter, her mind was filled not with her story, but with thoughts of Marc.

She said vaguely, "I put in a couple of hours on it today."

"Is it warm enough in the studio?" he asked her.

"Oh, yes. Now that the heating system's been reactivated it's downright cozy," Jennifer said. Inadvertently the thought of the old day bed in the studio crept into her mind, and sketched a picture of itself in full color.

They could make love in the studio, she and Marc. Jennifer had never thought of this before, and she was more than a little surprised at herself for thinking of it now.

It was late afternoon; Marc was calling her from his house. He'd told her that he'd put in a long day and had poured himself a Scotch on the rocks, then decided to phone her. He'd prefaced these remarks by asking, first, if he was interrupting anything. Jennifer had assured him that he wasn't. Silently she'd added to herself that Marc could interrupt anything she ever was doing as far as she was concerned. In her scheme of things, he took priority. She only wished he realized how much of a priority she gave him.

She asked impulsively, "Why don't you come out and have dinner with us? Trina's made a Spanish stew that smells marvelous."

"Don't tempt me," Marc protested.

"Seriously." She wanted to see him; she wanted to see him so much that she was willing to use any ruse to get him out to the house. "You know Julia would love to have you. She always does."

"A person can wear out his welcome," Marc pointed out.

Jennifer wished that he would materialize at her side physically, so that she could shake him.

"I thought about going into Pittsfield tomorrow to do some Christmas shopping," he told her. "I have to get packages off early, to my brothers and sisters and my parents. They're scattered in so many places. Would you like to go on a safari with me to the biggest town in the Berkshires?" he asked her.

"Yes," she said promptly.

He laughed. "You make up your mind faster than any woman I've ever known," he teased. "Suppose I pick you up around four o'clock. We can do some shopping and then have dinner somewhere, all right?"

To Jennifer, his plan was much more than "all right."

She was ready when he called for her the next day, bundled up in warm wool slacks and a matching jacket, an angora scarf wrapped around her neck and a bright red fuzzy mohair tam pulled down over her blond hair.

Marc said approvingly, "I think you're beginning to learn how to dress for winter weather in the hills."

"You've lectured me about it enough," Jennifer countered.

"Boots on your feet?" he asked.

She held out a well-shod foot for his inspection. "Will these do?"

"Nicely."

As they started out, Jennifer felt herself aglow with happiness. Just being with Marc was enough...well, almost enough, she amended. She smiled a secret smile. She'd confided in Julia just before Marc had come for her. "Don't be alarmed if I don't come home tonight." Then she had waited for Julia's reaction.

Julia had beamed and said, "I like hearing that." She'd added more seriously, "I've seen that distracted expression in your eyes of late, darling. I know Marc puzzles you. I think right now he's also puzzling himself. Give him a chance."

"I'll give him all the chances he wants," Jennifer had said.

The wide main street in Pittsfield was aglow with colored Christmas lights. Carol music wafted through the air, and as she and Marc window-shopped, walking along hand in hand, the beauty of the season mixed with her love for Marc to overwhelm Jennifer.

As they stopped to look in a toy store window, Marc asked suddenly, "Have you ever wanted to have kids?"

"I would," Jennifer said softly. "If I were married to the right person."

"You would have beautiful children," he told her so solemnly that she glanced up at him quickly. His eyes were deep sapphire, and there was a poignancy to his expression that made her want to cry. He added softly, "I think you look more beautiful tonight than you ever have before. I…"

Was he going to tell her he loved her? Jennifer waited to hear the magic words, but he didn't speak them.

She fought back a nagging disappointment as they moved along, coming next to a jewelry store window. Diamond engagement rings and wedding bands sparkled in the window, but Marc quickly bypassed this display to go along to the next store, a clothing shop for men.

They went in, and he chose an assortment of things for his father and his brother. Next, in another shop, she helped him pick out a nightgown and some bath powder for his mother, and then earrings for each of his sisters.

At this point he looked at her quizzically. "How about you?" he asked. "Aren't you going to do any Christmas shopping?"

She shook her head. "Not today," she confessed.

"Are you saying you came along just for the ride?" he asked her.

"Would that be so terrible?"

"No, of course not. But wouldn't you like to look around for something for Julia or maybe your father and your stepmother?" he suggested. "I know there are still a fair number of shopping days until Christmas, but the time does slip by."

"Yes, I know it does," she agreed. She hesitated. Getting anything for her father was always a problem. He literally was the man who had everything. Buying for her stepmother was equally difficult. Her father lavished gifts on Lisa; it was almost impossible to think of something that Lisa might want and not have.

As for Julia, Julia was easily satisfied. She was like a child when it came to gifts; she loved to open brightly wrapped presents. It wasn't necessary to give Julia anything "big." A couple of specially selected little things would be exactly right.

And what about a gift for Marc? She wanted to give him so much, and, she thought bitterly, she could afford to give him just about anything.

The realization of the difference in their financial circumstances, and how Marc would despise her if he knew the full truth, jabbed her.

Marc was watching her narrowly, and he asked, "What is it?"

"What do you mean?"

"You flinched just then, as if something hurt you."

"No," Jennifer said.

"Could it be hunger pains?" he suggested with a smile.

"Maybe." She smiled back, glad to get off the subject of Christmas presents.

"Then, we'll have to find a restaurant," he decided.

They ate in a charming old inn that was beautifully decorated for Christmas. Jennifer forced thoughts of everything but the handsome man sitting across the table from her out of her mind. When they clicked their wineglasses together, she offered the same toast Ricardo had proposed at Thanksgiving.

"To us," she said.

"I'll second that," Marc told her softly.

By the time they had finished dinner the shops were closed, and Jennifer was glad of this. She didn't want to go Christmas shopping twice in one day, and Marc had pretty well covered his own list.

As they drove back toward Thrussington she wondered if he might suggest that they stop at his house for a nightcap or coffee. If he didn't, she was going to have to find a way to take matters into her own hands.

When they entered the village and Marc kept driving straight ahead, Jennifer realized that it was his plan to take her home directly.

She began to feel acutely uncomfortable. She'd never in her life invited herself to a man's house.

At her side, Marc asked, "What is it, Jenny?"

"What is what?" she answered, really not knowing to what he might be referring.

"You're squirming," he accused.

"I—I'm sorry."

"You haven't said two words since we left Pittsfield," he told her. "What's on your mind?"

She drew a long breath. Then she said bluntly, "You."

"Me?" he echoed incredulously. "What have I done?"

"That's just it," she said. "That's it exactly. You haven't done anything."

He pulled the van over to the curb. With the motor idling, he looked across at her.

"What did you want me to do?" he asked her. "No, let me phrase that differently. What do you want me to do?"

He read the answer to his question in her face.

"My God, sweetheart," he said, plainly taken aback. "I had no idea. I mean...I thought you'd have to go along home. Julia..."

Jennifer's voice was very small. "I told Julia I might not be coming home tonight," she confessed.

He stared at her. "You told Julia that?"

She nodded.

A silence-filled minute that echoed like thunder in her ears followed. Then Marc admitted, "Jenny, I don't know what to say."

Her voice became even smaller. "Do you mind my having said what I did to Julia?"

"Mind? No, I don't mind. It's not a question of minding."

"Then what is it a question of?"

"I don't know," he said slowly. "I guess I feel strange to think that Julia would think—"

"Think?" Jennifer queried. "Why don't you come out and say that you feel strange at the thought of Julia knowing that we're...sleeping together?"

His mouth tightened. "I don't like that way of putting it."

"Why?" she challenged.

"You make it sound so casual," Marc said tightly. "It isn't like that with us. You know that as well as I do."

"So what would you have had me tell Julia?" she flung at him. "Nothing, I suppose. Which would mean that we'd almost never have a chance to really be together."

Again, Marc said nothing in the smothering silence. Jennifer felt that she was losing her breath in the midst of it.

Finally Marc said levelly, "You're misreading me."

"Am I?" Jennifer didn't know why she felt so hurt, but she did. It was as if he'd really spurned her.

A woman scorned, she said silently, and tried to convince herself that she was being ridiculous, that this was really silly. But the hurt still lingered.

"Jenny, it isn't that I don't want you—" Marc began.

She cut him off. "This isn't something you have to go into explanations about," she said.

"Jenny..."

"Take me home, please, Marc," she requested stiffly.

"I'll take you to my home," he said.

"No, Marc."

"Look, Jenny, you're reading this entirely the wrong way," he insisted. "It took me by surprise when you said you'd told Julia what you did. But—"

"Please take me home, Marc."

She meant it. Evidently her tone convinced him of that. She saw his face tighten, heard the engine roar as he turned the key in the ignition switch.

They were silent for the balance of the drive. Jennifer was aching all over, physically aching. Maybe the ache was all in her mind, she conceded, but it hurt as much as if it were real.

She stung with embarrassment as well when she thought of what she'd said to Julia, and of Marc's reaction to it.

Marc turned onto the lane that led to Julia's house and finally came to a stop in the driveway.

"I don't want to end the night this way, Jenny," he said quietly. "I don't want to leave you like this."

"I don't know what to say to that," Jennifer admitted. "Maybe I am overreacting but..." She sighed deeply. "I can't deal with this right now," she admitted.

"All right." Marc made no move toward her.

She thought sickly, *He isn't even going to kiss me good night.*

He said, "I'll call you in the morning. I want to talk to you. You and I need to talk about a lot of things."

She nodded, only half hearing him. She didn't wait for him to walk around and open the van door for her. She slipped out by herself, saying as she did, "Call me, then."

"I will," he promised grimly. "You're right. We belong together, Jenny. We belong in the same house. But not the way you inferred to Julia. I would hate like hell for anyone to think that there was anything cheap about my feelings for you."

Finally he said what she'd been yearning to hear him say.

"I love you, Jenny."

Jennifer nearly turned back, nearly climbed into the van again. But it was at that instant that she saw the front door open, saw Ricardo Castel silhouetted in the opening.

Across the intervening space, Ricardo called, "Is that you, Jennifer? Julia said she thought she heard a car."

"Yes," Jennifer called back. She turned away from Marc, wondering if she was imagining the odd note in Ricardo's voice. Something about his tone chilled her, and a sudden wave of apprehension swept over her.

Behind her, Marc said again, "We'll talk in the morning."

"Yes," Jenny nodded.

Ricardo was coming down the steps. She met him halfway and stared into his darkly handsome face. Suddenly she was frightened.

"Has something happened to Julia?" It was the first thing she could think of.

He shook his head. "No. It's your father, Jennifer," he said. "Julia will tell you about it."

As she stared at him he added, "There has been an accident."

Chapter Eleven

Hugh Chatsworth-Graham was dead.

Julia broke the word to Jennifer as gently as she could, but there was no way of really cushioning it.

The world-famous financier had been cruising off Majorca in a chartered yacht. Late at night, he had been returning to the yacht in a small motorboat. The details were unclear. Evidently, in transit between the smaller boat and the yacht, Hugh Chatsworth-Graham had slipped and plunged into the water.

Jennifer remembered, sick at the thought, that her father had been a very poor swimmer.

"We'll probably be able to read more about what happened in the papers tomorrow than we've been able to find out firsthand," Julia had said grimly. "It was Polly Mitchell, your father's secretary, who called, and she still didn't have all the details."

By then Julia had insisted that Jennifer sip some of the brandy Ricardo had brought to her. Jennifer had done so, feeling so numb that even the liquid's fire failed to scorch her throat as brandy usually did.

Julia had explained, "We've been trying to reach you at Marc's house, dear. I'm so glad you decided to come back here. We left word with the man who's handling Marc's alarm system tonight so that he'd have you call as soon as Marc made contact with him. Marc evidently phones in every now and then to make sure things are going all right."

Jennifer had nodded at this. Yes, Marc would certainly be one to phone periodically to be sure that all was well with the people to whom he'd entrusted his business.

"I wish Marc had come in with you," Julia had said worriedly.

Jennifer was very glad that Marc hadn't come in with her. Had this happened, Marc would have learned—far too precipitously—that she was the Chatsworth-Graham heiress.

Three hours after Ricardo Castel had given Jennifer the initial message that there had been an accident, she was finally able to climb the stairs to her room.

She was shaking all over. The shock was profound. She had never been close to her father, nevertheless he had been a dominant figure in her life.

It didn't seem possible that he was dead. As Jennifer climbed the stairs a new realization struck her. How could she hope to keep her true identity from Marc any longer? At some point, maybe not immediately, Marc was bound to learn all about her.

Jennifer undressed quickly, slipped into a long granny gown, and then climbed into bed. Usually she didn't bother with the electric blanket, but tonight she turned it on. Still, she couldn't get warm. The chill went through her, right to the bone.

She kept thinking about her father, remembering specific incidents when something in her life had happened in which he'd played more than a passing role. In retrospect, there had been far too few of them. So much of the time he'd been a figure in absentia, especially since her mother's death.

Regrets plagued Jennifer. Maybe she should have tried to reach out to her father. Certainly he'd never really tried to reach out to her. It was impossible to shut out the feeling that he had been a basically austere man, aloof. Had his wealth made him that way?

What would her father have thought of Marc? The question came inadvertently, and was answered. Hugh Chatsworth-Graham had been a snob. His only daughter couldn't deny that. She knew in her heart that her father would not have approved of Marc at all, at least in connection with her.

Marc wouldn't have been good enough for her in her father's opinion. He had tolerated Roger, primarily because Roger was the famous Julia Gray's son. Jennifer thought back to how many times her father and Roger ever actually had met. Less than a dozen, she'd say.

Jennifer knew that her bed was warm, too warm, yet she continued to shiver. Suddenly a longing for Marc swept over her that became so overpowering, it was all she could do to resist climbing out of bed and going into town and finding him. She wanted him so desperately. The wanting, this time, wasn't because of any sexual urge. She wanted him just to be with her, to have him hold her, perhaps to let her cry a little within the sanctuary of his arms.

Brooding about this, Jennifer recognized that her love for Marc went way beyond the physical, way beyond passion. He was the person with whom she wanted to spend the rest of her life.

She sank back against her pillows, stricken. She was one of the wealthiest women in the world, yet she was poor beyond belief. For she knew that once Marc discovered that she was the Chatsworth-Graham heiress, she would never have so much as a ghost of a chance of sharing her life with him.

The limelight came much sooner than Jennifer had thought it would. By late morning the next day a reporter from the *Berkshire Eagle* was knocking at Julia's door.

Jennifer finally had drifted off to sleep toward dawn. She was still drowsy when Trina entered her bedroom to tell her that there was a newspaperman downstairs who wanted to see her.

"Miss Julia thinks maybe you'd better come down," Trina added reluctantly.

Jennifer dressed quickly in slacks and a sweater. Julia was in the living room with the reporter. He stood as Jennifer entered, a tall, thin man with a pleasant, rugged face and a thatch of unruly brown hair.

"I'm Jack Thornton, Ms. Chatsworth-Graham," he introduced himself. Jennifer recognized the name immediately.

"You're Marc's friend," she said involuntarily.

He nodded. "That's right."

Jennifer stared at him helplessly. *Oh, my God,* she was thinking, *Oh, my God! Now there's no possible way of keeping Marc from finding out about me.*

"I'm sorry about your father," Jack Thornton said. The words could have been trite, but he made them sound sincere.

"Thank you." It was all Jennifer could do to answer him.

"Ms. Chatsworth-Graham..." He seemed almost as miserable as she felt, Jennifer noted. "I hate to intrude on you," he went on, and she believed him. "I've been deputized something of a committee of one to speak to you. Whatever you tell me can be relayed to the wire services. In other words, if you'll talk to me, maybe we can spare you a lot of other interviews for the time being."

"I've explained to Mr. Thornton that you'll be leaving for Boston shortly," Julia interposed. "Ricardo has booked an afternoon flight to New York for you. I've talked to Polly Mitchell again. She'll arrange for you to be picked up at LaGuardia and taken to your father's apartment."

The "apartment" that was a two-story Fifth Avenue penthouse, Jennifer thought dully.

"Lisa is flying back via Madrid with—" Julia struggled for the right word and then concluded "—with your father."

Jennifer nodded.

"Darling," Julia suggested valiantly, "do you want me to go to New York with you?"

Jennifer appreciated the kind of effort even this much travel would require from Julia just now. Her eyes misted at the thought that Julia would be more than willing to make the effort for her.

"No," she said. "Of course not, Julia. Look...I'll be all right."

"I know you will be. Mr. Thornton, be as brief with her as you can, will you? She has a lot ahead of her."

There was definite sympathy in Jack Thornton's brown eyes as he nodded. "We have plenty of background information in file about your father," he told Jennifer. "They will have even more, of course, in Boston and New York. You, however," he added, with a faint smile, "have kept a lower profile."

"I've tried to," Jennifer admitted. Inwardly she was churning with the questions. *What are you going to tell Marc? When are you going to tell him whatever you're going to tell him?*

She wished she had the courage to pose the questions aloud.

There was one question she did need to ask.

"How did you find me here?" she queried.

"Your Boston publisher told the news services where you were staying," Jack Thornton said. "Ours was the nearest newspaper. We picked the information up on the wire."

"How did you connect Jennifer Bentley with Jennifer Bentley Chatsworth-Graham?"

"Your father's secretary told the news service that you use the name Jennifer Bentley professionally."

"I see."

There was no point in damning either Jack Thornton or Polly Mitchell. Jennifer calmed, knowing that there could have been no long-term way of keeping either her identity or her location a secret.

"Am I right in assuming that you were Hugh Chatsworth-Graham's only child?" Jack Thornton asked her.

Jennifer had been deep in her own thoughts. She looked at him blankly. "Yes." Her answer was so quiet, he had to strain to hear her.

"And you are his heiress?"

She hesitated over this. She temporized by saying, "My father left a wife, Mr. Thornton."

"Yes, I know that. And I'm sure he has provided for her very comfortably. But as we hear it, you're to inherit the bulk of his estate. Is that correct?"

There was no point in hedging. "Yes," Jennifer admitted.

There was a curious note in Jack Thornton's voice, a disbelief, as he said, "That will make you one of the wealthiest women in the world, won't it, Ms. Chatsworth-Graham?"

At this Jennifer looked him straight in the eye. "I would say," she said distinctly, "that depends on how you define wealth."

Something glimmered in those brown eyes. Admiration? Jennifer wondered about that.

She formed her words without thinking them out. "Yes," she said, "as I understand it, I'm slated to be the Chatsworth-Graham heiress. But I wasn't raised to handle a vast financial empire, Mr. Thornton. Fortunately my father had advisors whom he trusted implicitly. I intend to rely on them. I have my own career, as you probably know. I intend to pursue it. What I'm trying to say, I suppose, is that I don't plan to alter my life-style. I've followed my own path, and that's what I want to continue doing."

And I want Marc with me on that path. She yearned to tell Marc's friend this.

Jack Thornton sounded regretful as he said, "I would think that would be a difficult thing to manage. You've been able to enjoy a certain anonymity of your own choosing until now. But within the next few days your picture is going to be splashed on the front page of every newspaper in the world. Your face is going to become so familiar on television that people who see you walking down the street will feel as if they know you."

"You think it's impossible that they will respect my desire for privacy?" Jennifer asked him. "Or that they will deny me the right to lead my own life?"

"Perhaps not impossible," he said honestly. "But doubtful."

And what of Marc? She wanted to cry the question out to him. Marc and this man had gone through college together, they were still very close. In some ways, this man knew Marc better than she did.

"I think you should realize," Jack Thornton said gently, "that when you get to Logan Airport there will be television cameras there, waiting to focus on you. You're going to be asked a lot of questions. It would be expedient to try to prepare some of your answers in advance."

Julia said quietly, "That's good advice, Jennifer."

"Yes." Jennifer nodded. Then she came out with it. She met Jack Thornton's eyes directly once again and said, "Marc doesn't know about any of this."

"You're saying that he doesn't know you're the Chatsworth-Graham heiress?"

"Yes."

"I suspected as much," he admitted. "Marc has spoken to me about you. He would have mentioned it if he'd known about your father."

He stood. "I won't delay you any further," he said. "I appreciate your talking to me." His smile was rueful. "I wish I could help you get through the next few days."

"Thank you," Jennifer said. "I wish you could."

"You'll see Marc before you leave for Boston?"

"I doubt it."

"Marc called earlier," Julia put in. "I told him you were still asleep. I said I'd ask you to call him later. He had to go out on business for a while." She hesitated. "I feel sure he hadn't heard about your father, Jen," she added.

"Thanks, Julia," Jennifer said. She already knew she wasn't going to try to reach Marc before she left for Boston. There were other things to be gotten through, other things that had to be done before she could hope to try to reach Marc again at all.

Jennifer had been twelve years old when her mother died. She still remembered the trauma of that time much too vividly.

On the flight to New York she reminded herself that she was considerably older now, far more able to cope with things. She kept trying to hammer this fact into her brain, over and over again.

Her father's secretary was with the limousine that met her at the airport. Polly Mitchell was a plump, pretty woman in her early fifties who had gone to work for Hugh Chatsworth-Graham straight out of business college, and immediately had fallen hopelessly in love with him.

Probably no love had ever been more unrequited, Jennifer thought as she greeted Polly. Yet Polly had been loyal to the end, even after her employer had clearly shown his feelings by marrying a woman only a few years older than his daughter.

Polly's eyes were red-rimmed, and Jennifer realized, with an attendant feeling of grief, that Polly had cried for her father considerably more than she had.

"The plane gets into Kennedy at six o'clock," Polly reported as they started for Manhattan. "Lisa will come directly to the apartment. The funeral is scheduled for the day after tomorrow at three in the afternoon. That will give people the chance to fly in."

"Fly in from where?" Jennifer queried.

Polly looked at her in surprise. "From everywhere," she said, as if this were something a kindergarten child should have understood. "People will be coming from all over the world to attend your father's funeral, Jennifer. Very important people."

She nodded. "Of course." Then she added, "Who are these people, Polly?"

Polly looked vaguely confused. "Business associates, the giants of the financial world, international bankers..." she began.

"Any friends?" Jennifer interrupted.

"What?"

"Did my father have any friends?" Jennifer persisted.

Polly was shocked. "Jennifer, what a thing to say," she protested. But Jennifer noted that her father's secretary didn't even try to answer her question.

Hugh Chatsworth-Graham had been internationally famous. The rich and the great would be flying to New York to attend his funeral. But Jennifer doubted if there would be a single friend among the mourners. Not even herself. Not even she had been her father's friend. Nor had Polly, for that matter. She had worshipped an imagined idol, not a man. Nor had Lisa, who had been interested in him for entirely different reasons, ever been a friend, in any sense at all. He had offered exactly what Lisa, who was a fairly good actress at the time they married, had coveted. For the rest of her life Lisa would have wealth and social position as the widow of Hugh Chatsworth-Graham. Lisa's position as his widow would, in fact, be a springboard toward making another advantageous marriage.

What a cat you are becoming, Jennifer told herself grimly.

The Fifth Avenue penthouse looked like a very expensive movie set. Nothing clashed; there was never anything out of place. But then, only a staff of servants ever lived there for any length of time, and they stayed pretty much within their own quarters.

Jennifer went directly to her room and asked that she not be disturbed until her stepmother arrived at the apartment. Jack Thornton had been right. She'd been met by a barrage of television cameras both in Boston and in New York. She had fended off questions, trying to get away in both instances as quickly as she could. As she had talked, waiting for the first chance to escape, she had wondered only if Marc were watching this.

Marc was watching. He was sitting in front of the TV screen, a glass of Scotch on the rocks in his hand, but so far he hadn't even touched the liquor.

He was still in a state of shock. When he had phoned Jennifer that morning, he had spoken to Trina, and she had said nothing to clue him in about what had happened. Returning to the house after a full day, he had wondered if Jennifer had tried to reach him. If so, she'd left no message on his recorder.

He'd called the Gray house anyway, and this time Julia had taken his call. It was she who had told him that Jennifer was on her way to New York because of her father's sudden death. Julia hadn't elaborated. Marc had at once asked for a phone number where he could reach Jennifer later, and Julia had given him one. But, strangely, he had postponed making the phone call.

Now he took the slip of paper with the phone number on it, struck a match to it, and watched the paper burn. It curled at the edges, then became a charred fragment and crumbled into ashes.

Marc felt an odd relationship with the slip of burning paper. Everything he'd ever wanted was going up in smoke with it. He could feel his inner self being pulverized into ashes.

He stared at Jennifer, trying to escape the press at LaGuardia, looking tired and stark and miserable as she fended off the TV reporters' questions.

He tried to tell himself that he hated her. But he didn't hate her; he loved her.

He grimaced, because loving her hurt even more than having his heart and soul pulverized. He'd never before felt such pain.

"Jenny, Jenny, Jenny." Marc spoke aloud, savagely. "How could you do this to me?"

In the midst of his agony Marc heard the doorbell ring. He ignored it. Then, a moment or so later, he heard the front door squeak as it was opened. He looked up to see Jack Thornton walking into the living room.

Jack strode directly to the television set and turned it off. "Enough of that," he said abruptly. Then, indicating Marc's glass of Scotch, he asked, "Any more where that came from?"

"Help yourself," Marc said roughly.

Jack left the room to return a few minutes later with a drink in hand. He slumped down into an armchair, and he said abruptly, "I can imagine how you feel."

Marc's laugh was derisive. "The hell you can!"

"Don't underestimate me. I interviewed her this morning. No," Jack corrected, "I didn't really interview her. I just talked to her...as briefly as possible."

Marc couldn't suppress his concern for Jennifer. "How was she?" he asked.

"Doing about as well as you are, I'd say," Jack opined. "When she heard my name I could see the questions spring into her eyes."

"What questions?"

"About you, idiot. I think she's scared to death she's going to lose you. No," he said as Marc raised a hand in protest, "hear me out. I'm serious. She was trying to tell me that inheriting her father's millions—I guess it's actually more like billions—isn't going to change her lifestyle. She was trying to convince me that she's been living the kind of life she wants to lead, and that's what she's going to keep on doing.

"I tried to tell her," Jack concluded, "that it won't be easy. In fact, that it's probably impossible. I pointed out that she's now—or is about to become—one of the wealthiest women in the whole world."

Marc finally took a long draft of the Scotch. Then he said thickly, "I don't want to hear about it."

"Look, Marc," Jack said, "she didn't ask for this."

"Spare me that." Marc's voice dripped with cynicism. "She could have told me her whole name. She could have told me who she was. She could have prepared the way for something like this." He waved vaguely toward the blank television screen. "I always knew she was out of my league. I told her so. But I'd about come to the point where I felt I was wrong about that. Today—would you believe this?—today I was going to ask her to marry me. I decided that last night as I was saying good-bye to her out at her house. Something had come up; we'd had a misunderstanding."

He broke off. "Hell," he said. He laughed shortly. "Suppose I'd asked her last night and she'd said yes? Where would that put me now?"

"I would think you'd be engaged," Jack Thornton told him.

"Engaged?" Marc scoffed. "Can't you picture the headlines? 'Chatsworth-Graham Heiress Pledges Troth to Crippled Ex-Cop.'"

He buried his head in his hands. His voice was muffled as he said, "Butt out, will you, Jack?"

"Marc..." Jack Thornton began anxiously.

"Seriously. Butt out, will you?"

Jack Thornton remained silent.

After a moment Marc looked up. "Tenacious, aren't you?" he asked.

"We've been through other things," his friend reminded him. "You stuck it out with me on some of those occasions. On others, I stuck it out with you. Why should this be different?"

"Because there's never been anything like this before, at least for me," Marc told him quietly. "Somehow, over these next couple of days, I've got to glue a lot of pieces together and get on with my life."

"As simple as that, eh?"

"I didn't say it was going to be simple."

Jack plunged. "What about Jennifer?" he asked.

"What about her?"

"Where does this leave her, Marc? You're going to glue together your pieces. Don't you think she's pretty much fallen apart herself. Don't you think she needs you to be here when she comes back to Thrussington?"

"If she comes back to Thrussington!"

"She'll be back," Jack said.

"What makes you so sure of yourself?"

"Let's call it a gut feeling."

"And your gut feelings are so infallible?" Marc challenged.

"This one is."

"Okay. Even if you're right, it's not going to make any difference," Marc said. As he spoke, the crazy love he had for her seemed to strangle him.

"She deceived me," Marc said slowly. "No, hear me out since you've put yourself in the middle of this. She told me her name was Jennifer Bentley. It wasn't Jennifer Bentley. It was Jennifer Bentley Chatsworth-Graham. She told me her father had remarried, and that she wasn't too close to either her father or her stepmother. She didn't tell me that her father was Hugh Chatsworth-Graham. If I thought she was out of my league in the beginning, where do you think that puts me now? She's in another galaxy, another universe. There's no place for me in her future, except maybe to install alarm systems at her various estates. There's no place for me with her, there never can be."

Marc's eyes were bitter as he faced his friend. "I was a novelty to her," he told Jack flatly. "Maybe she didn't even realize it, but I was something different. That's why I appealed to her. I was a cop who'd been phased out of business before his time. An ex-cop with a gimpy leg and a certain line of patter."

He said quietly, "I'm getting maudlin, and I haven't had that much to drink."

"Let me rectify the error," Jack suggested. "I'll freshen up both our glasses."

"No," Marc said. "I don't want to wake up tomorrow morning with a hangover. I need to be clear-headed for the next few days. I need to work things out before Jennifer gets back here...if you're right, and she does come back."

He added bitterly, "After that, I'll have the rest of my life to get drunk."

Chapter Twelve

Jennifer was in New York for nearly two weeks. She yearned to get back to Thrussington, but one obstacle after another arose to keep her from leaving the city.

The funeral had been a nightmare to her. It had been elaborate, crowded, and the sickly sweet smell of masses of flowers still assailed her nostrils and turned her stomach. She loved flowers, but she never again wanted to smell funeral flowers.

Worst of all, she'd lived through the day of the funeral saying all the right things, doing all the right things, but with the deep-seated knowledge that she, in her own way, was being just as phony as everyone else.

No one had really loved Hugh Chatsworth-Graham. His business associates and acquaintances around the world had seen not the man, but his money. To his only surviving child, this was the greatest tragedy of all.

A further difficulty had arisen when Lisa Chatsworth-Graham had not been nearly so compliant about her late husband's will as the Chatsworth-Graham attorneys had expected her to be. Lisa was being very well provided for, true. She would be able to have virtually anything she wanted to have and to live in the ultimate of luxury and comfort for the rest of her life. But this proved to be not enough.

Jennifer's share of the estate, in this instance, dwarfed the widow's share. Hugh Chatsworth-Graham, however, had been clever about that. He had required his wife to sign the necessary papers before their marriage, specifying her compliance to the terms of the will.

Now it became a question of Lisa being cut off entirely, or of agreeing to let the will go to probate without contest.

After consultation with her own attorneys, Lisa agreed. But the intervening days were painful and difficult for Jennifer. She was staying at the Fifth Avenue penthouse. So was Lisa. The place was large enough so that they could easily have avoided contact with each other. Lisa, though, was determined to be "civilized," and insisted that they share breakfast and dinner together. Jennifer matched her stepmother in politeness, and had the advantage of harboring no bad feelings toward her. The same couldn't be said about Lisa. At moments Jennifer felt that her stepmother really hated her, and this was a strain. She consoled herself by reminding herself that soon Lisa would be out of her life entirely.

The days after the funeral were spent in consultation with attorneys, business associates of her father's, executives in his far-flung enterprises—who flew from every corner of the world for the funeral, then stayed in New York in order to meet Jennifer and talk to her—and astute advisors ready to be of help to her in any way she wished.

She listened, she acted, but she had the odd feeling that she was watching herself from a distance as she moved through her necessary duties. It was another Jennifer playing the role of the Chatsworth-Graham heiress. The real Jennifer wanted only to go back to Thrussington...where Marc was.

Thinking about Marc became increasingly difficult. Jennifer had spoken to Julia on the phone several times. At first, she had asked Julia if she'd seen Marc. The answer, consistently, had been negative. Finally she'd stopped posing the question.

It hurt to think that Marc hadn't sent her so much as a sympathy note. She couldn't imagine what he must be thinking or feeling. She could appreciate that he, too, might be hurt, and confused about what possible direction a common future for the two of them could take. The problem was that she didn't know the extent of either the hurt or the confusion.

Was Marc so traumatized and so angry because she'd kept a secret from him, that he'd written her out of his life?

This was the question that haunted Jennifer when, ten days before Christmas, she flew from New York back to Boston.

She'd booked the flight under an assumed name, and she even tried a modicum of a disguise. She wore fake glasses with plain lenses, did her hair in a different fashion, donned a hat...and felt like an utter fool.

She told herself grimly that she didn't want to live this way, and was damned if she was going to.

Nevertheless, the disguise worked. At least no reporters hovered around her on the return trip as they had on the trip down.

Ricardo Castel met her at Logan Airport. He'd recently returned to Massachusetts himself after concerts in Chicago and Atlanta. Jennifer had told Julia her flight time, and had said that she'd plan to rent a car and drive back to Thrussington by herself. Having Ricardo come to meet her was a pleasant surprise.

Ricardo retrieved her single suitcase for her and drove his car around to the front of the terminal building. As they left the airport Jennifer heaved a sigh of relief so deep that he glanced across at her, startled.

"You sound like you're about to hyperventilate," he accused her.

She actually laughed. "No." She smiled at him, the first genuine smile that had crossed her face in a long time. "I'm so glad to get away from…everything," she admitted. She sobered. "I just hope I can stay away from it all. I hope the media isn't going to track me to Thrussington."

"I doubt they will, for the moment," Ricardo told her. "Jack Thornton was good to you in his story. He merely said you'd been staying in the Berkshires with a friend—he didn't name the town. He indicated it was a brief visit and that you'd been on the eve of leaving when word of your father's death reached you."

Surprised, Jennifer said, "That was nice of him."

"It may save you some grief at this point," Ricardo allowed. "That's one thing, Jennifer. The public forgets quickly. Yesterday's newspaper is used to wrap up today's garbage."

"What?"

"Well, that's what I always say," he told her. "To paraphrase it, front-page news gets stale very quickly. I admit you'll be good copy whenever you show yourself. But you'll learn how to handle the press with a minimum of annoyance to yourself. They're really not out to hound you. They have their jobs to do; all they want is a story. Give it to them, and they'll leave you alone.

"I know what I'm talking about," Ricardo added. "Over the years I've come under fire far too often myself. It began to seem as if every time I played a concert somewhere, someone accused me of getting involved with someone else's wife. The papers ate it all up."

Ricardo smiled bitterly. "Sometimes it's hell to be a celebrity," he confessed. "That's something you'll have to deal with. But my advice is to make it as small a part of your life as possible, and you'll do okay. Go on and lead the life you want to lead, and if you don't provide the papers with too much copy, there won't be anything for them to write about. I've kept a low profile on my concert tours these past couple of years, especially since I met Julia."

Ricardo's sudden grin was very endearing. "It took a hell of a lot to convince Julia that I wasn't just a playboy Casanova," he said.

Ricardo sold himself to Jennifer at that moment. She grinned back at him. "I think you've pretty well convinced her," she told him.

"Yes, I think I have. We plan to be married in February, Jennifer. I suppose I should have let Julia tell you. Maybe you and I might enter into a conspiracy and let her tell you anyway. But I can't keep it to myself any longer. I've never been so happy. We're going to be married February fourteenth. Valentine's Day. Schmaltzy, isn't it?"

"Very," Jennifer said, and loved the whole idea.

"I happen to know Julia wants you to be her only attendant."

"I think it would kill me if she wanted anyone else," Jennifer admitted.

"I don't have any family," Ricardo said. "Maybe some distant relatives in Spain and Italy; my parents came from

those countries. But I've been doing concert tours ever
since I was a kid, and I've been pretty much of a rolling
stone. I know a lot of people, but few that I consider real
friends."

"So who are you going to ask to stand up with you?"
Jennifer queried.

"I'm thinking about Marc Bouchard," Ricardo said.

A shock of surprise rocked Jennifer. "Do you feel you
know him that well?" she asked.

"I hope to," Ricardo said simply. "I ran into him in
town the other day. We had coffee together. Three cups of
coffee, as it turned out, and a lot of talk."

She waited, and when Ricardo didn't say anything more
she burst out, "You must know what you're doing to me,
Ricardo. Did Marc ask about me?"

"Yes."

"What did he say?"

"He wanted to know how you were. He said he could
imagine you must have your hands very full. I felt damned
sorry for him," Ricardo said.

"How...how was he?"

"He looked tired and miserable. He'd been working
very hard. He's installing the alarm system in the bank,
and it's a challenging task. It has to be absolutely foolproof, and he explained that it's a highly sophisticated
system. The very latest. He's been doing a lot of night
work on it because he can't do anything during the hours
the bank is open. Meantime, the president of the bank has
gone off to some island in the Caribbean and will be away
until after New Year's. Marc has to work with the vice-
president, someone named Paul Freyton...."

"He was against the new system if I remember rightly,"
Jennifer recalled.

"Exactly. Marc says Freyton has been a thorn in his side all along. The bank directors voted the system in despite him. Of course, LaFollette—the president—was in favor of it. Matters are complicated, though, because it appears that Freyton is LaFollette's son-in-law." Ricardo paused. "Do you really want to hear all this?" he asked her.

"I want to hear anything that involves Marc," Jennifer stated firmly.

"It's like that, Jennifer?"

"Yes, it's like that."

"Well," Ricardo said, "I would say that Marc, right now, is angry and bitter and lonely and unsure of himself. I think he loves you, but he's building a continuing series of mythical walls that are going to be hard to tumble down."

Ricardo paused. "Do you think you can tumble down walls?" he asked Jennifer.

It was not an idle question. The danger, she knew, was that Marc's mythical walls were apt to be built to last. The longer they stood, the stronger they would get.

"I don't know," she told Ricardo slowly. Then added, with a firm upward thrust of her chin, "But I can try."

Jennifer and Ricardo stopped for lunch at a "HoJos" along the turnpike. For the remainder of the drive to Thrussington they were silent for the most part.

With each passing mile Jennifer's thoughts became more and more involved with Marc and the problem of finding a way to reach him. Ricardo had painted a clear picture to her of Marc and his feelings. It was going to be up to her to find a way to attack the mythical walls and to blast them to pieces. Although she contemplated this bravely, she weakened when she realized what a difficult task it was going to be, and she wondered if she even had the tools with which to approach it.

What would the tools be? Love, for one thing, she decided, and she certainly had plenty of love to give Marc. Love, and determination, and courage...and perhaps patience and compassion as well. A lot of qualities, some of them intangible. Put together, they'd represent quite a force. But could she put them together?

They reached Julia's house late in the afternoon. Julia had progressed to walking with only a cane. Jennifer exclaimed with delight over this, then turned to catch Ricardo looking at Julia with a funny, guilty expression.

"I had to tell her," he said, and Julia laughed.

"Did you think I didn't know you would?" she challenged him.

Jennifer realized they were talking about their impending marriage, and she hugged Julia impulsively.

"It's wonderful," she said. "Really wonderful." She added, a wistful note in her voice, "I envy you both."

Trina served them tea and small sandwiches. "To hold you over till dinner," Trina said. When they had finished this repast Julia eyed Jennifer sternly.

"You look absolutely done in," she proclaimed. "How about taking a nap for a couple of hours? Then you'll be fresh and ready for dinner."

The vision of her inviting bed upstairs was too tempting to resist. But once Jennifer was snuggled down, restless thoughts came to plague her. Would Marc call? Was there a chance that he might come over? Or was she going to have to make the first move?

There was no way of looking into a symbolical crystal ball and getting any answers.

After a time she fell asleep. She was even more exhausted than Julia had surmised, and the combination of the long drive across Massachusetts and the wonderful fresh mountain air proved to be the perfect soporific.

It was well past the dinner hour when Jennifer awakened. She sat up in bed and stretched, and then was horrified when she saw the time on her bedside digital clock.

Downstairs, she found Julia and Ricardo playing cribbage at a card table set up in front of the fireplace.

"Trina put a plate with everything on it in the oven to keep warm for you," Julia said. "Bring it in and join us."

Jennifer put the plate of food on a tray and took it into the living room. She curled up on the couch and ate as she watched Julia and Ricardo arguing good-naturedly over the points in the cribbage game.

But when she finished her dinner she was more restless than ever.

"Has anyone used my car since I've been gone?" she asked suddenly.

"I've been turning the motor over each day for you," Ricardo said. "It should be fine."

"Good." Jennifer made a quick decision. "I want to go down to the village...for just a little while," she said.

The significant glance that passed between Ricardo and Julia didn't escape Jennifer. But Julia only commented, "Fine, dear. Be careful driving, that's all. At least the roads aren't icy."

The roads were bare, but a recent snow covered the fields and frosted the trees. There was bright moonlight, and Jennifer began to feel a sense of peace, from which she'd been far removed lately, as she drove through the silvered beauty of the woods to the main road.

All the houses had been decorated for Christmas. Again, Marc's comment that everything looked like a Christmas-card scene around here at the holiday time came back to her. Tears misted her eyes, and she brushed them away impatiently.

She thought of the old song about a little girl wanting only her two front teeth for Christmas.

Well, all she wanted for Christmas was the chance to be with Marc. Just to be with him and let him at least begin to realize how much she loved him.

Jennifer drove directly to Jack Thornton's house. It was a jolt to find it in darkness, with not even an outside Christmas light turned on.

For a terrible moment she wondered if Marc could have packed up and left Thrussington. But she dismissed this idea. Regardless of his personal feelings, she was certain that he wouldn't be that irresponsible where his business was concerned.

Then she remembered Ricardo saying that Marc had been working at the bank lately, installing the new alarm system. She drove on into the village, and when she came to the bank she saw Marc's van parked outside, and drew a sharp breath of relief.

There were a couple of other cars parked in the vicinity, probably belonging to the men who were working with Marc on the job. But the space directly in back of the van was empty.

Jennifer slipped her car into it, then shut off the motor and sat wondering what to do next.

She couldn't very well go up and pound on the bank door and ask to see Marc. She could do nothing, really, but wait.

She settled back, prepared for a vigil, but she hadn't counted on the cold. With no heat on in the car, it got colder and colder. For a time Jennifer turned the motor on and let the heater start its work again, opening her window a slit as a precaution against poisonous fumes. But she couldn't keep on running the motor forever. She shut it off, and the cold began to seep in again.

She was about to give up when she saw a side door to the bank open and several men come out. She recognized Marc instantly, in silhouette. He was taller than the rest, and then there was his telltale limp. It seemed more pronounced at the moment than it usually was, which meant that he was tired. Tired, and maybe irritable as well, and undoubtedly still angry where she was concerned.

It occurred to Jennifer that her timing was bad. But it was too late to retreat. Marc had to walk right by her to get to the van, and it was already too late to start up her car and pull away. Furthermore, a nearby streetlamp gave just enough light to make her car too visible. Knowing Marc, she was sure he would have checked out any car parked around the bank at this hour anyway.

He stopped, immediately abreast of her, peered, and then jerked his head up as if it had been tugged by an invisible rope. The other men went past him. As if in a fog, Jennifer heard them bidding good night to one another.

Finally she was sitting in her car and Marc was standing just outside it, and neither of them was saying anything to the other.

Jennifer broke the silence. She slipped out of the car so quickly that Marc was taken by surprise. He reeled backward, and as he had long ago in Julia's closet, went off balance. Jennifer saw him come down hard on his bad leg, and she heard him swear under his breath. Involuntarily her arms went out to him.

He froze under her touch, standing statue still.

Jennifer could feel his muscles tighten, and she became acutely aware of his hostility. Slowly she dropped her hands.

Her voice was thick as she said, "I have to talk to you, Marc."

"Why?" he asked. The single word was cold as an ice cube.

"You must know why. We have a lot to say to each other," Jennifer plodded on, determined not to let his attitude get to her to the point where she would give up.

"It seems to me," she went on valiantly, "that the last time we parted it was with the promise to each other that we'd have a serious discussion the next day."

"That no longer holds, Jennifer," Marc told her, his voice rough.

"I think it does," she insisted stubbornly. Something ignited inside of her, a spark flared. She gained the courage to say, "You are being hellishly unfair."

"I? How can you speak about anyone being unfair?"

"I've never been unfair to you, Marc."

"No?" He sneered the question. "Then our definitions differ," he informed her. Anger crept into his voice, tight and menacing. "You had your fun," he told her. "You made your pilgrimage to the other side of the tracks. Now let it go."

Jennifer stared at him, furious. "Damn you!" she exploded. "You're making a stupid cliché out of something that was beautiful! No matter how you feel about me now, don't destroy what we had, Marc."

Tension vibrated between them. Then Marc said, "Look, I'm bushed tonight. I don't have the capacity to deal with this. Maybe another time. I don't know. As I said, let it go for now. All right?"

He could not have defined the rift between them more devastatingly. The ragged edge of honesty in his voice snagged the fabric of Jennifer's innermost feelings, and she had never before felt so hopeless.

Whatever his feelings about her, Marc had managed to table them and go on with his own life. He'd put her on a shelf. Maybe sometime he'd take her down again. Maybe he wouldn't. Either way, it didn't seem to matter to him very much.

She turned and slowly got back into her car, closing the door carefully so that it thudded a dull thud.

As she pulled away from the curb she noted that Marc hadn't moved. He was still standing there, staring not at her but directly at the sidewalk as she turned the corner.

Jennifer thought she'd never seen anyone look quite so lonely.

Ricardo bought a beautiful balsam tree a few days before Christmas and they set it up in the corner of the living room. Under Julia's direction Ricardo and Trina brought down from the attic boxes of ornaments that had been in Julia's family for years.

One night they trimmed the tree together. Ricardo put tapes of Christmas carols on the stereo and glorious sound filled the house. They drank eggnog as they worked on the tree, and Julia hummed to the music. And Jennifer thought her heart would break.

Marc had not called, he had not come to the house. She was more than ever convinced that he had schooled himself to put her out of his life.

But despite her convictions about this, she still harbored the hope that he would find it impossible to let Christmas go by without saying or doing something. This, of all times, was the one that brought people together, healed wounds, mended misunderstandings. Wouldn't the magic of the season cause Marc to relent even a little bit?

Jennifer searched the stack of Christmas mail that came to the house daily for a note from him, or just a card signed with his name. She wasn't even asking for a message at this point. But there was nothing.

Julia didn't mention Marc, neither did Ricardo, neither did Trina. It was as if he had ceased to exist.

Finally Jennifer knew that regardless of what Marc did or didn't do, she couldn't let the holiday pass without a gesture on her part.

One morning Jennifer drove to Pittsfield by herself. It was a nostalgic trip. Each mile along the way reminded her of Marc.

She browsed along the main street, remembering the afternoon they'd looked at the toys in the shop window and had spoken about children. Marc had told her that she'd have "beautiful children."

She bypassed the jewelry store, just as Marc had then, and the men's clothing store, and the boutique where he had bought presents for his mother and his sisters. She wanted to find a new place, something entirely her own. She wanted something very special for him. But she had no idea of what it might be.

Finally, in a small art gallery on a side street, she found what she was looking for. It was a small oil painting, beautifully executed, that depicted winter in the Berkshires. It caught the spirit of the season, the spirit of Christmas. The artist had infiltrated the scene with a feeling that was exactly what Jennifer wanted to convey to Marc.

She had the painting gift-wrapped, then bought a card to go with it.

"May you keep the beauty and peace of this scene in your life and your heart forever," she wrote on the card. And added, "I only wish that you could have found it possible to let me share it with you."

Chapter Thirteen

The Thornton house was in darkness as Jennifer drove down the street past it. Relieved, she turned around at the next corner, drove back, and parked in front of it.

She wanted to leave the painting for Marc, but she didn't want to meet him face to face. She felt so emotionally shaky where he was concerned, she didn't think she could handle a meeting between them just now.

She had a felt-tip pen in her handbag. Switching on the dome light in her car, she used the pen to mark "Open Christmas Morning" in large letters across the surface of the brown paper with which the painting was wrapped.

This done, she made her way up the narrow walk to the house, and was about to prop the painting between the storm door and the front door when the front door opened so suddenly that Jennifer nearly screamed.

Marc towered above her. The house behind him was in darkness, so she couldn't see his face. But she could sense his coldness.

The bleak certainty that his love for her had turned to hate swept over her, and she felt sick about it. She tried to tell herself that if he'd been able to convert emotions so swiftly, it only proved he hadn't really loved her in the first place. But that didn't help.

"What do you want, Jenny?" Marc asked her, his tone flat, utterly emotionless.

Nevertheless, Jennifer's pulse thumped, and she began to feel the faintest glimmer of hope. In the past, Marc had called her Jenny only at those times when he felt tender toward her.

She said, stammering over the words, "I—I brought you something, that's all."

"Oh?" he queried in that same flat, cold tone. "What is it?"

"A Christmas gift," she said. She held the painting out to him, but he made no move to take it. "I wanted to leave it for you, that's all," she said. "I saw your van at the bank so I...didn't think you'd be home."

"I let a couple of my men take the van," he said. "They're doing some wiring work. It's a two-man job. I decided to cut along back here."

Suddenly the little foyer behind Marc was flooded with light, and she realized he must have pressed a wall switch.

He stepped back, and to her surprise he said, "Come in."

Panic gripped Jennifer. She really wasn't up to this, she thought frantically. Five minutes with him, facing his coldness, would bring on her tears. She would start crying her heart out right in front of him; she wouldn't be able to help herself. She couldn't stand the idea of putting on such a show of weakness. It would make him despise her all the more.

"No," she said hastily. "There's no need for me to come in. Just take this, please, and open it Christmas morning. All right?"

His silence made her look up at him. She noted, first, that his deep blue eyes looked hollow, and there were large, dark areas under those eyes that had never been there before. He looked terrible. Tired, unhappy. Her love for him overflowed, and it was all Jennifer could do to keep her hands at her side. She wanted so desperately to reach out to him.

Fortunately those hands were occupied with the painting. She held it out to him again, and she said, "Please. Take this."

He shook his head slowly. "I don't want any gifts from you," he told her bluntly.

She stared at him, shocked. Her words were pained.

"How can you be so callous?" she asked, a sob catching in her throat as she posed her question.

Again, silence descended like a pall. Then Marc said slowly, "I didn't intend to be callous. Look, now that you're here, come in, will you? I was about to try out some brandy a friend gave me for Christmas. Have a glass with me?"

It wasn't the most gracious of invitations, and pride alone urged Jennifer to refuse it. But then he reached out and laid his hand on her arm, tugging her slightly as he said, "Come on. The cold's getting in here. For that matter, you look frozen."

Jennifer felt frozen all the way through. But that had little to do with the winter temperature. She was dealing on an emotional rather than a physical level, trying hard to cope and very much afraid of failure.

Marc took the painting out of her hands and placed it against the wall. She realized that he must know it was some form of artwork, but he couldn't have appeared less interested in it.

He led the way into the living room. "I just got back myself," he said. "I came in the back way, that's why there were no lights on in front. I was about to put the outside lights on when I saw you. How long had you been sitting there?"

"What do you mean?"

"You had your interior car light on," he said patiently. "Why?"

"I—I was writing something on the package."

"I see."

Did he see? What did he see?

He struck a match as she watched, and lit the newspapers and kindling placed under the logs in the fireplace. The fire caught.

"I'll get the brandy," he said, and left her alone to gaze at the flames as she had the first night she'd known him.

By the time he returned, Jennifer felt so tense that she was afraid her nerves would snap if Marc so much as looked at her. She could no longer read him. She felt as if she no longer knew him at all.

She accepted the brandy and let its liquid fire scorch her throat. She sat down carefully at the far edge of the couch, averting her eyes from him. The silence fell again. It was heavy. She wasn't sure she could bear the weight of it.

Marc said suddenly, "I have an apology to make."

Jennifer's head turned toward him. He could not have surprised her more.

He was sitting in a chair near the fireplace, leaning forward, slowly twirling the brandy glass between his fingers, He said, "I'm very sorry about your father, Jenny. That's something I should have told you long before this."

She nodded, unable to answer him.

"I'm sorry about a number of things," Marc added, still staring at the glass between his fingers.

It occurred to Jennifer that it was as hard for him to look at her as it was for her to look at him.

Finally he took a sip of the brandy. She saw that his hand was shaking slightly.

He said, "You were right when you said the other night that we needed to talk. I should have had the sense to admit that. As a matter of fact, I intended to call you tomorrow." He looked up, and his eyes met hers directly. "I couldn't let Christmas go by with things like this between us," he said simply.

Jennifer felt a wild surge of hope. It would have been easy to let the hope take wings, but she fought down the natural urge to do this. Marc's expression was far too bleak for her to think that he had any intention of trying to pick up their relationship where it had left off.

"I always knew you must have money," he said slowly. "Everything about you told me that. The way you look, the way you dress, the way you act, the way you speak, the lovely things in your Boston house. They all told of your background. But for a while I had the crazy notion that maybe I could handle that." Marc seemed almost to be speaking to himself.

Again, his eyes met hers directly. "Why did you lie to me, Jenny?" he asked her.

Again, she was shocked. "I never lied to you," she told him.

His mouth twisted in a way that was painful to watch. "Jenny, Jenny," he reproved her gently. "You know better, I know better. Why, Jenny?"

Jenny's chin tilted upward in the way it did when she was sure of herself, and prepared to fight for her rights. She said, "I never lied to you. I've used the name Jennifer Bentley for years. I didn't tell you I was Jennifer Bentley with any intention of deceiving you. I told you I was Jennifer Bentley because, in my own mind, that's who I am."

This was true, as far as it went. But honesty compelled her to continue. "Then," she said, "after that—that first night here...I admit I didn't want you to know my full name. Not until you'd first come to know me. Does that make sense to you, Marc?"

"I don't know," he said. He repeated, "I don't know."

"There were dozens of people at my father's funeral," Jennifer said, forcing herself to keep her voice as steady as possible. "But there wasn't one person there—myself included—who gave a real damn about my father. They only knew Hugh Chatsworth-Graham. A figure. A symbol. A modern Croesus.

"That," she said, spacing the words slowly, deliberately, "is the way it always was with me, Marc, when I was known as Hugh Chatsworth-Graham's daughter. Sometimes I met someone who didn't know who I was and they found out and nothing was ever the same after that. After that they saw me as a symbol, not as a person, and the relationship between us, whatever it had been, disintegrated."

She looked at him imploringly. "I couldn't bear to have that happen with us," she confessed. "I prayed you wouldn't discover my full name. I hoped that if you came to know me first, if you knew *me*, then when you did find out who my father was it would no longer matter. I knew that sooner or later you were bound to find out. I hoped it would be later, that was all."

"How could I possibly believe that you ever could have been seriously interested in me?" Marc's words were like bullets finding their targets in Jennifer's heart.

She stared at him, overwhelmed by the question. She countered with one of her own. "How could you possibly think that I wasn't seriously interested in you?" she asked him.

"Because I know something about human nature," Marc told her, that dull, bleak tone back in his voice again. "I dealt with human nature for years in my work. I saw every facet of it. I was a novelty to you, Jenny. Knowing that doesn't do much for my ego, I admit, but I've come to terms with it."

His mouth twisted in a way that was painful to watch. "I'll never be able to say I'm sorry I knew you as I did," he confessed. "You were the most beautiful thing that ever happened to me. And, for a while, I had very high hopes for us. Would you believe," he asked with a crooked smile that further lacerated Jennifer's already torn emotions, "that I was on the verge of asking you to marry me?"

The smile faded, and an expression of ultimate mockery came to linger on his face.

"Can't you imagine the headlines?" he asked softly.

Jennifer shuddered involuntarily. She could imagine the headlines only too well. Then she remembered what Ricardo had said about the temporary effect of newspaper publicity. The headlines would be hard to deal with at the time, she was willing to concede that, but their impact would diminish with each passing day.

"I'd be considered the fortune hunter of the century, wouldn't I?" Marc asked deliberately.

She flinched at this. She hadn't thought of it that way.

If only he had asked her to marry him. If only they'd gotten married before this happened. If they were married now, she wondered what he would do.

Would he leave her? Would he insist on a divorce? Or would he merely retreat into a world all his own and let their marriage become a mockery?

It was impossible to know the answer to any of those questions. A waste of time and energy to even ask. But Jennifer's heart ached for what might have been. From the expression in Marc's eyes, she knew there was no way now that it was ever going to be.

He changed the subject. "What are you going to do, Jenny?" he asked her.

"What do you mean?" she hedged. She hadn't thought beyond now, beyond him. She had come back to Thrussington with Marc uppermost in her mind. Nothing else had mattered.

"Do you plan to take an active role in your father's business empire?"

"I suppose I must fulfill a certain role," she said reluctantly. "My father surrounded himself with very good people though. I intend to follow his example in that respect. I know that, regardless, it will make common sense to keep a personal eye on the different companies. I will do that to an extent, but I will largely rely on my advisors. I have absolute faith in them. As long as that faith is justified, there will be no need for me to play more than a token role."

She sighed. She hoped fervently that she would never be called upon to play more than a token role insofar as the Chatsworth-Graham empire was concerned.

"As for myself," she said, "I plan to stay here in Thrussington for the time being. Ricardo and Julia are to be married in February, you probably know that?"

"Yes," he nodded.

"They plan to go away on a long honeymoon," she said. "Ricardo is refusing any concert tours for at least four months after their marriage. I've assured Julia that I'll stay on here with Trina. I have my own work to do."

"You plan to keep on writing and illustrating your books?" he asked, sounding faintly surprised about this.

"That's my career," she said stiffly. "Of course I plan to continue with it."

Marc was surveying her narrowly, a fact of which Jennifer was intensely aware. She heard him say, disbelief evident in his voice, "You seem to think you can go on as if nothing has happened."

"If you mean that I plan to go on living without altering my life-style—yes, that is exactly what I intend to do," Jennifer said, and hoped she sounded more convinced about this than she felt.

Marc said softly, "I wish you luck, Jenny. From what I've heard, most heiresses have found it pretty difficult to lead private lives as they might wish. Maybe you'll be an exception."

Marc made it plain that he doubted very much if this would be the case.

Their conversation dwindled. Jennifer announced that she should be getting back to Julia's house, and Marc made no move to change her mind. He walked her to the door, and she wondered if he knew that her heart was breaking more and more with every step.

Neither of them noticed the painting propped up against the wall. Jennifer glanced at Marc to see that he was staring straight ahead as he opened the door for her, his eyes fixed on the Christmas lights twinkling on an outdoor tree across the way.

"If I don't see you again before Christmas, have a good one," he said.

"Yes," she managed. "Yes. You too."

All the way back to Julia's the wheels of Jennifer's car seemed to be chanting a single word. *Strangers. Strangers.*

She hated the words.

The next morning Jennifer got up so early that even Trina wasn't stirring. She made herself a mug of hot tea and took it with her out to the studio.

She forced herself to plunge into work. At first, it didn't come easily. Every word that she wrote was ground out of her. Her phrasing was stiff and awkward, and she realized her copy would need a lot of editing. But she plowed on. She was willing to work it over and over until it was right. Just now, the main thing was to work at all.

Kenneth Trent had been calling her almost daily since her return from New York. Like Marc, Ken had doubted that she would want to continue with her career. This had annoyed her thoroughly, and she had decided that once she had delivered her present book to Ken she was going to look around for a new publisher.

She was intensely serious about her work. She needed a publisher who would recognize that, and would see her as a writer and an artist rather than a potentially frivolous heiress.

She also decided that her next publisher would be middle-aged, if not elderly, and perhaps female as well. She wanted no more personal involvements on any level.

At one in the afternoon the intercom sounded. It was Trina, sounding worried.

"Miss Julia said I shouldn't disturb you," Trina admitted, "but I happen to know you haven't had a bite to eat so far today. How about if I bring you out a sandwich and a piece of cake?"

"I'll come in the house and have it there," Jennifer compromised.

Trina had been baking Christmas cookies. The kitchen smelled of vanilla and spices and a wonderful blend of less identifiable aromas.

Jennifer urged Trina to pour out a cup of tea for herself, and to join her at the kitchen table as she munched her sandwich. She yearned for company.

Trina agreed readily enough. As she was spooning sugar into her tea, she said, "I went into the village this morning to do some shopping, and I ran into Marc Bouchard. He looks awful. Like he hasn't slept in weeks, and is dropping pounds." Trina fixed her eyes accusingly on Jennifer.

Jennifer smiled sadly. "It isn't me, Trina," she said. "There's no need to look at me like that. Our being apart is Marc's doing, not mine."

Trina frowned as she got the message. "Oh, Jen," she protested, "if you're saying what I think you're saying— well, anyone with half a brain would know that just getting richer than you used to be isn't going to go to your head."

Jennifer nearly laughed at Trina's simplistic, but very accurate, way of putting things.

"Would that you could convince Marc of that," she murmured regretfully.

"I just might try," Trina said grimly. "I've seen you look a lot better than you've been looking since you got back from New York. I just thought it was because of the trouble you've been through." Trina shook her head. "Men!" she exploded. "Sometimes you have to give them a good shaking up before they come to their senses."

Jennifer couldn't imagine what she could do that would give Marc a good shaking up. He seemed to have developed the capacity in a very short time to be impervious to her.

At least, she reminded herself as she finished her lunch, he hadn't returned the painting to her. Not yet, anyway.

She wondered if he was abiding by her request to wait till Christmas morning to open it.

Chapter Fourteen

It's that Mr. Thornton from the newspaper on the phone, Jen,'' Trina said. ''He says it's urgent.''

It was Christmas Eve. Ricardo had put carols on the stereo, and their lovely strains wafted through the beautifully decorated rooms of Julia's house. Presents had been placed under the tree, aglow in one corner of the large living room. The scene was unutterably lovely, and all evening Jennifer had been sad. It was all she could do to keep up the pretense of sharing in the holiday spirit.

Each time she glanced toward Ricardo and Julia she felt especially alone, despite their efforts to include her. They were so much in love with each other. Their quiet happiness glowed like the lights on the Christmas tree.

Ricardo said quickly, ''I'll take the call for you if you like, Jennifer.''

''No,'' she said, standing up slowly. ''That's all right. I'll speak to him.''

At that moment Jack Thornton represented a link with Marc. It didn't matter that he was probably after a story that strictly involved the Chatsworth-Graham heiress, and had nothing to do with Marc at all.

She went to the phone and quickly found out that she couldn't have been more wrong.

"Jennifer?" Jack Thornton sounded distraught, and she doubted if he even realized he was calling her by her first name.

"Yes," she said, sudden apprehension flooding her. She had the awful premonition that something had happened to Marc, something terrible. She clutched the phone receiver tightly, and her heart hammered as she waited to hear what Jack Thornton had to tell her.

"Jennifer, I think Marc's in real trouble," Jack said.

"What kind of trouble, Jack?"

"Something's haywire at the Berkshire-Hudson Bank and Trust Company," she was told. "Look, I'm heading down to Thrussington from Pittsfield right now. Want me to pick you up?"

"Yes," she said. "Oh, yes."

She was waiting at the door when Jack Thornton pulled up in an aging station wagon. She was down the front steps and into the wagon in a flash.

"Tell me," she urged as he headed out of the driveway.

"I know Marc planned the alarm system switchover tonight," Jack said as he drove down the narrow dirt lane, trying to avoid the potholes. "My parents wanted him to come over to our place for eggnog, and he said he couldn't. At first, I thought he was being antisocial. Marc's tended in that direction recently. But he explained that he was planning to work tomorrow, starting bright and early...."

"Christmas Day?"

"That's right. He said it was the ideal time to switch the systems at the bank from the old to the new. Seems that at the last minute, with everything installed, this becomes a fairly simple procedure, something he could do all by himself. The main risk was in leaving an interval of time when the bank would be without an alarm system at all. Marc figured a certain element of surprise in his planning. Only he knew exactly the hour when the switch would be made."

"But?" she urged, noting the hesitation in Jack's voice.

"A few of the bank's inner echelon knew the change-over would be made tomorrow," Jack admitted. "Not exactly when tomorrow, but at some point. Maybe they leaked the word, I don't know about that. I do know that Marc went over to the bank tonight, apparently to make a final check. I tried to reach him, and I happen to know the person who answered his phone—one of his employees, monitoring his business tonight. He told me Marc had decided to swing by the bank, but should be back shortly. That was two hours ago."

"That doesn't necessarily mean anything," Jennifer pointed out. "Marc could have checked out the bank and then gone on somewhere."

"Marc is very fond of my parents," Jack said stubbornly. "If he were to spend his Christmas Eve with anyone, I think it would be with them. He refused their invitation because, as he put it, he intended to go to bed with the birds so he could get up in the wee hours and take care of the bank job. I don't think he was lying to my parents about that."

"I'm sure he wasn't," Jennifer said placatingly. "Nevertheless, he could have changed his mind. Or, he could have met someone along the way who persuaded him to stop for a drink or something." Even as she spoke,

Jennifer recognized that she was rationalizing because she didn't want anything to be wrong. She didn't want Marc to be in trouble.

"Not Marc," Jack said so definitely that she could mount no further argument.

She looked across at him, her worry increasing. "Jack," she demanded, "what do you think has happened?"

"I phoned the bank about an hour ago to see if I could persuade Marc to change his mind about coming out to our place," he admitted. "I felt he needed to be with people tonight a lot more than he needed extra sleep. I guess you know how down he's been."

"I can imagine it," she said quietly. She was just beginning to imagine it. She was just beginning to realize that she'd been selfish of late, in a sense. She'd been thinking primarily of her own pain because Marc had shut her out of his life. She hadn't stopped to think that he could be suffering every bit as much as she was.

"The bank has a telephone," Jack said. "If Marc had been there, and could have, he would have answered it. He'd told the man covering for him where he could be reached if he were needed.

"I tried to phone the bank three different times," Jack continued. "There was no answer. I called the Thrussington cops and asked them to swing by the bank and take a look—to see if Marc's van was there. It was. I asked them to knock on the bank's side door to see if they got any response out of Marc. They did as I asked, and no one came to the door. If Marc had been able to, he would have looked out a window when he heard a knock on the door. He would have seen the police cruiser, and he would have gone to the door."

"You keep saying that Marc would have answered the phone if he could have, or that he would have gone to the door if he were able to."

"Exactly," Jack said tersely. "I know the guy, Jennifer. Sometimes I think I know him better than anyone else does. He's a professional; he reacts professionally. No matter what his private feelings, he'd react professionally as long as there was a job to be done.

"I have the gut feeling," Jack told her, "that Marc has been worried about something in connection with this bank job. And that's why he went to the bank himself." He hesitated. "I think he walked in on something. Maybe a robbery in progress," he concluded.

Jennifer stared at him, horrified.

Jack shrugged. "What the hell," he said wearily. "It isn't my imagination. I've talked to the local cops. They agree with me. They also think Marc's in there, and that there has to be a super good reason why they can't rouse him."

Jennifer shuddered. "You're serious," she whispered. "You really do think there's a robbery in progress."

"Yes," he agreed heavily. "Yes, I do. And I think Marc's been caught in the thick of it. Can you imagine a better hostage?"

"Oh, God," Jennifer murmured, and this was a prayer. She turned toward Jack, desperation in her lovely gray eyes. "This can't be happening," she implored him. "If the bank really was being robbed and Marc walked in on it, they—the robbers—they can't hold him hostage. Marc's been through too much. He couldn't fight back." She ached as she said, her voice very small, "He's lame...."

The word trailed off. Jack snapped tersely, "Marc is strong as an ox, and capable of handling himself in any situation, Jennifer. You underestimate him."

"I'd never underestimate him," she retorted sharply. "I love him too much."

She felt Jack Thornton's eyes sweep her face. He said, as if not quite believing her, "Are you sure about that?"

Her thoughts were already on the bank, on the chance of Marc being in that bank, held hostage by a group of thieves. Fear for him gripped her as she asked, "Am I sure about what?"

"Are you sure it's love you feel for Marc?"

She turned toward him, lashing him with her scorn. "You too?" she asked bitterly. "Marc doubts I love him. Now you, his best friend, doubt it too? What can I do to prove myself? What can I ever do to convince him that I'd give up anything else in the world if he'd take the love I have to offer him!"

She flung the words out, and at the moment it was a rhetorical question. Still, Jack Thornton gave her a long and singularly comprehensive look before he turned to concentrate fully upon his driving.

They met up with a police car a block from the bank. Jennifer recognized the emblem on the side of the Thrussington cruiser, and she saw one of the police officers standing by it who had come to Julia's house on that first, fateful afternoon when she'd set off the alarm.

Jack pulled up his car, and the police officer came over to it.

"Anything happened?" Jack asked.

The police officer surveyed first Jack and then Jennifer before he answered. "No. Except that he's in there all right. Bouchard's van's the only vehicle parked in the immediate vicinity of the bank. Stands to reason, though, that if he was alone, he would have made the fact known by now.

"We're calling the bank phone at five-minute intervals," the officer continued, "but no one's answering. Every now and then one of us goes up and bangs on the side door. But there's been no response there either. The place is locked up like a vault—there's no easy way in. If this is a robbery situation, anyone who tries to go in will face a direct line of fire, and that won't help Marc. But," the man added, "the alarm's not on."

"The hell you say!" Jack Thornton exploded.

Jennifer's mind was racing. Jack had said that Marc planned to switch the alarm systems at some point during Christmas Day, evidently early in the morning, because Marc had indicated to Jack that he planned to get up very early.

The new system hadn't been activated yet, but the old one wasn't working. This didn't make sense, because the transition was to have been smooth from the old to the new, so that the bank would have consistent protection during the changeover.

"Brent Cranston's on his way down with Chief Andrews," the Thrussington police officer volunteered, and Jennifer remembered the state police lieutenant who had come to Julia's house at the time of their robbery.

Jack nodded. Then he said, "Look, Bill. I'm going to move on closer and park near Marc's van. I don't see what harm it could do."

"I don't know," the police officer said doubtfully.

"If the chief or Cranston object, I'll move," Jack promised.

A moment later Jack Thornton was driving down the remaining block to the bank.

There were red Christmas lights in each of the bank's many windows. Jennifer would never have thought that Christmas lights could look sinister, but these did. She saw

Marc's van, and her fear grew, becoming an invisible monster that clawed at her.

She asked under her breath, "Do you suppose anyone has looked inside it?"

"Looked inside what?" Jack asked her.

"The van. Marc—" She hesitated. "Marc could be inside. Maybe he...well, maybe he got sick or something."

Jack took her seriously. "I'll check that out," he promised.

He did, once he had parked, only to quickly return with word that the van was empty. He stared toward the bank moodily. "He has to be in there," he said. "God, I wish I knew what was going on."

Jennifer silently echoed his sentiment and magnified it a thousandfold.

A state police cruiser pulled up directly in front of Jack's car, and Brent Cranston got out and walked over to them.

"Jack," he greeted, and then peered more closely and said, "Miss Bentley, isn't it?"

"Yes," Jennifer said.

"Do you know anything about Bouchard being in there?" the state police lieutenant asked her, gesturing toward the bank.

"No," she said.

Jack Thornton said quickly, "I called Jennifer when I couldn't rouse Marc. Brent, he's got to be in there."

"I agree," Brent Cranston said quietly. "What we've got to figure out is what to do about it. Marc may have met with an accident, he may be hurt, unconscious. That may be all there is to it. On the other hand..."

"I think he walked into something," Jack insisted. "I know Marc. If he was hurt, he would have gotten to a phone if he had to crawl."

"Unless he is unconscious," Brent Cranston pointed out.

"Yes," Jack admitted reluctantly.

"Let's find out," the state police lieutenant suggested. "I've got a bullhorn in my car, suppose you use it, Jack. Marc will recognize your voice. If he's able to, he'll respond to it. I have an idea."

"Yes?"

"Ask him to go to the front of the bank if he can, and unscrew the red light in the right front window. That way we'll know he's in there and okay. We can take it from there."

For the next few minutes Jennifer held her breath. Unable to tolerate staying in the car, she got out and sat on the hood, watching Brent Cranston instruct Jack in the use of the bullhorn.

Jack's voice rang out, magnified. "Marc? This is Jack," he called, his words echoing in the dark, cold night. "Are you in there? Are you okay? To answer both questions, go to the front of the bank and unscrew the Christmas light bulb in the right window."

Time passed. An eternity of time. Then the red light in the bank window suddenly went out.

"Oh, my God," Jack said, his voice stark.

Jennifer realized that like herself he had been hoping against hope that Marc wasn't in the bank. That he'd gone somewhere else, to do something else. That he was safe.

The enormity of what was happening to Marc struck her, and terror made her shiver involuntarily.

Dimly she heard the Thrussington police chief talking to the police officer they called Bill. "Put in a call for mutual aid from all the towns in the area. We'll need to surround this place. Call the state police barracks. Tell them Cranston says we need help. Set up a roadblock on every path into town, and another within a two-block radius of the bank. We need to establish a network..."

Then a miracle happened.

The police chief beckoned urgently and she followed. Jack and Lieutenant Cranston went over to join him at the side of the police cruiser. Through the car's open window they heard Marc's voice coming over the police radio. It rang out clearly, and his tone was almost conversational.

"You've flubbed this, Freyton," he was saying casually. "They know I'm in here. You had to let me give them that much information or they would have blasted their way into the place. Now, how do you think you're going to get out?"

"The same way we got in," came a second voice. "Through the back door. With you leading the way, Bouchard. You don't think they'll try anything when we're holding you right in front of us, do you? One move, and you'll be dead. They'll know that."

"They may consider it a calculated risk," Marc said, still casual.

"I doubt that," the other man answered. "You'd die a hero, Bouchard, but it would make the cops look like dirt. They'll try to figure a way to let us slip through and then catch up with us. And that's where we'll have them."

"Do you plan to take me with you?" How could he sound so cool, Jennifer wondered frantically, when it was his life hanging in the balance.

"To a point," came the enigmatic answer.

"Murder's heavy stuff," Marc observed.

"So is bank robbery," the answer came.

"Not in the same league."

"Close enough. My life would be ended."

A silence fell. Jack whispered to Brent Cranston, "That has to be Paul Freyton he's talking to."

"I know." The state police lieutenant nodded.

"Somehow Marc's managed to activate the new system."

"Somehow," Cranston agreed.

Marc had told Ricardo that the alarm system he was putting in the bank was a highly sophisticated one, Jennifer recalled. She had no idea how such a system might be activated, but somehow Marc had managed whatever was necessary so that it was like having a broadcast being played in public of what was going on inside the bank.

They heard Freyton say, "I didn't ask for this, Bouchard. You stuck your nose in. That was your bad luck."

"Possibly," Marc admitted evenly.

"I've never wanted to kill anyone," Freyton said. "All I wanted was the money. I tried to block your damned system. Now, it's unfortunate that you felt the need to come over here tonight. Why? Can you tell me that?"

"I guess you'd call it a gut feeling," Marc said. "Little things, now and then. The way you've acted. Your resistance to the change, especially when you knew better than most people that the old system was obsolete. Your field was electronics before your father-in-law offered you the job in the bank. To get you out of debt, or to keep you where he could watch you?"

Freyton actually laughed. "Maybe a little bit of both," he conceded.

"What about your two friends here? Are they as adverse to killing as you are?"

"I think the answer to that's an easy no," Paul Freyton said. "But then, you've had more experience in that line, haven't you, guys? I owe them, Bouchard," he added frankly. "I owe them more than I could make in several lifetimes of working for my father-in-law. Lately they've been getting itchy for the money. They've gotten some of it back through the places around the area we've robbed. But not much. I guess you realize those robberies were primarily a diversion.''

"Yes," Marc said quietly.

"We wanted to give the impression there was a professional gang operating in this area. A lot of the stuff we stole, though, wasn't negotiable."

"That's what made me wonder about what was happening," Marc confessed.

"Okay, I suppose it wasn't smart of us. We concentrated on hitting places that belonged to famous people, like Julia Gray. We thought it would draw more attention to what we were doing."

"It did. What did you do with what you stole?" Marc asked out of curiosity.

"Most of it is stashed in a barn on a farm my cousin owns a few miles from here," Freyton said. "Not that it matters. The robberies were only to pave the way for tonight. I knew how to handle the old system; this was my last chance to play with it. Tomorrow you'd have your system in here, and one reason why I gave you so much flack was to find out as much as I could about it and how it could be broken into. I hand it to you, Bouchard. It appears to be foolproof."

Freyton's voice grew serious. "How did you identify me?" he asked. "I thought I'd fool my own mother with this stocking cap over my head."

"Your hand," Marc said.

"What about my hand?"

"Did you happen to take piano lessons when you were fairly young?"

The man sounded dumbfounded. "Yes." He laughed shortly. "Yes. My mother wanted to make a kid prodigy out of me. What put you on to that?"

"There's a certain list to the center finger on your left hand that one observes sometimes in people who played the piano at an early age, while their bones were still in the formative process," Marc said. "Ricardo Castel also has it, but his skin tone is quite different from yours. An olive cast, whereas yours is on the pink side..."

That was as far as Marc got.

Jennifer heard Brent Cranston say softly, "Now." Then, suddenly, searchlights went into play on the police cars surrounding the bank, sweeping the building, crisscrossing back and forth against the windows.

The lieutenant's voice rang into the night. "Okay, Freyton," he said, "we've heard it all. You'll make life easier for yourself and your accomplices if you quit now. Are they armed, Marc?"

Marc's voice came back. "Yes."

Jennifer shuddered.

"Freyton, give your guns to Bouchard," Brent Cranston ordered. "There's no way you can get out of here, regardless of what you do to him. It will go a hell of a lot harder with you if you do anything to him at all. We've got the building surrounded, and every road and path out of town is blocked. Marc?"

The moment of silence that followed was nerveracking. Then Marc said, "Okay, I have the guns."

"Make them go in front of you, Marc. Hell, I guess I don't have to tell you that. Head them toward the main door." Cranston paused. "Don't try anything, Freyton," he urged. "Maybe you'd better keep your accomplices in front of you, for safety's sake. Now, get marching!"

Jennifer lived through a thousand years in the next few minutes. Then, as the searchlights continued to crisscross the building, she saw the front door open slowly. Three men appeared in the aperture one by one, stocking masks pulled over their faces, their arms extended over their heads.

Behind them was Marc. As police officers converged on the men who had been holding him hostage, he moved forward slowly, looking very tired, his limp pronounced. But there was a grim smile on his face.

Brent Cranston started toward him, but Jennifer ran ahead of the state police lieutenant. She sped toward Marc as if her feet had wings, caring about nothing but reaching his side. She threw her arms around him, tears streaming down her face as she clutched him. She prodded his chest with her fingers as if to be sure that his heart really was still beating, and she kept murmuring over and over again little words that were unintelligible even to her.

Only then did she realize that more than the police searchlights were focused on them. Those other lights were coming from portable TV cameras.

The media had reached the scene, and were about to take full advantage of the drama being enacted on this Christmas Eve.

Chapter Fifteen

Jennifer would never have believed that she could be capable of putting on a performance in front of television cameras. But now she found that performing could be easy.

There was a subtle difference between performing and acting, and she wasn't acting. Her emotions came strictly from the heart. She was deliberate, though fully aware that Marc was going to be furious.

She flung her arms around his neck and pressed her lips to his. At first, he made no response. His mouth was closed to hers. Then, despite himself, he yielded, and his lips told her things she knew he'd never even considered saying to her.

His lapse was a brief one. His hands became like steel bands as he tried to force her away from him. She only pressed herself closer.

"Oh, thank God, my dearest," she mumbled brokenly. "Thank God you're safe!"

It was a performance worthy of an Academy Award but, again, Jennifer wasn't acting. What she was telling him was the essence of truth, and it was no effort at all to succumb to emotion so that tears filled her eyes and trickled down her cheeks.

She heard Marc mutter something low and fierce in her ear, but she paid no attention to him. She clung to his arm, knowing he couldn't shake her loose without making a scene about it. The media was moving closer, a cameras was literally thrust into her face as a reporter asked, "How did you happen to be here, Ms. Chatsworth-Graham?"

Jennifer had never in her adult life used her father's hyphenated name. She bristled, but she contained her irritation and said sweetly, "Mr. Bouchard and I are engaged." She heard Marc's angry hiss at this, but went on steadily. "A friend of his—Jack Thornton, who is a reporter for the *Berkshire Eagle,* incidentally—called and told me he was convinced there was something wrong down at the bank. He brought me here with him."

There was an excited buzz at this, and Jennifer knew that Jack would be coming in shortly for his share of the limelight.

Meanwhile, the media continued to focus attention on Marc and her.

"How did you foil the bank robbers as you did, Bouchard?" Mark was asked.

Jennifer was sure that Marc was reaching the end of his fuse, but she knew that the resulting explosion was due to be directed not at the media, but at her. His voice was barely under control as he said, "A new alarm system I had installed in the bank was due to be activated tomorrow. Essentially it was ready to go; it needed only to be turned on via a small hidden button whose location, of course, I cannot divulge. I was able to reach this location, and to press the button. This, in turn, activated the highly sensitive new sound system. The more modern of the bank security systems are sound and voice-activated. This means, for example, that if bank robbers attempt to drill holes into or sledgehammer a vault, the sound-activated system will go on silently. The intruders will never be aware that it is on."

"And that's what happened here?" one reporter queried.

"Precisely," Marc said. "The hidden and supersensitive microphones that have been installed in the bank pick up all sounds. They are automatically transmitted via phone lines to police headquarters, and simultaneously are taped and broadcast over police radios in the area. That is what was done here tonight. I can't tell you exactly how I accomplished this. I can say that the alarm system had just been activated at the time Jack Thornton spoke over the bullhorn so the local police station was already beginning to receive a transmission of what was happening inside the bank. When I went to the window to disconnect the light, as Jack requested, I was able in transit to also activate the loudspeaker system. After that, my conversation with Freyton became police property, I guess you could say.

"You know the rest," Marc finished abruptly. "Now, gentlemen, if you'll excuse me..."

Jennifer was still clinging to his arm. He tried to push her away, but she clung harder so that he couldn't succeed without being very obvious about it. She saw Marc grit his teeth, and then to cap things one of the reporters said, "Do we take it there are wedding bells in the offing for you and Ms. Chatsworth-Graham?"

Before Marc could snap back an answer, Jennifer said sweetly, "We haven't set a date yet, but we plan to shortly."

The media drew back, and Jennifer made her way toward Marc's van with him. They were joined by Jack, Brent Cranston, and Chief Andrews.

"We'll need to go over this step by step with you, Bouchard," Cranston informed Marc.

"I wouldn't mind a story for my paper now that you've blabbed the best parts to the TV guys," Jack complained.

"Go on over to the house and once I can shake myself away from Cranston and company I'll give you one," Marc gritted in tones meant for Jack's ears only, and Jennifer's, since she was standing right next to him. "First paragraph will consist of a fervent denial of a few things."

"All right," Jack said evenly, but he was looking at Jennifer as he spoke, not at Marc. She caught an expression of compassion in his eyes.

In an even lower tone Marc suggested, "Since you evidently brought Jennifer down here, would you kindly see that she gets home?"

Jennifer followed Jack over to his car and huddled into the corner of the front seat. She had never felt smaller. She wished she could sink into the ground and disappear from sight. There had been such scorn in Marc's voice, such downright dislike. But, she thought miserably, she'd had it coming. She had taken advantage of a situation, hoping to force Marc to take her into his life again.

She had failed.

Marc wasn't that afraid of headlines. He'd make his own, if necessary, in order to rebuff everything she had said.

She was so lost in her thoughts that she came to with a start when Jack Thornton suddenly stopped the car. She looked up to see that they were parked in front of the house Marc was renting.

She had no idea what Jack had in mind, but she said weakly, "Please take me back to Julia's, will you?"

A ghost of a smile crossed his face. "I don't think so," he told her.

"Jack, Marc will only be all the more furious if he comes back to find me here," she implored.

"Are you sure about that?"

"Of course I'm sure about it," she retorted, puzzled. "Could he have made it any plainer?"

"Personally I think that he was protesting too much," Jack drawled. "Anyway, I also think you both owe it to each other to watch yourselves on the eleven o'clock news. And I mean to be together when you watch yourselves."

"You're out of your mind," Jennifer sputtered.

"Maybe," Jack allowed. "But I don't think so. I saw the expression on your face as you looked up at him. He didn't. He was avoiding your eyes. I think maybe once he sees that expression he may experience a moment of truth."

Jennifer shook her head. "I wouldn't have thought of you as an incurable romantic," she told him.

"Neither would I," he answered with a grin. "As a matter of fact, I've always considered myself a realist. I think I'm being a realist in this instance. Maybe a romantic realist? How does that sound?"

Despite the emotional toll exacted by the evening, despite a fatigue deeper than she'd ever felt before, Jennifer had to smile back at him.

Jack Thornton was a very engaging person. Also, it occurred to her that though he knew she was the Chatsworth-Graham heiress, there was a strong chance he liked her strictly for herself. He even seemed to feel that she and his best friend belonged together.

As if to verify this, Jack said, "The guy loves you, Jennifer. I know Marc, and I'd swear on my life that you mean much, much more to him than anyone else ever has. I know how he views himself—he has a lot of crazy complexes because of the things he's been through. But you know what?"

"What?" she asked faintly.

"I think you can get him over his hangups. I think the two of you have a chance for a great life together. I'm not saying it will be easy. You'll have to face up to a lot most people never have to think about, but I believe you can handle it. You are quite a person, Jennifer Bentley Chatsworth-Graham," Jack concluded sincerely.

Jennifer's eyes misted, and she groped for a handkerchief. "This is getting to be a habit," she said.

"Well, you're pretty even when you cry," Jack told her magnanimously. "Come on, now, into the house with you."

She shook her head. "Please, Jack." When she saw that he was adamant, she said impatiently, "Very well, then, I'll hitchhike."

"The hell you will!" Jack contradicted. "I've a good idea of what the full fury of Marc's wrath could be, and I have no desire to experience it personally. He'd have my hide if he thought I let you start off for the Gray place on foot at this hour."

He added, "I can't force you to go in the house. So okay, we may freeze to death. But we can just sit here and wait for Marc to come back, if that's what you prefer."

She hesitated. "You'll stay with me if we go in the house?" she asked him.

"Yes," Jack said.

"Promise?"

"Promise. After all, I have to phone something in to the paper for the Christmas-morning edition, and the deadline's right on top of us. The paper will be going to press early, but your story has to make the front page or the TV stations will really be putting us to shame."

Jack was climbing out of the car as he spoke, and Jennifer followed him reluctantly up the path to the house. Jack inserted his key in the lock, pushed the door open, and all hell broke loose.

The hideous sound was much too familiar. It transported Jennifer back to an autumn day when she'd stood in Julia's kitchen, thinking that she'd go crazy if the wailing banshee didn't stop. Then, for the first time, she'd heard Marc Bouchard's voice....

She clapped her hands over her ears, and saw that Jack was doing the same thing. The incredulous expression on his face would have been funny under any other circumstances.

"How the hell do you shut the thing off?" he shouted to Jennifer.

"There's a code number. It has to be punched in. There's a numbered plate somewhere," she shouted back. "But if you don't know the code..."

"How the hell would I know the code?"

Jack was moving around the living room, scanning the walls. Jennifer went out to the kitchen and did the same thing. The sound rose and ebbed around her, ear-splitting in its intensity. She found a small, familiar-looking panel and started punching numbers at random, hoping that somehow she'd hit upon the right combination. She didn't, and the wailing continued.

She headed back to the living room, her head beginning to ache from the piercing wail. Then suddenly the sound stopped, and at the same moment she pitched, head-on, into a human wall.

Marc snapped furiously, "Just what do you think you're doing? Is this an attempt to demonstrate that history can repeat itself, as if that would prove anything?"

Before she could answer, Jack loomed in the living-room doorway. "Exactly when did you install an alarm in here, Bouchard?" he demanded.

Marc swung on him, and then suddenly had the grace to look abashed. "I put it in a couple of weeks ago," he said. "It occurred to me that you have a lot of nice things in here and I've added a few of my own. I had visions of being at the receiving end of a robbery, and thought how ridiculous that would be. So I rigged up a system. I meant to tell you, Jack. I guess I forgot."

A telephone rang, and Marc strode to answer it. Jennifer heard him repeat a series of numbers into the receiver, and then she heard him say, "It's okay. A false alarm, that's all. Everything's fine."

He was still looking slightly abashed as he looked back toward them. "Honestly, Jack," he said, "I'm sorry about that."

"My eardrums have probably been damaged beyond repair," Jack grumbled. "To say nothing of Jennifer's."

Marc turned toward Jennifer, and she saw his shoulders stiffen. She stared at him helplessly, wishing desperately that he would let her make his way easier for him. Their way, she amended. Somehow, he had to be convinced that it was going to be their way from this night forward.

Wearily he asked, "Why did you come here, Jennifer?"

"I brought her," Jack answered for her. "I have to get a quick interview with the two of you and phone it in, Marc. As I explained to Jennifer, the paper will be going to press early tonight. I'll be lucky to get a couple of paragraphs on the front page.''

Marc glared at his friend. "Have you lost your mind?" he demanded.

"Not at all," Jack said cheerfully. "I won't be able to beat out the eleven o'clock news, needless to say, but our readers will expect something in the Christmas-morning paper."

Marc's tone was ominous. "I think you know what you can do about your readers..." he began.

Jennifer found her voice. She was surprised to hear herself ask calmly, "Don't you think you're being unfair, Marc?"

"No. I'm damned if I am!"

"Jack's right," she persisted. "He does need to phone in a story. They know, at his paper, that he started for Thrussington because he felt you were in danger. Jack's the one who alerted the police to that danger, so that they were able to surround the bank before the robbers could carry out their threat and take you hostage. He deserves something from us."

"From *us*?" Marc stared at Jennifer as if she were crazy.

She nodded, determined not to let him ruffle her to the point where she'd turn to jelly right in front of him. Despite her outward coolness, she had never felt more weak-kneed.

"Why don't you begin, Jennifer?" Jack suggested. "Just a simple statement about how you met Marc."

Jennifer actually managed a smile. "My mother-in-law was in the hospital last fall," she told Jack, "and she asked me to drive out to Thrussington to get some papers she needed. She forgot to tell me that Marc had installed an alarm system for her and I walked right into it, just as you and I did here tonight. When I answered the phone, I didn't know the coded number combination that would have identified me. It was Marc who called. I told him who I was, but he didn't believe me. He called the police, and they were on the verge of carting me off to jail when Marc appeared...."

Memories of that golden autumn day overwhelmed Jennifer as she spoke, and suddenly her courage deserted her. "I'm sorry," she said brokenly.

She made a sudden resolution. "I'll give you a statement, Jack," she said recklessly, "and I want you to print it. In fact, I insist that you print it! Marc and I aren't engaged, as you already know, I'm sure, but I want to say it for publication. That was a sad ploy on my part tonight, and you can put it that way if you want to. There will never be a wedding. I love him, and I think he loves me, but I'm too rich for him. He can't believe that I'd give every cent I have away for his sake—as I would if I could, but I can't. There are too many people dependent upon the Chatsworth-Graham empire. If I were to try to get rid of all the holdings, there would be a great danger of my creating a panic in the financial world. Thousands of people would suffer who wouldn't deserve to suffer...because of my capriciousness.

"So," Jennifer continued, "I'm stuck with my money. But having more money than I want or need isn't new to me. A long time ago, I inherited a trust fund from my grandmother that would make me seem wealthy in most people's eyes. I've used only a portion from it for myself. The rest has gone to charities of my choice. I don't need that much money. Certainly I don't need my father's kind of wealth. What I want out of life is really very, very simple, but—"

Jennifer came to a stop. She couldn't go any further. "Is that enough?" she asked Jack in little more than a whisper.

He nodded, his usually genial face serious. "Plenty," he said.

In the doorway he turned. "I asked Jennifer to stay and watch the eleven o'clock news with you, Marc," he said. "I'm asking the same thing of you. Do it, will you?"

Marc didn't answer him.

The door shut behind Jack, and it was all Jennifer could do to keep herself from running after him.

She'd tossed her coat and her mittens and a knit hat she'd been wearing on a chair in the little foyer. Now she went to get them, and she was slipping them on when she heard Marc's voice behind her.

"Where do you think you're going?" he asked her.

"Home," she said, and amended, "to Julia's."

"How do you plan to get there?"

"It's only a few miles, and it's a clear night," she told him. "I plan to walk."

"Do you seriously think I'd let you do that?" he demanded.

"It's my choice."

"Your choice or not, I have no intention of standing by and letting you start off out into the country in the middle of the night," he informed her.

He'd stepped toward her as he spoke, and now he was towering over her. The sight of him, the nearness of him was too much for her. Jennifer's lips began to quiver. "Please, Marc," she implored. "I've had it. Just let me go."

"Don't you think I've had it too?" he asked her.

"Maybe," she conceded.

"Don't you think I have any feelings, Jenny?" he persisted.

It registered that he had called her Jenny, but it also occurred to her that maybe that really didn't mean anything anymore.

"Yes," she said, ignoring the fluttering sensation that was beginning deep down inside her, like butterfly wings surging up to the surface. "Yes, of course I know you have feelings, Marc."

"Do you really?" he asked, and the irony in his voice forced her to look at him. At once, she wished she hadn't. He looked so damned tired. The fatigue also gave him a certain vulnerability. The combination was almost more than she could bear.

"Do you really?" he repeated. "How the hell do you think I felt when you stood up there in front of those TV cameras and kissed me square on the mouth and then told those reporters you and I were going to be married? You were making your announcement to the whole world, that's what it amounted to, Miss Chatsworth-Graham. Our picture is going to be plastered on TV screens all over the world."

"I suppose so," she agreed dully.

"You suppose so? Okay, I'll ask you again. How do you think I felt when you did that?"

"I—I don't know," she admitted.

"You don't know?"

"No," she said, "but it doesn't matter. I've made it right, Marc. When Jack's story is printed, everyone will accept that...that I was way off base."

He surveyed her. "Way off base," he said reflectively. "That's a funny way to put it. Regardless, everyone won't know, because Jack's story will never be printed."

"What are you saying?"

"Jack will never write the story you gave him. He gave me a big wink behind your back when he left here. I got the message. I know Jack. Even for the sake of a top front-page story like that, he wouldn't do it. He wouldn't embarrass you."

"I deserve to be embarrassed," Jennifer said, tilting her chin. "I'm the one who set out to make a fool of myself. Giving that story to Jack was only my way of righting a wrong."

"Really?"

"Yes. Yes, of course."

"Again, may I ask the question. What about me?"

"What about you?" Jennifer asked, puzzled.

"Do you really think I'd let you off the hook so easily, Jenny?" Marc asked her. "Hell, you said you were going to marry me in front of cameras that will translate your message to the entire world. I'm not about to let you jilt me now."

"Jilt you?"

"It's as good a word for it as anything that comes to my mind at the moment," Marc told her, and actually grinned.

Jennifer stared at him, nonplussed. She saw his grin fade, and a number of other emotions were left in its wake to play across his expressive face. He said frankly, "I'm scared to death of this. I have no idea how I'm going to handle it...or you. I've faced some risks before, and they seem puny compared to this one. But I love you. I love you so much, the rest of my life would be dry as a bundle of straw without you."

He drew a deep breath. "That fact hit me this morning when I opened your Christmas present. I couldn't stand waiting until tomorrow, Jenny. That package has been tormenting me; this morning I had to find out what you'd gotten me. When I saw the painting and read what you'd written about wishing I had let you share the beauties of this place with you, well, I felt like a thousand kinds of a fool. You'd offered me the greatest gift a woman can give a man, a gift that has nothing to do with money. You'd offered me yourself, your heart…and I'd been so blind.

"Tonight, when I saw you as I started out of the bank, I thought maybe I'd rocked out of my mind. Then you came and threw your arms around me and I felt the reality of you. I still couldn't accept it. I still couldn't accept you…and then Brent Cranston said a funny thing."

"What?" Jennifer whispered.

"He said he wished once in his life he could hope to have a woman look at him the way you looked at me when you were talking into the TV cameras. All of a sudden I knew I could never give you up. Say what you will about it, that's the way it is, the way it will always be as far as I'm concerned. I don't want your damned money, all I want is you. I hope I can support you and give you the things you want. If I can't, I suppose it would be wrong to keep you from getting them for yourself. But, one way or another…"

"One way or another," Jennifer said softly. These were petty details he was talking about, small matters they'd have years in which to work out.

Marc glanced at his watch, and he said, a smile quirking the corner of his mouth, "It's almost eleven."

"I should call Julia," Jennifer said swiftly. "She and Ricardo will surely be watching the eleven o'clock news and she'll wonder—"

"Cranston said he'd call her and fill her in," Marc said. "I told him to warn her you might not get back home tonight."

"You did what?"

"I was ninety percent sure I'd find you here with Jack," Marc confessed. "It was a calculated bet."

"And suppose you'd lost that bet?"

"Then," he said, "I would have come after you."

There were no shadows in Marc's smile. Despite his fatigue, his eyes were bluer than they'd ever been, and to Jennifer he had never looked quite so handsome.

"The news will be on in a minute," he said. "But personally, I don't think we need to watch it. I can think of a much better way of ushering in Christmas."

"So can I," Jennifer told him, and the butterflies that had been tormenting her vanished. A warm glow suffused her. It started at her toes, and became a melting current that spread through her body and flowed right to the top of her head. Marc was responsible for the glow. He held her happiness in his hands.

Did he know that?

As she started up the stairs with Marc to the little bedroom under the eaves, Jennifer promised herself that if Marc didn't realize the power he had over her, she was going to make sure, tonight, that he found out.

This was a lesson she was determined to teach him. A beautiful lesson she'd never let him forget.

READERS' COMMENTS ON SILHOUETTE SPECIAL EDITIONS:

"I just finished reading the first six Silhouette Special Edition Books and I had to take the opportunity to write you and tell you how much I enjoyed them. I enjoyed all the authors in this series. Best wishes on your Silhouette Special Editions line and many thanks."

—B.H.*, Jackson, OH

"The Special Editions are really special and I enjoyed them very much! I am looking forward to next month's books."

—R.M.W.*, Melbourne, FL

"I've just finished reading four of your first six Special Editions and I enjoyed them very much. I like the more sensual detail and longer stories. I will look forward each month to your new Special Editions."

—L.S.*, Visalia, CA

"Silhouette Special Editions are — 1.) Superb! 2.) Great! 3.) Delicious! 4.) Fantastic! . . . Did I leave anything out? These are books that an adult woman can read . . . I love them!"

—H.C.*, Monterey Park, CA

*names available on request

Author JOCELYN HALEY,
also known by her fans as SANDRA FIELD
and JAN MACLEAN, now presents her
eighteenth compelling novel.

With the help of the enigmatic Bryce Sanderson,
Kate MacIntyre begins her search for the meaning behind
the nightmare that has haunted her since childhood.
Together they will unlock the past and forge a future.

Available at your favorite
retail outlet in NOVEMBER.

If you're ready for a more sensual, more provocative reading experience...

We'll send you **4** Silhouette Desire novels **FREE...**

and without obligation

Then, we'll send you six more Silhouette Desire® novels to preview every month for 15 days with absolutely no obligation!

When you decide to keep them, you pay just $1.95 each ($2.25, in Canada), *with no shipping, handling, or additional charges of any kind!*

Silhouette Desire novels are not for everyone. They are written especially for the woman who wants a more satisfying, more deeply involving reading experience.

Silhouette Desire novels take you *beyond* the others and offer real-life drama and romance of successful women in charge of their lives. You'll share precious, private moments and secret dreams... experience every whispered word of love, every ardent touch, every passionate heartbeat.

As a home subscriber, you will also receive FREE, a subscription to the Silhouette Books Newsletter as long as you remain a member. Each issue is filled with news on upcoming titles, interviews with your favorite authors, even their favorite recipes.

And, the first 4 Silhouette Books are absolutely FREE and without obligation, yours to keep! What could be easier... and where else could you find such a satisfying reading experience?

To get your free books, fill out and return the coupon today!

Silhouette Books, 120 Brighton Rd., P.O. Box 5084, Clifton, NJ 07015-5084

Silhouette Special Edition

COMING NEXT MONTH

SUMMER DESSERTS—Nora Roberts
Blake Cocharan wanted the best, and Summer Lyndon was a dessert chef *extraordinaire*. She had all of the ingredients he was looking for, and a few he didn't expect.

HIGH RISK—Caitlin Cross
Paige Bannister had lived life from a safe distance until she met rodeo rider Casey Cavanaugh and found herself taking risks she had never thought she would dare.

THIS BUSINESS OF LOVE—Alida Walsh
Working alongside executive producer Steve Bronsky was a challenge that Cathy Arenson was willing to meet, but resisting his magnetic charm was more than a challenge—it was an impossibility.

A CLASS ACT—Kathleen Eagle
Rafe had always thought that Carly outclassed him, but when she was caught in a blizzard nothing mattered other than warming her by his fire…and in his arms.

A TIME AND A SEASON—Curtiss Ann Matlock
Two lovers were thrown together on a remote Oklahoma highway. Katie found Reno easy to love, but could she embrace life on his ranch as easily as she embraced him?

KISSES DON'T COUNT—Linda Shaw
Reuben North hadn't planned on becoming involved, but when Candice's old boyfriend threatened to take her child away, Reuben found himself comfortably donning his shining armor.